A CHRISTMAS WISH

A CHRISTMAS WISH

STARLING BAY, BOOK 9

SIENNA CARR

AUTHOR'S NOTE

A Christmas Wish is a STANDALONE romance in the ***Starling Bay*** series. While you do not need to have read any of the earlier books in this series, it might enhance your reading experience if you do because many of the characters in this book appear in the other Starling Bay books.

Starling Bay Series:

Whirlwind Kisses
Winter's Kiss
Maid for Him
Love Letters
Escape to Starling Bay (Books 1-3)
From Faking to Forever
Winter's Vow
Guarded Hearts
Table for Two
A Bouquet of Charm
A Christmas Wish

CHAPTER 1

"I'll be home a little later tonight. I've got another appointment." Leah waited for her sulky teen son to say something, but Peter's eyes were glued to his cell phone.

"It's my last one," she added, but if she was waiting for support—some excitement even—from her son, she didn't get it. It was delusional to think so. "You don't have anything to say?"

Her teenage son glanced up, his mouth twisting in mild resentment at the interruption. "Cool."

"My last one, hopefully," she said carefully, knowing that he didn't like to talk about these things. "That should be a good thing, no?"

His shoulders, specifically *one* shoulder, lifted, then dropped, and he went back to his cell phone again. She couldn't gauge his reaction. Was he pleased for her? Did he even care?

Maybe if she'd had a daughter, her response might have been different, but it was no use wondering about such things. She wasn't going to have any more children.

Not now.

So, she would never know.

Her family was complete; it was just her and Peter. Before

this, she'd hoped to meet someone. She'd been eager to find a life partner, someone reliable and dependable, someone who could be a good father to her boy. Someone with whom she could share her life. A man who would make her happy. But it hadn't happened. She'd been unlucky, and now there was no point in looking.

Her goals had changed.

Life had changed, and she no longer possessed the energy, or the desire. She no longer had such trivial dreams.

Life now, was about survival.

Yet life with Peter had changed. She missed the lovely, adorable little boy her son had once been. Now in the midst of puberty, this teenage version was so very different. She wasn't even sure she liked him much on some days. She loved him with all her heart, as any mother loved her child, but *like* him? Some days, no.

"There are leftovers from yesterday in the fridge," she continued, slowly getting up from the table. "Do you want Hyacinth to check in on you?"

He glanced up at her from his cell phone, momentarily. "Nah." It was a grunt, with a word wrapped around it. He went back to his phone.

Her parents had left Starling Bay and moved to Iowa—they had visited her, briefly, to see how she was—and her brother kept in touch via texting. A little more support would have been helpful, but she'd long known she couldn't rely on others, not even her family, too much. People disappointed more often than not; after her husband initiated divorce proceedings, when Peter had been five years old, Leah had learned to depend on no one but herself.

But Hyacinth Fitzsimmons, her latest employer, a hitherto formidable woman, became one of the few people she relied on for support in these difficult times. The woman had her moments. She'd been bossy, always believing she was right, and she didn't pander to others, but when it mattered, Hyacinth came through for her.

Leah put her dishes away in the dishwasher and then turned around, the ball of simmering resentment in her belly starting to smoulder. "How many times have I told you not to bring that device to the dining table?" She hated Peter's cell phone, more to the point, she hated his usage of the device. She'd only given it to him so that he could reach her if he ever needed to in an emergency.

"Peter!" she cried, when he didn't respond. His eyes were still glued to the home-wrecking device; that's what these things did, in her opinion. They stole children from their parents, and for children, they stole their time, their attention, their concentration. "Peter!"

"What?" Her son possessed the ability to infuse a word with so much anger.

"Don't you *what* me," she snapped.

He glared at her and pushed the phone away, then stood up, leaving his half-eaten bowl of cereal. He was jabbing all of her buttons this morning, and she didn't need this. Not now. Not today.

"What do you want me to say?" he growled. "You told me what you're doing, and you asked me if I wanted Hyacinth—"

"She's Miss Fitzsimmons to you."

"Whatever."

Push, push, push went her buttons.

"Do what you want." She marched out of the kitchen, got her things, and before she left the house, she caught sight of herself in front of the mirror.

At only thirty-one years, she looked and dressed more like a middle-aged frump. She was more tired than ever, not enough to make her curl up and lie in bed all day. She was lucky, and maybe her age had something to do with that, but she could still function.

She could still go to work and cook and clean and be there for the son who didn't really care if she was or not.

As a single mom, she didn't have the luxury of taking it easy. There was no one else to depend on. She was the sole breadwinner, and it was down to her to keep a roof over their heads and food on the table, even for the boy who didn't seem to appreciate it all.

Disgusted with what she had become, dressing for comfort, for invisibility, now that there was no reason to catch anyone's eye, she walked out, but just before she closed the door, she thought she heard a 'Good luck.'

Maybe not. It was possible that she was hearing things. Mustering her limited reserves of energy and strength, she held her head high and put on a brave face, reminding herself that today was going to be a good day.

It was, because she'd lived to see another day.

CHAPTER 2

Brody Holt sat by his mother's bed and held her hand. Hodgkin's lymphoma patients had a high chance of survival. Ninety-four percent, the doctors had told him.

He'd been coming here with her for over a month for her outpatient visits and she'd been doing well with chemo but being immunocompromised, she'd caught a serious infection and had been hospitalized.

He caressed her hand and willed her closed eyes to open. He needed to see those blues. Instead, all he could do was stare at her as she lay peacefully sleeping.

Now as he sat by her bedside, he prayed and wished and willed her to recover. He leaned forward and lifted her hand, pressing his lips against her soft, warm, limp skin, silently imploring her to wake up.

A hand settled on his shoulder. "Why don't you go stretch your legs, Brody? Get something to eat. I'll take over." He hadn't even heard Jackie come in.

"You sure?" He stood up, towering over her. She looked as tired as he felt. She'd flown over from California a few days ago, having left her home and family behind.

"Go," Jackie told him.

He walked out, feeling his legs slowly unstiffen. He'd been here since early morning and planned to be here for a few more hours before heading back to work. Luckily, his boss was flexible. Understanding, too. He could go back and put in a few hours later now that Jackie was here.

He headed towards the vending machine, and as he approached, he saw a woman jabbing the buttons on the machine.

"You took my money," he heard her mutter. She jabbed the buttons again.

He recognized her, even from behind. That's what happened in this place. You got used to seeing the same faces, week after week. All the regular people who needed treatment frequently quickly became familiar. "Is it stuck?"

She turned around, her eyes widening as her gaze swept over his face. "Yes. It's jammed and I can't shift it." She thumped the window. He saw the issue at once. The bottle of water was stuck in the vending machine arm at a slight angle. He gave the machine a heavy thump with the flat of his hand. The bottle shook, but didn't release.

"See what I mean," she said.

He thumped it again. This time it fell. He bent down and plucked it through the wide flap. "Released. Here you go."

"Thank you. I obviously didn't hit it hard enough."

"There's a knack to it."

"A knack?"

He nodded. "You have to give it a big thump."

"I'll bear that in mind." She unscrewed the lid of the bottle but didn't take a sip. They stared at one another for a few moments. He had seen her here many times, but she'd always been by herself.

"How's your mom?" she asked. "I haven't seen her around here lately. Has she finished with her treatment?"

He leaned back against the wall, as if he needed the steadiness of it to take his body weight. "She's caught an infection."

Her eyes grew wider. "I didn't know. I'm sorry to hear that. How is she?"

"It's not looking too good."

The woman placed a hand to the wall, needing to steady herself. Surprised that this news had appeared to hit her so strongly, he pushed away from the wall and turned to her in concern. "Do you want to sit down?" Maybe *she* was feeling unwell.

Maybe this wasn't about his mom's news. In all the time that they'd become familiar strangers here at the hospital, passing in hallways, near the water cooler or vending machine, or sitting in the waiting room, he was still none the wiser as to the cause of her illness.

"I'm fine." She wiped a hand across her face. "Sorry. I haven't eaten breakfast, and I've come from work. I'm always slightly stressed out when I come here, but your mom's news has shocked me. She's going to be fine, though, isn't she?" The way she said it sounded like a plea.

His mother would be touched and he hoped to tell her as soon as she was well again. "I hope so. I think maybe her body just got weak. The chemo has weakened her. Neutropenic sepsis is what the doctors told us."

The woman took a sip of her water. "I wish her well. I'm so sorry."

"It came as a shock. Completely unexpected, especially as she seemed to be doing well with the treatment."

"That's the thing about this disease, it hits out of the blue and then it makes things worse." She looked away, speaking more to herself than to him, and then she chugged down some more water.

"Is that your experience of it?" He waited, hoping she would elaborate and tell him about herself. He knew nothing, not even her name and in the cold and clinical hallways and waiting spaces of the hospital, making small talk with a stranger was something to cling on to. A distraction and diversion from the worry that plagued him.

What if his mother didn't make it?

He had always seen her by herself. That must take some strength. Going through 'something,' which she clearly was, alone made his protective side kick in.

"I can't explain, I don't have the words to express my experience of it. I try to take one day at a time."

He nodded. "Of course. I always see you here by yourself. It can't be easy." His words hung awkwardly in the air. He hadn't meant to pry, people in this place didn't. They respected boundaries.

She shrugged. "Everyone's busy, and I don't like to impose."

Impose? This was an odd choice of word. Did she have no family? No husband? No friends?

"I wouldn't want my son to come here with me, and there's really no need for anyone to be here with me. I don't want to make such a big deal of it."

"You have a son?"

"Peter. He's thirteen, and therefore a teenager, grumpy and miserable. I hope this is just a phase."

"That sounds about right for a teen."

"Do you have children?"

He shook his head. "No. Nothing like that." He was about to ask her something, when his phone rang. It was Jackie.

"Where are you?" she cried. "Something's not right. Come back." The terror in her voice made the hairs on the back of his neck stand at attention.

"I have to go. Good luck." He rushed away, not knowing what he was wishing her good luck for, but everyone who came to the hospital needed some kind of luck.

CHAPTER 3

When he rushed off looking worried, she hoped it was nothing serious. But what were the chances of that in a place like this?

He'd seemed nice enough, now that she'd had a chance to talk to him. She had been on her second month of radiation treatment when she'd noticed him and his mother. She didn't even know his name, nor had she spoken to him or his mother much, apart from the usual greeting. They were sick strangers who passed one another in the waiting room or in the hallways, and by virtue of their illness, they shared a code of sorts.

She'd only known that the woman he came with was his mother because she'd heard him call out 'Mom' one day when he'd walked away to look for a nurse. His mom had started to wander off in the opposite direction and luckily, she'd seen this and had gotten up and led the elderly lady back to her son.

It had got her thinking. Would Peter be there for her like that, when she got older?

If she got older.

When she'd first discovered the lump in her breast, she hadn't thought it was anything, until it had started to get painful. For a woman who prided herself on never going to the doctor, she had rushed to make an appointment right away. A flurry of tests had confirmed her worst fears and a biopsy showed the lump to be malignant.

It was cancer. They'd caught it early, the doctor reassured her. A lumpectomy had followed, and then two months of radiation. Five days a week, from Monday to Friday, she'd been coming to the hospital.

"Just keep an eye out for any lumps or bumps, and if you have any concerns, be sure to make an appointment."

She could barely contain her joy. No more radiotherapy for now. Hopefully not ever again. She smiled, her insides quivering like wobbly jelly.

"Otherwise, we'll have to schedule you for the routine three-month scans."

"Thank you." She prayed that this would be the last of it. She prayed that she would have her life back and she could continue as if nothing had happened. She wanted to put this scary episode behind her and move on with her life.

Faced with the fear, the knowledge, the certainty that death was not guaranteed to be a far-off event had given her a fire in her belly.

Time was not infinite.

Life had to be lived.

She walked out of the hospital room almost gliding on air. "No more treatments," she said to herself as she strode purposefully out of the treatment room, and headed for the main doors.

Despite Hyacinth telling her that she could take the afternoon off— the way she always did—Leah wasn't ready to go home but back to work. Taking time off daily for treatments mounted up. She didn't want to lose this job, even if her gut instinct told her that Hyacinth would never fire her no matter what happened. Also, she never felt too bad after her appointments, and she needed the money.

Hyacinth had been good to her, and she wanted to stay in the older woman's good graces. It was odd, how she now had a different perception of the woman who at one time had been such an ogre to work with. She'd seen a side to Hyacinth she had never seen before.

As she headed down the hallway leading to the elevator bank, she saw him again; the man who had slammed her water bottle free from the vending machine.

She wanted to ask him if everything was okay, given that he had rushed off, but he had his back to her as she walked towards him. Filled with joie de vivre that had been lacking from her life lately, she was about to tap him on the shoulder playfully, but she heard the crying.

It wasn't him, but the woman he was cradling in his arms. His head was bent as he tried to comfort her.

Leah's heart sank. When people cried in a hospital, it was because of loss.

His mother.

She wanted to say something, but it seemed too soon, the shock and the emotion so raw, like a bleeding wound that had no time to heal. She walked past then glanced over her shoulder to see that he and his wife were consoling one another.

Suddenly, the older woman's face flashed before her eyes. It hadn't been too long since Leah had seen her and smiled and said 'hello.'

Her heart was heavy. The happiness she'd felt as she'd walked out of her treatment room deflated like a lead balloon. The good news about her last treatment meant nothing, in light of this, and the loss of a woman she barely knew signaled that her good news was fleeting, not permanent.

There was no guarantee of a happy every after. Just because her own treatments had now finished didn't mean a thing. It was a mild reprieve for now and only time would tell, with more tests and vigilance, whether something might be wrong.

That was the thing about cancer, once it invaded your body, the fear of it never went away.

She made her way back to the town hall feeling somber. All she wanted was to sit in her tiny office at work and hide. Unfortunately for her, she had to walk past Hyacinth's office to reach hers.

"Leah!" Hyacinth had a voice which could not be ignored. Leah stopped, turned and walked back and into Hyacinth's office.

"My dear, how was it?" the older woman asked, her face beaming, as if she were asking about how her date might have gone, instead of her radiation treatment.

"Why are you still here, Hyacinth?" This woman did not sit in her office all day long. Hers couldn't be construed as a desk job. Hyacinth made it her mission in life to poke her nose all over the town hall—indeed all over Starling Bay when she could—talking to people and making their business *hers*. She had her fingers in so many committees, and subcommittees, and had lots of tiny projects going on, it was a wonder that she found enough hours in the day to do everything. This elderly lady—some said she wasn't far from seventy years of age--didn't cut herself any slack.

"I had some things to finalize before the monthly town hall meeting on Wednesday," Hyacinth replied. Though Leah sensed this wasn't the real reason her boss was still here. "You look … relieved." She seemed to be waiting for Leah to say more.

Leah leaned against the door jamb. "It was the last treatment, for now," she answered softly, not wanting to jinx thing. The next few weeks and months would be the litmus test, and she wasn't going to feel free to breathe until then.

"It will be the last one, forever." Hyacinth marched over to her like a general wading into war.

"You can't say that, not with this disease." Leah thought about the guy at the vending machine. It was so infuriating not to know his name, and now she never would. Her heart ached for what had happened. Nothing good.

"You need to have faith, my dear. It's what all you young people these days seem to lack."

"Faith." Leah snorted. Since when had faith ever helped her? She'd had faith when she'd exchanged vows with her husband.

"When you have faith, you need never be afraid. Expect that things will work out and you'll find that they almost always do."

Leah almost rolled her eyes. People of Hyacinth's generation and disposition had an alternative view of the world. They didn't live in reality. She swanned around the town, giving orders, dictating to people about things they needed to do. Somehow or other, things got done. People might have moaned about Hyacinth behind her back, but things got done.

"Just like our beloved Christmas pageant, my dear. You'll be in charge of that again, as usual, now that Dylan Fraser has washed his hands of it." Hyacinth rubbed her hands together excitedly. "I can hardly wait. This year, I want it to be bigger and better than ever."

"It's August, Hyacinth. *August.*"

Leah's dumbstruck impression didn't hinder Hyacinth from talking about her vision. "We're getting more people visiting us not only in the summer, but at Christmas time as well. I like to think it's because of the effort we put into promoting our town, and the Christmas market, and the town square, and all our lovely little shops. And our Christmas pageant."

"It's far too early to be thinking about Christmas."

The older woman looked at her intently for a while. "But it will come, and you will be in charge of it again."

Leah shifted uneasily. An elderly woman she had regularly seen at the hospital had passed away. She didn't have the reservoir of faith that Hyacinth seemed to have by the truckload, but she was in no mood to talk about Christmas or the pageant. That event was months away, and she needed to take each day as it came.

"I would like to get Hailey Ross involved." Hyacinth adjusted her suit jacket, and dusted her brooch with her fingers, the way she always did.

"Hailey Ross?" Leah's eyes widened. Hyacinth had a tendency to dream a little too big and crazy at times. As if the movie star would ever want to be associated with a Christmas pageant. "I don't think a Hollywood movie star is going to take you up on that offer."

"Have a little faith, Leah."

"Surely you're not thinking of asking her agent?"

"Her agent?" Hyacinth picked up her shiny black handbag and smoothed a hand through her hair. Leah wished she'd ease up on her pink lipstick. It was far too bright, and far too gaudy, yet, in an odd way, she couldn't imagine Hyacinth in any other color.

"I don't need to go through an agent to get to her. I've known her since she was a baby."

"You know her?" Leah moved away from the door.

"I know everyone in this town."

The eyeroll couldn't be helped, but luckily Hyacinth had walked out. "I'm going to talk to the people in the planning department."

"Do you need me to come along and take minutes?" Leah asked.

Hyacinth waved her off. "It's not a meeting. Nothing so formal. We have some work starting here next week. Painting, and rewiring and the general upkeep of the building. It will last a while and I need to make sure the workmen have a designated area outside." She sighed. "There's never a right time for these things, but I suppose they have to start at some time."

"I'll finish up what I was doing before." Leah started to walk towards her office.

"You should go home to your son, my dear. I don't understand why you insist on coming here, especially after what you've been through."

Leah smiled appreciatively. She liked to come to work because she wanted to be busy, and because it was here that she had control of things. She suspected that it was the same for Hyacinth, who seemed to enjoy being a busybody. As far as Leah was aware, the woman was single, had never married, and had no children. She needed to fill her days with something that gave her a reason to be.

As for herself, cancer had ravaged her body and invaded the part of her that made her a woman. She hadn't had a mastectomy, and her body was intact, yet she didn't feel whole.

She felt *less*.

Less feminine.

Less confident.

Less sure of herself.

Being at work made her feel in charge of something, and given that she had no control over her health—and therefore her life—coming to work gave her meaning.

CHAPTER 4

He left Jackie inside the florist shop and stepped out, finding it all too much. They were looking at funeral wreaths for their mother's funeral next week.

It was all happening at lightspeed, and he felt helpless to do anything. His mother had gone in with cancer, yet the doctors had reassured them that the prognosis was good.

It didn't make sense. One week later and he was still reeling from the giddiness of it all. The foundations of his life had been rocked and he hadn't yet regained his full senses. Numbness allowed him to get through each day, to follow Jackie around and do what she said. She seemed to have taken charge of the situation, which was a good thing because he was struggling. Jackie's family had come over yesterday, and her husband and their four children were all staying at his mother's house. It was strange to see that house be such a hive of activity even though his mother was no longer there.

Jackie waved at him to come inside, but he shook his head. He didn't want to get involved with flowers. He wanted a funeral wreath in the shape of 'Mom' and he'd left his sister to take care of the details.

When someone tapped him on the shoulder, he turned around.

"Hi." It was the woman from the hospital, the one he'd run into at the vending machine.

"Oh, hey," he said slowly, adjusting to seeing her in a place that wasn't the hospital.

"I walked past you last week after my appointment at the hospital and ..."

"I know. I remember. The water bottle."

Her expression tightened. "I heard you ... uh ...and ..." She seemed to be falling over her words, her uneasiness palpable. "Is everything okay? You rushed away ... I was worried about your mom."

He stared at the floor. She didn't know. Of course she didn't. He rubbed his hand along his jaw, the skin feeling extra rough and stubbly because he hadn't shaved in days. He cleared his throat. "She passed away, that very day." It still felt odd to say that.

She passed away.

"I'm so sorry for your loss. I did think something bad had happened. I walked past you after my appointment, and I heard. I saw you and your ... I'm so sorry."

"So am I." He leaned against the wall, thinking about that day, and how sudden and unexpected it had been. One minute he'd been sitting with his mother, and the next he'd gone out to take a break. By the time he'd rushed back in, when Jackie had called him, he suspected that something was wrong. His darling mother had passed away and he hadn't even been there.

Now he was drowning in guilt, knowing that he hadn't been by her side at that final, terrible moment.

"I didn't know her too well, we didn't really talk, but I could tell she was a lovely woman. She was always smiling. She would catch my eye sometimes, and I'm sure I saw a hint of mischief in them."

He let out a long breath. "That's what my mom was like. She

made the best pound cake. She was a great cook, she was a great mom. She's left a hole so big that me and my sister are lost, partly because it was so unexpected. You think you have more time, and then suddenly, you don't."

What he didn't tell her was that his mother had commented that Leah often came alone, and, as she was sometimes prone to do, had hinted that she might be single, and then she would look at him, with that same hint of mischief in her eyes that this stranger had just mentioned.

"I miss her. She wasn't supposed to go. She wasn't, and she wouldn't have if she hadn't ..." If she hadn't caught the damn infection. That was what made it all so tragic. His mother had battled the cancer, and was doing well, but something out of the blue had blindsided her and now she was gone.

If ever there was a sign to him of how fleeting and fragile life was, it was this. What happened with his mother should have been a different and happy ending.

"I'm so sorry." The woman looked distraught, as if she was trying to hold herself together. For the longest time, she looked at the floor, then away, anywhere but at him. Inhaling a long deep breath, she turned to him again. "I thought she would be okay. She didn't ..." The woman stopped talking suddenly. Lately, he'd noticed that many did this—especially since he'd started announcing the sad news to friends and family. People would be about to say something and they stopped.

"What were you going to say?" He was interested to find out.

The woman shifted uneasily on her feet. "She didn't look too sick."

He could have said the same about Leah. She still had a full head of hair, and she didn't look to him to have any signs of chemo.

"I thought she would be fine. I expected her to be," she said, her voice so quiet he barely heard her.

Her warm brown eyes stared back at him, temporarily mesmerizing him. It was easier to lose himself, if only for a few seconds, in something that took his mind away from the misery of life.

"It happened when you and I were talking," he told her. "I rushed off and that's the reason why."

She brushed a lock of brown wavy hair away from her face. "I wondered if that might have been it. I've been thinking about your mom a lot lately because I wasn't sure what had happened. I had a feeling it wasn't good. At least I know now." She shook her head. "I didn't expect to see you again."

"I didn't expect to see you, either." Truth was, this was a weird coincidence.

"There won't be any more hospital visits for me." He'd looked forward to taking his mother, because he got to spend more time with her, that he wouldn't usually have. She'd become pensive lately, talking to him about her fears that he'd end up alone. These talks were so different than the conversation when he used to go over for dinner, or to fix something in the house, or to take her shopping for groceries. He wondered if she'd had a sense that things could go wrong. She'd talked a lot about being afraid for him, that he would grow old and have no one to take care of him the way he had taken care of her.

"Nor for me. I had my last appointment that day."

"You did? No more?"

She didn't reply right away, and then, "I hope not."

"That's great. I'm happy for you." He felt genuinely happy for her. She was one of the luckier ones.

She raised a tentative hand to the shoulder strap of her handbag. "I hope so. I'm glad I ran into you again. I was worried after the last time, and as it turns out, I had reason to be. I'm sorry for your loss. Moms are irreplaceable."

"Yes, they are." A lump mushroomed in his throat and lodged

there. He cleared his throat. A tapping noise made him look over his shoulder. Jackie was signaling for him to come inside.

"You're being summoned."

He turned back to face the woman. "It looks like it. I don't even know your name. I'm Brody." He put out his hand.

"Leah." She shook it.

He nodded. She seemed nice enough, and he was touched that she'd given her condolences regarding his mother.

CHAPTER 5

She rushed to the bookstore to buy a croissant and a cup of hot chocolate. She'd brought sandwiches to work, and had decided to treat herself to a little afternoon pick-me-up.

What a strange turn of events to see that man again. *Brody.* It had lifted her spirits, even though the news he had shared was sad. Now she couldn't get his mother's face out of her mind.

At least she now knew his name.

There was a time in her life when someone like that would have been on her radar. Once upon a time when she was single and life was hard and she didn't want to end up alone, she would have eyed a man like that as a possible father figure for Peter, and a partner for her.

But things had changed now.

This year had hit her like a tornado, scattering her hopes and self-esteem across the landscape of her dreams. She was still single, and life was still hard and, as recent events had shown her, life wasn't even guaranteed. She was more conscious than ever of its limits.

She was no longer interested in trying to find her soulmate. She didn't want to be a burden to anyone.

And Brody had a wife. Or a girlfriend, possibly, given that she hadn't seen a ring on his finger. She'd checked. Of course she'd checked. Some habits died hard.

These days, Leah didn't have the time and space in her life to think about a relationship. She wasn't even sure she wanted to commit to the Christmas pageant that Hyacinth was obsessed by. She was loath to make commitments or promises she wasn't sure she could keep.

It was a negative attitude, but life had taught her to be pragmatic.

She walked into Books & Buns, and headed for the coffee and cake corner, but even as she approached that section, she saw a group of women sitting at one of the tables. The shop owner, Leigh, was also sitting with them. It was their laughter that first drew her attention. They *looked* happy. They *sounded* happy, chatting away as if they didn't have a care or a worry in the world. It was like a slap in the face for her to walk in and see them.

She knew the other. Merry was the-one-that-got-Dylan-Fraser, and she'd met Jenna when she'd started working at the town hall.

She walked past their table, praying they wouldn't notice her.

Unfortunately, her prayers were in vain. "Leah!" Jenna called out her name. She turned around, but didn't move from the counter, where she pretended to be busy looking at the selection of cakes and pastries on display.

"Hey, Jenna." She waved. But Jenna motioned for her to come over, and so she begrudgingly did.

"Are you still working for Hyacinth?" Jenna asked. The other ladies at the table stopped talking and Leah felt suddenly out of place, the contrast between her and them never more sharp. She felt like an outsider standing on the side-lines looking in; not part of the club, but a loner all by herself. She didn't have a group of women she could confide in.

Maybe she'd been too needy, too clingy, too desperate back in the early years, and had frightened other women off. Hyacinth was her closest confidante, a woman who was easily four decades older than her.

"I am."

"Hi, Leah," Merry piped up. When Dylan and Merry had gotten married, the news had flown around Starling Bay like a grade ten hurricane, trashing her heart, her feelings and delicate self-esteem.

She had seen this woman as a competitor once. Merry was the out-of-towner who had captured the heart of the man Leah had long set her sights on. Unfortunately, Dylan Fraser hadn't felt the same way about her.

Leah hadn't made many friends when she'd moved to this town soon after she and her husband divorced. The sad fact was that Merry had been a single mother too, as Leah had later learned when both their children had taken part in the Christmas pageant years ago.

Not only had Merry made friends, she'd found a herself a husband, too. She'd fit right into Starling Bay. Now, as Leah watched her, sitting with her friends and enjoying life, she felt like a failure in comparison.

"How is the old dragon?" Jenna asked.

"Jenna!" Merry cried. "You leave Hyacinth alone."

"She's not a dragon when you get to know her," was all Leah could think of to say. Hyacinth was her friend, her support system and her boss, and she would defend her to the death.

"She's very fussy with her cakes," the coffee shop owner remarked.

"Don't get me started," Jenna cried. "The number of times she refused to drink the cup of tea I made her. She would ask me to make her a drink and then she would complain." Jenna rolled her eyes dramatically. "Don't you agree? She's so difficult. So trying.

Such a pain in the bu—?" And when Leah stared at her blankly, Jenna continued. "Doesn't she give you hell?"

Leah shook her head. "No, and no, she's never asked me to make her tea."

"Are you still in the small office next door to her?" Confusion made Jenna's brows squish together.

"I'm still there, and not only has she never asked me to make tea or any other drink for her, she's never asked me to get anything for her."

"Never?" Jenna's face turned incredulous.

"Never." But it got her thinking why that might be. She hadn't been sick until a few months into her job. So, while Hyacinth had been demanding, and with a sense of self-importance in the beginning, all of that had changed soon enough. But she'd never given Leah any tasks to do like the ones Jenna had mentioned.

Leigh stacked all the dirty plates together. "She doesn't like you because Reed didn't name the movie theater after her."

"He named the pizza place after her," Jenna told her. Leah felt uncomfortable standing there as the women talked among themselves and seemed to forget all about her.

"So he did! I remember that." Merry laughed. She was wearing a large baggy jumper and Leah couldn't tell, couldn't see given the way she was sitting forward against the table with her arms folded, but alarm bells started going off in her head.

Merry was pregnant.

She had to be.

She couldn't see the bump, but the woman was glowing, looked as if she'd put some weight on her face. A sixth sense caused a shiver to trickle down her spine. Even if Meredith Nicholls wasn't pregnant *yet*, Leah was sure it was only a matter of time.

A wave of pity enveloped her. The past year for her had been awful; a nightmare that had unexpectedly crept up on her, and now even her son seemed distant from her. But for Merry, life had never been better.

"I need to rush, so … I'll leave you ladies to it," she said, eyeing the counter, and glancing at her watch.

"I forgot to tell you about Shay," Jenna cried. "She's going on another vacation."

"Again?" Leigh asked.

"She's always on vacation," Merry cried. "I'm jealous."

"Me too," Jenna said, slumping back in her chair. "Reed's always busy working."

"You get to go away," Leigh retorted. "What about the last-minute surprise trip to the Bahamas?"

The grin on Jenna's face widened. "I forgot. But Shay has been vacationing a heck of a lot more lately. What's with that?"

"Reed told Dylan that Blake's business is doing really well," said Merry. Leah slipped away discreetly, feeling as if they'd even forgotten that she as there. As she placed her order at the counter, the women were still talking animatedly among themselves. They hadn't even noticed that she'd left.

Or maybe they had, but they didn't care.

And why should they?

They weren't unfriendly, but they were together. A tight-knit group. A clique even.

She was of no importance to them.

She was a nobody, and now, she'd never felt more alone.

CHAPTER 6

He'd asked for a few days off after the funeral, but after Jackie left with her husband and their children, his mom's place was as lifeless as ever. It was eerily quiet, uncomfortably so.

He couldn't take it any longer, sitting around in his mom's empty house, going through her things, staring at the walls. Because staring at the walls meant looking at the photographs his mother had lovingly put up. Photos chronicling her life with their father and him and Jackie. Memories of a happy childhood and a time gone by, of childhood days filled with fun and laughter.

The photos had always been up, but it wasn't until he'd sat down on his mother's couch—the one on which she used to sit and read for hours—that he'd looked at them properly, and *really* seen then. Now he noticed them like never before. His mom and dad's faces smiling back at him made the truth all the harder to bear. It was an odd feeling to have no parents, and to suddenly be an orphan.

It would all be so very different from this point on; his mother would never again walk into this house, nor would he come over to visit her, or smell the delicious aroma of her cooking. He would never hear her tell him excitedly that she had made him his favorite meal.

He couldn't think of his mother and not remember the things she'd said to him, and how she'd kept hinting that time was ticking on, and that she wanted to see him settled down and have a family.

He'd let her down.

"You sure you're ready to come back?" Carlyle asked him. His boss examined his face carefully as they stood with their cups of coffee, ready to start the day.

"Yup." Brody lifted his cup to his mouth. "I'm good. You don't need to worry about me. I've got everything under control." Although he reported to Carlyle, who had overall responsibility for the project, Brody was in charge of the men. He wasn't as hands-on as he used to be, and seemed to spend most of his time dealing with admin and paperwork, as well as listening to the men's never-ending gripes.

"If you need to take time off, just let me know."

"I won't."

"Okay. If you're sure."

"I'm sure."

Carlyle nodded and walked away.

Brody had taken time off, not because he needed it to sit around and mope, because he wasn't the moping type, he was a doer. He'd taken time off to go through their mother's belongings.

He and Jackie were supposed to do that after the funeral, but a few days of sifting through his mother's things, of smelling her scent, touching her clothes, sitting on her bed, feeling her presence in the air and every room, yet knowing that she wasn't nor would she ever come back home, Jackie had broken down. She changed her mind and said she needed to go back home in order to grieve.

They'd agreed to take care of everything later on, maybe at

Thanksgiving or at Christmas time when they would all get together again as a family, only without mom.

A few days later, he was walking back to work after having bought a can of soda, when he heard what sounded like a loud argument near the steps of the town hall. As he walked closer, he realized it was the woman from the hospital.

Leah.

He kept running into this woman at the most unexpected of times and places. If he didn't know any better, he'd think his mother was looking down, causing mischief and matchmaking.

"I *will* pick you up," Leah demanded. She hadn't seen him yet, because she had her back to him, but her teenage son didn't seem to agree with her.

"I don't want you to pick me up," he snarled. "I want to sleep over."

"Not happening, Peter. I'll pick you up."

"Why can't I stay? Everyone else is. Why can't I?"

"Because I said so." She wiped a hand across her face, and all at once Brody could see that she looked weary.

"Why do you have to be so strict? Denny says it's okay. His mom says it's okay. Why do you have to be so strict?"

"I don't care what Denny or his mom say—"

"You don't mind when his mom helps you out by dropping me back home from away games."

The boy was rude, interrupting his mother like that. Brody watched, impatience bristling under his skin as he found himself unable to walk away and mind his own business.

"I don't want you to stay over," Leah shrieked back. "*I'm* your mother, and what I say goes."

"It sucks. Everything sucks," the boy yelled and Brody didn't like it. No one should speak to their mother like that. He never had.

"I. Don't. Care," Leah bit out slowly.

The boy walked away. "Peter! Peter. Don't you dare walk away. Don't you dare. I *will* pick you up at eleven," she shouted to her son.

Brody started to walk up the few steps that led to the entrance of the town hall. He was too close to them now to back away, and just as he turned to look away, Leah turned and stared at him; an embarrassed expression sweeping over her features.

"Midnight. Pick me up at midnight," he shouted back.

She turned around. "Eleven thirty."

The boy's nostrils flared and he quickly disappeared out of sight.

"I need Denny's address!" she shouted, but he had walked away. "Teenagers," she muttered under her breath; she was near enough that he heard. Her cheeks turned pink as she glanced at him.

She looked humiliated, but she had no reason to be. This was on her boy, not her. He was out of order to create a scene right outside her place of work.

"What are you doing here?" she asked him, the shakiness in her voice giving away her calm exterior. They walked into the town hall together.

"I'm working here."

She stopped, blinked, then side-eyed him. "You work *here*?"

"Here. What are the chances of that?" He tried to make light of the situation but her lips never broke out into a smile. Not only did she not look pleased, she made no attempt to mask her displeasure. "It seems we keep walking across one another's path," he said. If he'd thought meeting her outside the florist shop was bizarre, this took things to a whole other level.

"This so unusual. You working here, at the same place."

He gave her a smile. "I couldn't believe my ears when I heard your voice."

"I'm sorry about that. Peter is going through some sort of phase." She threw her hands up in defeat.

"You said he was thirteen?"

"In his head he's twenty-six, but in real life he's thirteen."

They laughed at that, and he noticed that she looked different today. Maybe being away from the hospital environment had something to do with it. Her big brown eyes, the color of dark melted chocolate, gazed up at him.

"That's right. I remember that's what you said. That's not an easy age to navigate."

They stared at one another, each waiting for the other to say something. The conversation stalled in an unfamiliar setting.

"My boss mentioned that there was work going on in this building. Is that what you guys are doing?" she asked.

He nodded. "The town hall needs a touch of refurbishment and new wiring, some plaster work, too. It's a very old building, and it hasn't been touched in decades."

"You'll be here for how long?"

He could read her face like a book, and it wasn't a happy story. She didn't look at all pleased and he wasn't sure what he'd done to elicit that reaction.

As far as he was concerned, he didn't mind that he'd run into her again. There was something about her, being there on the day his mom passed, and in the weeks before, and now, that made him curious.

He wasn't a superstitious man, nor prone to believing in miracles, but even he found it odd that they kept running into each other. "A couple of months, maybe a little more. It depends on how bad some of the plaster work is. How long have you been here for?"

"A while now. I work for … you wouldn't know her."

"Try me."

"Hyacinth, she's a—"

"The old bossy lady who struts around with her handbag and attitude?"

"That's the one."

He blinked. "You work for *her?*"

"She's not so bad once you get to know her."

"She's probably around the same age as my mom, but there's a world of difference between them. This one thinks she owns the place."

Leah's face turned somber. "Last time we met, you were getting ready for the funeral. Did it … did it go okay?"

"As well as funerals can go."

She squirmed. "Sorry, I didn't know how to ask."

"That's okay."

"I still can't believe it. It happened so fast," she said, as if reading his mind. There were days when he woke up and for a few blissful moments, he forgot that his mother was no longer around.

"One minute she was here, and then the next she was gone," he said, agreeing. He shoved a hand into his pocket.

"Cancer will do that to you." Her gaze stretched far away into the distance. He sensed she had slipped up, given away more than she had intended.

"Is that what you were there for?" he asked softly, surprised to hear her confession. She'd kept a lid on her illness, and he'd never known what she'd had. She turned her head towards him, not nodding or acknowledging his question.

"I feel better now that the radiation treatments have stopped. I hope they caught it all."

His interest piqued at the roundabout way she had answered his question. "That's a good thing, Leah. Hell, that's a great thing."

"Time will tell. With this disease, you don't really know." A hollow sadness touched her voice.

"You're going to be okay. You're young."

Leah looked at him, fear flashing across her eyes. "Age has nothing to do with it. We're all living on borrowed time but some of us don't know it until something like this happens."

"You make a good point." She was far too serious and contemplative, like his mother had been recently. Maybe that's what happened when people were forced to confront their mortality.

"I never thought about death much before, but now I find myself thinking about it all the time."

"But you're better now," he said, trying and failing to find something that might cheer her up, or at least deflect her attention from this depressing topic.

"For now," she answered, far too breezily for him to believe that she was okay with it, talking so casually as if it didn't matter. "This disease lurks and lingers, and it weakens you. It mutates your cells and wreaks havoc inside, and then the treatment for it poisons you even more." Her voice tapered off, and he could hear the worry in it.

"Hey." He moved closer, touching her arm, wanting to provide her some of the comfort she so desperately craved. No longer was she a complete stranger to him. Now, she was someone who was clearly hurting, and someone who looked very much alone.

In a flash, her expression changed. "Look at me, getting all whiny and complaining. I'm sorry. You're the one who needs comforting, not me. You're the one who lost someone close to you. A mom. I don't know why I went off at a tangent. I don't usually talk to anyone about this."

"Maybe because we shared something?" He couldn't think of the right word. Being in the hospital, going through a difficult time, there was something about their shared experience of being at the hospital together—him with his mother, and Leah suffering alone—that bound them together, like cement. Solid and hard. A wall of comfort. "We do keep running into one another."

"That's true."

He felt touched that she had been able to say what she had. The idea of her not having anyone to share her news with couldn't have been easy for her and if she felt she could open up to him, it could only be a good thing.

"People survive from this thing," he told her. "What happened to my mom isn't going to happen to you. My mom caught an infection. It wasn't the cancer that killed her."

"I worry about Peter, about leaving him all alone."

All alone? She had no husband, then? "You won't." He seemed more sure of that in this moment. He didn't believe that someone as young as her would not come out of this just fine. She was maybe in her early thirties, he guessed, which made him almost a decade older than her.

"How can you be so sure?" she asked, staring up at him.

"I … just …" he shrugged. "Sometimes you have to have faith."

Then she blinked and snapped out of it. "That's what Hyacinth says," she puffed out. "She talks about faith a lot."

"Is that your boss woman? I didn't think we had anything in common."

"Apparently, you do."

He'd made her smile, and that had to mean something. "We're two people who are going through a bad time, Leah."

She pressed her lips together, and he wondered what thoughts she was trying to keep inside. "But your loss is greater."

They said nothing for a while, and then he looked out into the distance. It didn't seem right that his mom was buried, and he was continuing with life. Only last night, he'd gone to his mom's place to keep an eye on it and make sure everything was intact. He found it sad being there and he couldn't wait to leave.

"The workmen started work here last week, but I haven't seen you here until now."

"I took some time off. Jackie and I needed to go through Mom's things, and then she found that she couldn't deal with it just yet. The kids were getting restless, time off school and all that, and they had nothing to do. It all became too much, and Jackie wanted to be alone to grieve."

"How many kids?"

"Four."

"Four?" Her eyes almost popped out of her head. "Here's me struggling with the one."

"Jackie always wanted a big family. Dealing with my mom's estate took a toll, especially as it was so soon after Mom passed. So, Jackie went back."

"Went back?"

"To California."

"You don't live together?"

He wasn't sure what to make of this. "She's my sister."

"Your sister? Oh, I assumed she was your …"

Now he understood. "My sister," he replied firmly. "I have two nephews and two nieces, and my brother-in-law was here, too. I could cope then, and by 'cope' I mean I could get up, make coffee, eat. The busyness of the day helped, as you can imagine trying to keep four kids aged from eight to fifteen busy is quite a task, especially when you're numb inside and trying to get to grips with what's happened."

"I can imagine."

"Jackie found it difficult, so she went back, leaving me to deal with things. Problem was I couldn't stare at the walls much longer. Couldn't sit in my mom's house and her not to be there. It was surreal. I kept thinking any moment now she would walk in."

Leah's eyes grew large as she listened, seeming to hang onto his every word. "It must have been so difficult."

"It was. I had to come to work. I had to do something." It was easy talking to her, telling her, even though a part of him didn't understand why he was in full-blown confessional mode, pouring out his life story.

He was usually a reserved man. Talking to strangers, and women, no less, about private matters close to his heart was something he never did. He was more broken than he realized.

"I understand that. It's why I used to always go back to work after the hospital appointments, even though Hyacinth told me not to."

So that was why she'd said she needed to go back to work. He hadn't before been able to figure out what was wrong with her, but discovering now that she had cancer, he looked at her with admiration.

"Keeping busy helps," he agreed.

She glanced at her watch. "I should get back."

He could have talked to her for hours. Something about her not being family, but being loosely connected through their mutual experience, seemed to bring them together in a weird way.

CHAPTER 7

She had palpitations in her chest by the time she returned to her desk. For the next twenty minutes, she couldn't focus on anything, or even eat her sandwich. Instead, she sat at her desk, going through the conversation with Brody.

The idea that Brody was working in this same building was somehow exciting and left her a little on edge. Their conversation had turned deeper faster than she'd intended. She never told anyone about her cancer, aside from Hyacinth and Denny's mom, and that was only because she'd absolutely had to.

Now she'd gone and told a complete stranger. Yet, Brody didn't feel like a complete stranger. Talking to him came easy. It was like confiding in a friend. To think that she'd even shared with him her fears about death.

He'd even overheard her arguing with Peter.

And she'd discovered that the woman she'd seen him comforting wasn't his wife, but his sister.

He hadn't spoken of having anyone else in his life. Everything he'd told her pointed to him being by himself, just like she was. Now that she knew he didn't have a wife, she wondered why he was still single. She assumed he was, but she could be wrong.

Tall, broad-shouldered, a good few years older than her, and yet rugged, rough and well worn, he was a catch. He looked sexy even in his dirty work clothes, and with that tool belt around his waist, her imagination started to wander.

She gave her head a quick shake. This line of thinking would lead to no good. The pre-cancer Leah would have been scheming by now. She would have taken running into this man as a sign that he was meant to be in her life.

But she was a cancer victim now.

Survivor.

She'd had cancer, and had hopefully beaten it.

But she didn't know from one day to the next what the future held, and she couldn't risk getting involved with anyone. Peter was her focus now, as well as her need to stay fit and healthy.

A man like Brody … she had to forget. Post-cancer Leah had only one thing in life to do, and that was to survive.

By the time she'd come home from work, the house was empty. Peter had left and gone to Denny's house early, hours before the party. He hadn't called her, nor had he checked the text messages she'd sent him to confirm that she would be picking him up at eleven thirty as planned.

She ate the leftovers from last night's dinner watching TV. As the hours went by, she kept checking her phone, and calling and messaging him, but to no avail. The time for picking him up approached, and with it a sense of panic when she realized that her son hadn't given her Denny's new address.

The family had moved to a new house a few months ago and she had no idea where they now lived. She called Denny's mother and left a message on the voicemail, asking for their new address. Shame crawled over her that she was so out of touch with everything in her son's life.

As time wore on and she didn't hear back, she wondered who else to call. She knew a few of the other moms, but she hadn't called them in years. Once kids reached a certain age, mothers didn't keep in touch, unless they were friends, and she wasn't friends with anyone. She felt more out of the loop than ever.

Frustrated and anxious, she called Andrew's mom. Peter had been friends with Andrew for many years, but she wasn't so sure they were now because she didn't recall Peter mentioning him much.

But it was almost midnight and she didn't know what else to do. She called and then panicked when a sleepy-sounding person answered. She'd woken them up. Feeling guilty, she slammed the phone down, not having the heart to explain who she was and why she was calling them at this time of night.

She paced the room. Her lack of friends, and the shock of not knowing much that was going on in Peter's life, hit her like a shockwave. She'd been so consumed by her illness—had been desperate to keep as much of it away from Peter—that she'd been in her own little world. She'd wanted to protect her son from the ugliness of her disease, but she'd ended up failing him instead.

Scratching her head, wondering what she should do, she picked up her keys, but she couldn't leave because she didn't know where to go. When her cell phone rang, she rushed to answer it, desperate to hear the sound of Peter's voice.

"You called my number?" The gruffness at the other end startled her. She looked at her cell phone, at the caller ID. It was Andrew's mother's number, but this was a man's voice.

"I'm sorry. It's Leah, Leah Shriver, Peter's mom. Our boys went to school together a long time ago. I'm sorry to call you so late but I was wondering if you know where Denny lives? He's having a party tonight and I don't have the—"

"Lady, we moved away a year ago. Andrew's at another school."

"He is?" The air whooshed out of her lungs. "I'm sorry for waking you up—"

But the man had hung up and she was talking to a dead line. Feeling weary, she sank onto the couch and lay there. She didn't dare call anyone else, and instead racked her brains trying to figure out what to do next.

She checked her phone again to see if Peter might have miraculously checked his messages, but he hadn't.

That boy.

Rage bristled under her skin. She couldn't wait to give him a good talking to. But in the meantime, she had to leave him be and hope that he was okay. She was being overly protective.

If Peter wanted a sleepover after a party, was that such a bad thing? Why not let him stay the night at his friend's place?

But he was only thirteen.

Teens experimented and did all sorts of things at that age. Worry wrapped itself around her neck like a piece of rope.

She didn't want him to stay over, it was as simple as that. Yes, she was a clingy, needy mother and more so lately, but he was her only child. What was the worst that could happen, aside from drugs, and alcohol and sex?

Her mind roared into overdrive.

Peter was a normal healthy teen.

Which meant he would have interest in alcohol and drugs and …

No, no, no.

She couldn't think of that. Those thoughts didn't help. She called him again, and then again and then a few more times after that. In a pique of frustration, she threw her cell phone at the other couch but it bounced off and landed with a thud on the carpeted floor.

She would wait up for him. That's what she would do. That's all she *could* do.

She picked up her phone, and sat back on the couch, putting a blanket over herself as she settled down to watch a movie to take her mind off things, but all the while, she was on edge as she waited for her boy to call.

It was the cold that woke her up the next morning. She rubbed her eyes and shivered under the flimsy blanket. She was still on the sofa, and she'd slept through the night. She bolted upright, grabbed her phone and checked. No calls from Peter. He still hadn't read her messages.

Fear coursed through her veins. A whole night and Peter was still out. In a panic, she called him, and then her heart dipped when she heard his phone go off upstairs. Jumping off the couch, she raced upstairs and pushed his door wide open.

Peter was asleep in his own bed.

She let the phone ring, her insides roiling with rage. In his bed, her son stirred, his hand reaching out for the phone to turn it off.

She called again, and let it ring again.

This time his eyes opened. "Mom?"

"You came home and you didn't even tell me?"

"You were asleep." He yawned loudly.

"But I was waiting up for you," she cried. She was happy and relieved that he was here, safe and in his own bed, but she was also foaming at the mouth with rage, and his further disinterest and lack of knowledge about how much he'd worried her fueled her anger.

He rolled onto his side, turning his back to her. She prodded him, her fury making her finger jab harder than she'd intended.

"Mom!" he yelled, turning around and sitting up. "What's wrong with you? Why are you bugging me?"

"I waited up all night for you. I called and texted you. I didn't have Denny's new address. How was I supposed to pick you up?"

"I was at a party."

"And we had a deal for me to come and pick you up."

He slid under the bedspread, hiding his face.

She yanked it down.

"Leave me alone, Mom! I'm tired."

"You're tired now, are you? I was worried. I was worried *all* night, and you didn't even care."

"I was having a good time. For a change."

"What's that supposed to mean?"

He pulled the bedspread back up again under his chin. "I wanna sleep, Mom. Can't you let me sleep?"

"I was worried about you!" She hadn't meant to shout, but this careless, self-absorbed boy didn't seem to care that she'd been so worried she'd fallen asleep on the couch. "What time did you get back? *How* did you get back?"

"We got a lift. Someone else's strict parent picked them up from the party and gave me a lift home."

"What time?"

He shrugged. "I dunno. Maybe three."

"THREE?" she yelled. "We had a deal."

"But you didn't come to get me."

"And how would you have known? Were you waiting for me outside? You didn't pick up my calls. You didn't read my messages or else you would have known I didn't have the address."

"I set my phone to silent and left it in my pocket all night. We were having a good time. I deserve to have a good time, don't I?"

"Yes, you do, but I didn't want you to sleep over, Peter. We had a deal, and I asked you for Denny's new address before. I haven't been in contact much with any of the moms. In case you hadn't noticed, I've had things to deal with."

He gave her a poison dart of a look which make her insides curl.

"What?" she barked, her anger getting the better of her. "Why are you looking at me like that? You have no idea how freaked out I was. Denny's mom didn't answer and so I called Andrew's mom for the address and—"

His face turned angry. "Andrew? What'd ya go and do that for?"

"Why do you think? I needed Denny's address."

"He left the school, you'd know that, if you weren't so obsessed about your own problems. You'd know what was going on in my life."

His words froze her to the core. Venom dripped from Peter's words, and if looks could kill, she'd be curled up and lifeless on the floor.

She was so shocked, she forgot to speak. Her anger melted and was replaced by quiet worry. What had happened to her sweet little boy?

"You should sleep," she said, moving towards the door. She didn't know what to make of him and his outbursts. Overnight, he seemed to have turned into a monster. He didn't say a word but turned his back to her again.

Deflated, she went to her bedroom and crawled into bed. It was still early morning, and she needed to catch some quality sleep.

Even though she was in her comfy bed with a warm bedspread, she couldn't sleep. She couldn't get her son's angry expression out of her mind.

It was almost as if he hated her.

CHAPTER 8

He'd visited his mother's grave at the weekend, and sat there silently for a while, contemplating the vast void she had left behind.

Other than that, he'd spoken to Jackie. Worked out a bit. Done some work on his place, and gone over to his mom's house, just to make sure everything was in order. An empty house had to be watched over. He'd need to keep doing this until he and Jackie decided what to do with the place, which had once been home but now it was only walls and empty rooms.

When Monday came around again, he couldn't wait to get back to work.

"Good weekend?" Carlyle asked as he poured himself a cup of coffee from the pot.

"As good as." Brody waited his turn to get his coffee.

"Okay, then."

He liked that none of his fellow workers made small talk. He preferred things that way. Would he see Leah today? He'd been thinking about her and wondering if he'd run into her again. It was highly likely given that they now worked at the same place.

He didn't know whereabouts in the town hall building she was, other than that she worked for the bossy old woman.

But two days passed, and still he hadn't seen her. Yet, come midweek, his luck turned. As he stepped out of the town hall, he caught sight of her ahead of him. He rushed to catch up. "Hey."

She turned, her eyes growing round and large. "Oh, hi!"

"Haven't seen you around here lately." He had slowed down to match her stride.

"I've been here all the time. I haven't seen you either."

"I've been here." They smiled at one another. It was good to run into her again. Memories of his mom surfaced. "Where do you work exactly?"

"Next to Hyacinth's office. On the ground floor. Why?"

"Just wondering." Though it was a pointed question to ask.

"I guess you're all over the building."

"All over it, like a rash."

She frowned at that.

"Your boss wants us to get our work done super fast and be out of the way."

"Hyacinth is worried about optics. But you guys have a job to do, and I'd be more concerned that it was done safely and properly, so you take all the time you need."

"I plan to." He continued to walk, but wasn't sure where she was going. It didn't seem to be in the direction of the stores and he wanted to get his lunch from the diner.

"No fixed office then, huh?"

"Unfortunately, no. I'm not an office guy." He waved his hand at himself, indicating his dirty clothes. He'd removed his helmet and tool belt before coming out to lunch. "I tend to be a handyman walking around in dirty clothes fixing things."

Her eyes started to rake down the length of him, but she stopped, giving him a half-hearted smile. He didn't mean for her to think he was coming onto her. He wasn't. It was nice to have someone to talk to. She was familiar, and at this point in his life, it was comforting to be around someone like that.

"Office work is overrated." She stared ahead of her, giving him a chance to admire her side profile. Her soft wavy chestnut brown hair fell around her shoulders. She looked well, and if he didn't know any better, he would never have guessed she'd ever been sick. "Don't you like what you do?"

"I love what I do," he answered. "I'm thankful that I have a job."

"You sounded defensive about what you do, so I was just saying …"

"Ah. You were taking pity on me." He grinned.

"I was being empathetic." She stared up at him with a hint of amusement in her eyes. She was short, and with his huge frame, he towered over her.

He was glad he'd run into her today. She added a touch of something different to his otherwise boring day. "Where are you going?"

"I was going to the beach, to sit down. I sometimes have my lunch there because it's nice and peaceful."

That sounded like a good idea, only he didn't have his lunch with him, and he didn't want to ask her to come along with him so that he could buy some, in case she said no and he lost the opportunity to talk to her. "Mind if I come along? A walk by the beach sounds great."

"Be my guest."

So, they walked towards the seafront together.

"What happened with your son? Did you pick him up from the party?" He'd even thought of her on Friday night and was curious to know how that event had played out.

"That's a whole other story," she groaned.

"Not good?" He braced himself.

"It didn't go well at all. It turned out even worse than me going to pick him up."

"What happened?"

"Do you have time to hear me whine and moan?" she asked.

He laughed. "It isn't whining and moaning if you're offloading to a friend, even an acquaintance," he added quickly.

"I suppose you deserve to hear what happened, seeing as you heard our argument." She sat down on one of the empty deck chairs along the seashore. He joined her then waited as she pulled out a small package from her bag. She unwrapped the tin foil and hesitated before pulling out what looked like a sandwich. "Did you already eat lunch?"

"I … eat at odd hours. I had a bacon and egg biscuit for breakfast. I'm good for now." He was starving, and that bacon and egg biscuit had been consumed early in the morning. "Tell me, what happened with your son?"

She recounted the story of how she didn't have the address of his friend who was having the party, and how she'd called up another friend's parents at midnight only to discover that the kid had left the school years ago.

"No way." He cringed on her behalf.

"Yes way. The boy's father hung up on me. I don't blame him."

"What did you do?"

"I called Peter a million times but he didn't pick up or read any of my messages. I got more and more worried as time went by."

She proceeded to tell him how she'd woken up in a panic, realized it was the next day, called her son and heard the phone go off upstairs.

"He had it switched on the entire time?" That boy seemed to be putting his poor mother through the ringer.

"I don't know. He said he'd put his phone on silent the entire time I was trying to get a hold of him, but on Saturday morning it clearly wasn't on silent because I could hear it. I don't know what to believe sometimes." She told him how her entire weekend had been ruined because her son was in a mood with her. "He said he didn't want to wake me, so he left me sleeping on the couch."

"I can understand that."

"You can?" She turned to him, her eyes questioning. "But I was worried about him. The least he could have done was woken me and told me he was back."

"But you were sleeping, and you wouldn't have been the wiser." He could see the boy's point of view. She was sleeping. Why bother to wake her up and tell her that he was back? He would have done the same as Peter, but he wasn't thinking like a mom, and his mom would have reacted the same way that Leah did.

"I know he's growing up, and he wants to be independent, but he doesn't seem to like me much at the moment."

"I'm sure it's his hormones. You did what any mom would do." He tried to reassure her and make her feel better, because she looked completely downbeat at the moment.

"Maybe I'm being overprotective? He is thirteen, after all, and on the cusp of wanting to be independent."

He scratched his jaw. That might be so, but the boy still had no business talking to his mom like that.

Leah sighed and set down her barely eaten sandwich. "I'm just … ever since I got sick, I want to hold onto him. I feel as if I lost control with my own life, but I can at least hold onto my boy." She took a nibble of her sandwich.

He could see that she was worried. "I understand that. I do. You don't have to feel guilty for being a good mom."

"You think I'm a good mom?"

Her question took him by surprise.

"You sound like a good mom. You're setting boundaries,

you're concerned. You want to know where he is and you want him to be safe. Yes, you're a good mom." Had nobody told her?

Her eyes turned glassy; so very slightly that he wasn't sure if it was the sea wind or something else.

"I don't know anymore. He seems to have become angry and bad-tempered, ever since I started going for my treatment. I thought he'd be more understanding."

Brody had been thinking about this very thing. He didn't have children, but he had an idea on what that might be. Anger was sometimes fear clothed. It wouldn't surprise him at all if the boy was scared, but didn't have the words to tell his mom that's how he felt. "He's probably going through a phase, as you said. Teens, boys especially, have a lot of stuff going on with them at this age. Lots of feelings and emotions that are new. He's maybe also scared."

"Scared?"

"Of what's happening to you. It's scary for a child, even though he's a teen, to see his mom going through treatment like you did. Cancer scares people. I was scared when we found out that my mom had it, and I'm a grown man. I'm supposed to be strong and be able to handle it."

Her brows pushed together. "I hadn't thought of it like that. He does seem very angry with me."

"Maybe he's worried about you as much as you're worried about him."

She seemed to like this idea. "That would explain a lot." Her eyes twinkled with relief. "You'd be very good at parenting."

He laughed. "I have four nephews and nieces, remember. We don't see each other as often as I would like, but when we do, I get my parenting practice in."

"You never thought about it?"

"About what? Having kids? Nope. Never." Not even when he'd had his nephews and nieces around. To want to have kids, well, you had to have someone you wanted to have them with, and he had yet to meet such a woman.

An unpleasant silence fell.

"What did you do on the weekend?" she asked.

"I visited my mom's grave. I was at her house cleaning up and checking in on things. I missed her, and I wanted to be close to her, so I went to the cemetery."

She gave him an apologetic look. "It's peaceful there, I bet."

"It's peaceful, and pretty. It gave me space to think, out in the open. Like this." He nodded at the sea. "This is nice."

"I come here a lot."

At least he now knew where to find her.

"My mom and I used to talk, after she was diagnosed, and she would say that her body had been good to her all her life, but now that this was happening, she felt as if it didn't belong to her anymore. What with the chemotherapy, then being sick, she felt like she'd given up ownership of her body to the doctors. So, I understand a little of the demons you might have been battling, and I don't think you should be hard on yourself about being a mom."

She lifted a bottle of water from her bag, and still had the sandwich in her other hand.

"Want me to get that for you?" he asked, reaching out. She handed it over and he unscrewed the lid then handed the bottle back to her.

"Thanks." When she'd finished drinking, he held his hand out again, screwed the top on and kept a hold of it. She ate slowly and it seemed to be taking her forever to get through that small sandwich.

"Sounds like neither of us had great weekends."

"It does, doesn't it?" she agreed.

"Did you go to Hailey Ross's movie premiere when it was

held there a few months ago?" he asked, seeing the Knight Movie Theater in the distance.

"Peter wanted to go, and yes, we did."

"You were there?" It seemed strange now, to know that she had been there with her son and he'd been there with his mother.

"A premiere in Starling Bay with one of Hollywood's biggest stars? Of course we went. Peter didn't want to admit that he was excited, but I could tell that he was."

He chuckled. "Hailey Ross seems to be every teenage boy's dream, I guess."

Leah made a face. "I imagine she is. Yours too from the sounds of it?"

"Hailey Ross is a little too young for me. I'm forty-one," he told her, giving her information she probably didn't want, but in case she was wondering.

"But you came anyway."

"Because of my mom."

"Your mom?"

"She said she'd never been to a premiere before, and it seemed like the perfect opportunity given that this was on our doorstep. We went and Reed Knight gave us tickets. You must have heard of Reed Knight?"

Leah rolled her eyes. "I don't think it's possible to live in Starling Bay and not know of the Knights."

"His company refurbished the movie theater."

"He's named it after himself," she pointed out.

"He spent a lot of his own money on it."

"You're defending him!" she cried.

"I've done a lot of work on his properties, not just his mansion, but the guy owns plenty of properties around here and neighboring towns. A guy like me earns good money doing all these extra jobs."

Something seemed to go off in her brain and she stared at him as if she was going to ask him something. He had that reaction when he told people what he did.

"That's good to know," she said slowly.

"What needs fixing? I'd be happy to help."

"Nothing."

He tilted his head. "Nothing?"

"Nothing." She smiled and finished off her sandwich.

"If you ever have anything wrong with your place, and need anything to be fixed, you can let me know."

"I'll bear it in mind. Thanks."

CHAPTER 9

"Ou didn't contribute anything towards this trip, Tom. Not a cent."

"I can't. Be a bit more understanding, will you? We need to buy things for the new baby."

"The new baby isn't here yet and it won't be for a few months. Peter's trip is in a few weeks. I've paid for all of it. I don't ask you for much, but a little something from you would enable me to buy him a few things he needs."

"What more does he need? And why did you leave it so late?"

"I was preoccupied at the hospital. Not that you'd care." In the background, she heard his wife calling him. That woman always found a way to cut short his conversations with her.

"Go running to her," she snarled. "Be the little lapdog. I had to put up with you being the bulldog."

"That's not fair."

"Life isn't fair, Tom." She hung up.

"Was that Dad?"

She turned around in shock. She hadn't even heard Peter walk in. "It was. How long have you been listening?" She hated for him to know just how stingy his father was becoming, though she had an idea that her son knew.

She sighed as she stood up, knowing that she could put it off no longer. With Peter's school trip coming up, she needed to buy a few things for him but she'd been waiting for the sales to start at the outdoor store. The problem was the store hadn't run a sale yet. Now she'd have to go shopping and buy those things anyway.

"What did he want?" Peter growled, his tone startling her.

"Nothing, sweetheart."

"You needed some money and he wouldn't give it."

She clenched her jaw. He'd heard everything. "He's a little tight for money at the moment, what with the new baby on the way …"

"But he lives in this great big house with all the latest cool stuff, and you should see his new car."

"I don't want to know, Peter. Please don't tell me these things."

"But he's living like that and he left us this shitty little—"

"It's a roof over our head. Let's be grateful for that."

"You haven't seen his new place. You don't have to see his new life with his new wife and his new kids."

Peter didn't know it, but his words landed like punches.

"He's got a good job, doesn't he?" Peter asked.

"He was high up. He was always traveling a lot."

"Is that how he met her?"

Her face clouded over. "How do you know this?"

"Because I've got ears, Mom. I hear things. You think I'm a child, but I'm not. I'm growing up."

She needed to say less, especially when she was talking to her ex. In the past, she hadn't been able to hold back, and Peter had obviously heard her arguing with him on the phone. It was rare for their conversations to be amicable. She still hated him for falling for the secretary in the Arizona office.

"We've got a home, Peter. It's a lovely home. Be thankful for that."

"Lovely? It's falling to pieces! Look around you, Mom. He left us this shitty little house—and…"

"Peter!" Shock rippled through her. Not only was he miserable, he was ungrateful too. "You will not use such words, do you hear me?" She hadn't brought him up to speak like that. Taking a deep breath to calm her nerves, she told him, "You don't appreciate what you have."

"It's been like this forever. The paint is peeling. My room is horrible. I can't ever ask my friends over for a sleepover because so many things around here don't work."

"What doesn't work?"

"The light switch in my room, for one."

"I'll try to get things fixed maybe when you go to your dad's at Christmas." She didn't want to promise him too much. The calendar months to her were no longer about the seasons and events, but about going the distance, in weeks and months, and staying cancer-free.

"I don't want to go there. This summer was bad enough, I'm not going there for Christmas. Or Thanksgiving"

"For a few days, maybe?"

"I don't wanna go at all." He sounded dead set against it. "He doesn't care about me."

"He loves you. You're his son. He does care about you."

"No, he doesn't, Mom. Just like he didn't care about you. That's why he left. He didn't care about us, and he still doesn't. And with this new brat on the—"

"Peter!"

"It's true. He's more interested in his new family."

She didn't like him when he was like this. A volcano waiting to erupt. "You can't use that word. Not for a baby, Peter. Children and babies are pure."

"He hates me, Mom."

She watched her son's face turn ugly. "If you don't want to go, you don't have to."

She yawned. Today had been a long day. She didn't have the energy to make dinner, but she had to. There was no slacking off for the single mom. "I'm going to make dinner, it won't take long. Half an hour max."

"It's because of him that you're sick."

Her son's words roped her back into the room. "What?" Where was this coming from. "Peter, that is not true."

"Stress causes cancer," he maintained.

She scoffed at that. "We don't know what causes cancer. This isn't your father's doing, Peter. I don't want you to blame him for what happened to me."

"You're always working, even when you went to the hospital you'd go back to work afterwards—"

"Because I could. I had radiation therapy, and it didn't make me so sick that I couldn't get back to work. Hyacinth has been good to me."

"Denny's mom says you're a hero."

Her eyes almost popped out of their sockets. Denny's mom was the only school mom she had told about her illness. This little compliment boosted her spirits. "Me? A hero?"

"She says it can't be easy, and you still do all the things."

"Not all the things. I don't take you to your games at the weekends." Partly because with working, and fitting in the treatments, she left all of her household chores to the weekends.

"That's no big deal. Denny's got a mom *and* a dad, they can do that between them."

CHAPTER 10

"He was complaining about the light switch again," Leah explained, as she pulled an apple out of her bag.

Call it luck or good timing, but he'd seen her on one of the benches around the front of the town hall as he went to get his lunch with a work colleague. He ditched the colleague and went to talk to her instead.

"Who was complaining?" he asked, curious.

"Peter. I think he was in a bad mood because he heard me on the phone to his father asking for his help."

"Help?"

She was about to take a bite when she stopped. Her eyes shuttered down as if she'd said too much. "About … him … not contributing as much to Peter." Her words were guarded, the information hesitantly given.

"I'm sorry."

"It's not your problem. I hate that Peter overheard me. His relationship with his father is strained. It's not Peter's fault, but I want him to have a father figure. A boy needs someone to look up to." She took a bite of her apple, then chewed thoughtfully for a while. He waited.

"But Tom never bonded with him from the start," she said. Then jerked her head back, her regretful eyes searching his. "I have never said that out aloud. Please don't ever mention that to anyone. I don't want Peter to ever know."

He rushed to reassure her. "Of course I won't. I would never."

She'd said too much, and now she regretted it. Whenever he was with her, there seemed to always be something floating between them; a current of electricity, or knowing, something he couldn't put a name to. It was as if he'd known her for much longer than he had, because he found it so easy to talk to her and, as she'd just shown, she did too. She'd overshared without meaning to.

She groaned. "Peter has a school camping trip coming up and I need to get him a few more things. I was asking his father to pay for them."

"Camping trip?" He tapped his chest. "I have some almost new camping equipment."

She gave him a dubious stare.

"I swear. You can come home with me now and check if you don't believe me. I bought it for Jackie's kids this summer, but my mom got sick so they didn't go camping in the end. But they used the tent and camped out in the yard. Peter is welcome to borrow whatever he wants."

"Are you sure? He doesn't need a tent. The school is providing those, but he doesn't have a lot of the other things."

He lifted his hands, palm out. "What am I going to do with it? Yes, I'm sure. It'll make me happy to know it's being used."

She sighed as if a huge weight had been lifted from her. "Thank you. I'll let him know. I'll make sure he brings it back clean and as good as when you lent it to him."

"Sure." He scratched his chin. "What's wrong with the light switch?"

"The light switch?" Her brows knitted together. "Oh, the light switch! It sometimes takes a while for the light to come on after you've pulled the cord."

"You've got one of those?" Brody asked, surprised that they had something so old. "I didn't think many places still used those."

"We live in an old-style house. Nothing has been updated, but it's home. Though the way Peter was complaining, you'd think we were on the streets."

He sensed another disagreement between them. "He was complaining about that? Why?"

She bit into her apple and chewed for a moment. He much preferred spending time talking and listening to her than any of the guys he worked with. He no longer saw her as a stranger. They might not have known each other before, but they were getting to know one another now. She was someone he could talk to about his mom—not that he did it too often. The wound was still raw, and he was still cut up about her passing.

At least Leah knew about his mother, and she was empathetic, and listened. It was the thing he needed.

"Sometimes when he pulls it, it gets stuck. I don't know if I'm explaining this well."

"You are. I know exactly what you mean."

"It's a minor thing, but—"

"I can fix it for you."

She was about to lift the apple to her lips again. "I didn't mean to tell you so that you'd fix it. I was just telling you because—"

"It doesn't matter. I'm an electrician. I can fix these things with my eyes closed."

She seemed to hesitate.

"It won't cost a thing," he told her, hoping to push away any concerns she might have.

The grimace on her face told him he'd messed up. "I can afford to get it fixed. I just never got around to finding anyone who could do that."

"I'm your man."

The line between her brows deepened. He was so not saying the right things.

"What I need is an electrician," she said, as if she needed to make that distinction.

"As before, I'm your man. That's what I do, Leah."

"Okay. I'll pay you the going rate. No favors are needed."

He understood. "Deal. I can fix it, if you want me to."

"Let me think about it."

She still needed to think about it?

"I don't want to be a burden."

"A burden? How can you be a burden? I'm only offering to fix the light in Peter's room. I'm not offering to rebuild your house."

"Leah." They both turned.

"Hey, Heather." Leah's voice was guarded.

"What are you doing?" Heather asked.

"Having lunch." Leah bit into what now remained of her apple. The moment stretched out to an uncomfortably long one. Brody smiled back at the woman who seemed unable to shift her gaze away from him.

"This is Brody, he's, uh – one of the guys who—"

Heather flashed him the biggest smile. "I've seen you around. You're one of the workmen."

She was making a move on him. He could tell by the way her eyes roamed over him and lingered over his biceps ravenously. He took it in his stride, sat back, cleared his throat. "I am."

"How about you come over and take a look at Peter's light?" Leah asked him suddenly.

"You've made up your mind?" That was fast.

"If that's okay with you."

"You know it is. Happy to take a look."

"Are you coming back?" the woman asked Leah. She stood there, like a rod in the ground, stubborn, inanimate and refusing to move.

"How about we go for that walk now?" he suggested. He could see what was going on here, and he was willing to turn things up a notch, or four.

Leah stared at him, then blinked. "Uh…"

"You said after your lunch." He watched in amusement as her reaction went from confused to irritated.

Two could play that game.

If she was going to put on an act for Heather, he was more than willing to help her. Even if she didn't look all that happy about it.

She got to her feet slowly, wrapping the apple up in her sandwich waste, ready to throw into the trash. "See you later," she said to her friend as the two of them wandered off. "What walk?" she hissed, when they were out of earshot.

"This walk." He smiled to himself as they headed towards the beach. "Isn't this view pretty?" He looked out at the shimmering water. Leah wasn't looking at that. Her eyes were boring into him. "What are you doing?"

He stopped and turned to face her. "Tell me what happened just now?"

"N-nothing happened."

"You instantly changed your mind about the light. What's that about?"

She pursed her lips and stared at him defiantly.

"I get that you wanted to make her jealous—"

"Jealous?" She laughed. "W-what makes you think … I mean, why would I—"

Her incoherence told him enough. "Then let's rephrase it. You wanted her gone."

"She can be annoying. Interrupting our lunch and refusing to move."

"Yeah," he agreed.

They didn't say a word, but walked along the seashore on their familiar path. "This is nice," he said finally, watching the expression on her face.

"It is nice." She faced the sea, and took a long breath in.

"You don't have to pretend to be my boyfriend."

This shock out of nowhere tasered him. "I'm not pretending to be your boyfriend."

"What you did in front of Heather…"

"She wasn't moving. I sensed she was irritating you. Was she?"

"She wasn't there because of me," Leah replied pointedly. "You must get that a lot, women flocking to you."

"I can't say that I've noticed." He wasn't going to give her the book on it; women did have a thing or ten about a man in dirty working man's clothes, and tool belts and helmets, too.

Had he used this to his advantage in the past?

Did men have red blood?

Heck, yes. He gotten hit on of plenty of times and he considered it a working hazard. Sometimes, he'd ended up in a short-term relationship, lasting as long as the work at any particular site lasted.

But as a rule, he didn't like to mix work with pleasure. He scratched his stubble, which was getting way too itchy. He'd have to find the time to have a proper shave tomorrow. Too bad he hadn't been sleeping too well ever since his mom had died.

"You never got married?" she asked.

"Never." It had never happened because he hadn't met anyone he saw himself spending the rest of his life with. For that to happen, it had to be one hell of a woman. "What happened to you and Peter's dad?" If she was asking him personal questions, then he was going to do the same.

"He was a workaholic. I was the homemaker. And when a man spends a lot of time working, and doesn't come home much, and you have a young child on your hands that he doesn't seem too interested in, that man isn't worth holding onto."

"I'm sorry to hear that. For your sake and for Peter's."

"I'm not. He's happy now. He'd met someone when we were still together."

"He cheated on you?"

"I guess."

What sort of an answer was that? Either he did or he didn't.

"Shall we head back?" She didn't like the questioning, and the probing into her personal life, but she shouldn't have asked him anything in the first place.

"I'm sorry that happened to you," he said, his jaw tightening at the thought.

"I have sworn off men," she said, mistaking his silence for a need to explain. "I don't need them, and I won't let anyone treat me the way my ex did. Peter deserves better."

You deserve better.

No one ever knew what went on behind closed doors, but what he had come to know of her made him feel sorry for her. Hearing her son talking to her like that didn't sit right with him, and especially not when she was recovering from an illness. The poor woman needed a break.

"I'll come over and fix the light. You just let me know when."

CHAPTER 11

"Hey," he said walking into Leah's kitchen. Her son stared at him as if he were an alien. "You must be Peter."

"Yeah." The boy's voice gave gruff a new meaning. Leah braced a smile.

"Peter, this is Brody. He's going to fix the light in your room."

"Why?"

Brody shuffled as he looked around the kitchen. He could see what she meant about her awkward and unfriendly teen. Leah smiled at him apologetically. "Because you were complaining about it. It gets stuck sometimes, right?"

"But it's been like that for ages."

"That's way too long," Brody answered, setting his toolbox on the floor. "I can fix it so you won't ever find it to be a pain in the butt." The boy continued to eat what looked like the biggest plate of pasta he'd seen.

"He's just come back from a game of football at the school."

"You play football, huh?" he asked the boy.

"Yeah."

Talking to him was like getting blood out of a stone. "Are you okay for me to go into your room, Peter?" he asked, wanting to get the boy's permission. Teen boys could be territorial like that.

"Yeah."

He thought it was a 'yeah,' though it sounded more like a grunt.

"I can show you the way," Leah said brightly. "Did you clean your room, Peter?" she asked, a tightness in her voice.

Another grunt.

"Let me show you to the room," Leah offered, leading the way. He picked up his toolbox again, since he clearly wasn't going to get much conversation out of the boy. "I don't want this to take up too much of your time."

"I told you I don't mind." He followed her to the boy's room where Leah opened the door, her gaze quickly scanning the room. Clothes lay in small piles on the floor. She looked horrified. "He said he'd cleaned it up." An angry frown drew lines on her face. She rushed to the boy's unmade bed and hurriedly tidied it.

Brody chuckled. "This is probably his version of clean. I wouldn't worry about it." He pulled the pull cord, and it took a while before the light came on. "I see the problem. Do you have a ladder?" he asked.

"It's in the utility room. I'll go and—"

"I'll get it," he said smoothly. Her mind was on her crotchety boy and the mess he'd left. Clearly, she was embarrassed, but she had no reason to be. He wanted to put her at ease, not have her running around like an anxious doe. "Just tell me where it is."

"I'll get it for you." She was stubborn too. Didn't like to depend too much on people. He shrugged, then followed her. The ladder was almost as tall as her, folded down. He reached for it and carried it back, then busied himself with his toolbox. This wouldn't take long at all.

"Are you going to watch me?" he asked, seeing the way she was staring up at him.

"No." She almost jumped back, shifting her gaze away, but not before he'd caught her checking him out. He smiled inwardly. He wasn't in his work clothes today, but was wearing a clean pale blue T-shirt and dark jeans. The tee, hanging out, showed off his physique more than his work clothes did. He'd spent a few seconds longer than usual deciding what to wear today.

"I'll be … uh … I'll be in the kitchen. Call me if you need anything."

He smiled to himself and got on with the job.

Her heart was giving her palpitations as she left Peter's room. The big man climbing on the ladder looking so cool might have had something to do with it.

It was impossible not to notice the expanse of his shoulders, and the way his torso narrowed to a V at his waist. She could tell, even though his T-shirt wasn't tight, but the way it hung on him, the way his biceps and triceps and all kinds of ceps filled it out, wasn't lost on her man-starved psyche. He was the sexiest forty-something she'd ever seen.

She was about to mention to Peter that his room was a mess, but she didn't want to get into an argument with him, not while Brody was in the room next door.

Luckily, her son offered her a great solution. "I'm going out with Denny and the boys." He stood up and looked at her. "If that's okay," he added tentatively.

"That's a great idea." It would be good for them both. She reached into her purse and pulled out ten dollars. "Here you go. Have some fun."

He balked, refusing to take it. "It's okay. I still have some left over from the money you gave me before."

"Take it, sweetheart." Money was tight, but she worked hard, and they were getting by. They were more than getting by. She waved the bill at him.

He shook his head. "I don't need it, Mom."

She ground down on her teeth. "I'm sorry if I make it sound as if we don't have a lot of money. We don't have a lot, but we have enough."

"I don't care about the money."

"Then what is it? Why are you always so angry?"

But he'd moved away to grab his jacket. She rushed to his side. "Take the money, please. I'm on a good thing working for Hyacinth. We're okay now." They were, compared to how things had been before when she'd had odd jobs, doing a few hours here and there. A steady nine-to-five job with all the perks had been a game changer.

She'd been lucky to get it because staying at home and raising Peter, being a homemaker, made for an empty resume. Meanwhile, her husband was thriving. The early years hadn't been easy. She'd hit gold finding work at the town hall, and Hyacinth didn't seem to care so much about her empty resume.

Peter looked at the bill and took it. "Thanks, Mom."

After he left, she started cleaning up the kitchen. Brody was quiet and she didn't get a peep out of him, but the thought of him in the other room made her body temperature rise. She tried to keep herself busy, otherwise she'd do nothing but think about him and get all hot and bothered for no reason.

No reason.

The lie poked its great big nose at her in jest. She'd always wanted to have someone in her life, someone to share it with, someone who was kind and good, sexy and good-looking.

And now here was such a man, in her home, fixing her son's light. He ticked all the boxes.

But now the timing wasn't right. She didn't want anyone in her life. She couldn't. Not like this. Not while she was recovering from cancer. It wouldn't be fair.

When she'd finished cleaning up and the kitchen was spotless, she leaned back against the countertop.

"You look as if you've got a lot on your mind." Brody walked in with his toolbox in his hand. She looked up at him, and forced herself not to give him the once-over, again.

"Are you finished already?" Her hopes deflated like a dying balloon at the idea that he was leaving.

"All done. Told you it wouldn't take too long. Come and see."

She followed him into Peter's room. He'd replaced the pull cord. She gave it a tug and the light came on immediately.

"That's wonderful. Thanks so much."

"Not a problem."

"Thanks for coming to fix it on a weekend."

"Glad to be of help." He leaned against the door jamb, her gaze darting to his muscles and imprinting the outline of his bicep on her brain. She forced her gaze back to the pull cord, as if it was the most interesting thing in this room. For added emphasis, she pulled it a few times. "It's great. Thank you. How much do I owe you?"

He let out an exasperated gasp. "It really didn't cost much. I had a spare cord lying around."

"Lying around?" She eyed him with suspicion. He moved out of the way, clearing the way for her to leave the room. She headed into the kitchen where she reached for her purse again. "That's not fair, Brody. I won't ever ask you to fix anything for me again if you don't take payment."

"Leah… this isn't needed. It's a simple cord."

"And your labor? That must account for something."

Ten dollars? He felt silly taking ten dollars from her, and as for his labor, as if he had anything better to do this morning. "How about you buy me lunch one day?"

"Buy you lunch?" she cried. "That doesn't sound like a fair exchange."

"Why not? I like your company." He held up his hands. "I heard what you said the other day about not looking for anything." He shrugged. "I'm having a hard time getting over losing my mom and the truth is, talking to you makes everything seem a little brighter."

She forgot to breathe. His words fell on her like sunshine, warm and comforting.

"It was unexpected, and it was quick. I feel like I've been punched in the stomach, and the punches keep coming. But you, spending a few lunchtimes with you makes it all seem a little bearable."

Was that a confession? He was telling her something, no? It wasn't just normal banter. This meant something.

He needed her. He liked her company. He wanted to be her friend. This was something new; something to be cherished. She wanted this, too.

"Can I at least give you some payment?" The price of a sandwich didn't seem to be a balanced compensation fee.

"How about we sit down and eat at the diner?"

"Sit down at Roxy's?" she asked, the idea was as strange as fish flying through the air.

"We've walked along the beach. I feel like I know that stretch of land like the back of my hand. How about we try something different?"

"We could sit down," she answered slowly. It was a simple enough request. Nothing grandiose. And yet …it felt ... odd to her. Sitting down at a table with Brody. A man she barely knew.

"That would be better than a sandwich by the sea," he said.

"It would?"

"Yes."

"Lunch at Roxy's then, one day next week."

Sit down with him, over lunch, only the two of them? The thought caused her heart to swell with joy.

CHAPTER 12

"Ｔhis place is always busy these days," she said as they walked into Roxy's Diner. "It's because of that show on TV, the one about the chef, what's his name, Mason something or other."

"I know the one. I think they finished filming just as we started working at the town hall," he told her. "Did you watch it?"

"Did you?"

They stared at one another, an understanding becoming clear in a split second. They'd both had a lot going on to pay much attention to such things. She watched TV, but none of it went in. She'd tune into soap operas and romcoms, but her restless mind would soon wander.

"We can grab a sandwich and go to the beach." Brody's gray-blue eyes resting on her.

They could do that. But he hadn't taken payment from her for fixing the light, even when she'd insisted. All he'd asked her for was lunch. It was the least she could do.

She hesitated, but felt free, exhilarated, as if she were riding a wave she was scared of but wanted to. After the last horrendous few months, it was exactly what she needed.

Just as they were hovering around the door, three tables of people got up and started to get ready to leave. As some of them filed out one by one, she saw an empty table by the window.

"There's one." She pointed to it, and soon enough, they were both sitting down. A few tables away behind Brody, Dylan, Merry and one of their friends were sitting together. She couldn't stop staring, and she was sure she'd heard the other guy, a familiar-looking man whose name she didn't know, mention something about sleep deprivation. Cocking her head, she tried desperately to snatch snippets of their conversation; she was sure she heard mention of a baby. This news caused her insides to riot.

She reached for the menu and opened it, but her gaze kept going back to the happy trio.

"Someone you know?" Brody asked, a hardness to his voice that she hadn't heard before. She couldn't tell from the way Merry was sitting, but her eyes were riveted at the happy trio. "Leah?"

She darted her attention to Brody.

"Do you want to go over and say 'hello'?" he asked.

She laughed nervously. "No."

"Your menu is upside down."

She laughed even more nervously, then turned it right side up. "Silly me."

Brody shut his menu and put it down. "You seem more interested in their conversation than in anything I have to say."

"I know them, the couple sitting together."

Brody turned to look. "Then go over and say hello."

"I don't know them *that* well." She knew of them, and they knew of her, but they weren't in one another's friend groups.

"If you don't know them that well, then why are you so obsessed by them?" Brody growled.

His tone made her jolt back in shock. He sounded moody and miserable, nothing like the Brody she knew.

"Why are you so grumpy today?" she asked.

"We had to see the lawyer about mom's will. I hate dealing with stuff like that."

"I'm sorry." This was a man who was grieving, and sometimes she forgot that. "I'm sorry, Brody."

He waved his hand dismissively. "We should order."

"Yes. We should. We don't have long."

"Does Hyacinth go on the warpath if you're a few minutes late?"

"Hyacinth has been very good to me," she told him as the server came over to take their order.

They talked about the weekend and what they'd been up to. He opened up some more about his mom and how Jackie was dealing with things, and that she was already dreading Thanksgiving and Christmas.

"She's thinking about it already," he groaned.

"She's probably dreading it because your mom isn't here. It can't be easy for her, processing what's happened and having to move on with life knowing that the people you love aren't here."

He eyed her for a few long, silent seconds, as if she'd made him think of something. "I guess … yeah, maybe that's it."

"You weren't angry with her, were you?" Peter couldn't empathize with her illness and her fears, and Brody seemed to have the same kind of problem, albeit that his situation was slightly different.

"I'm not heartless. I listened, but I'll take your advice on board."

She smiled. If she could help him, in any small way, it made her feel good. "Peter is happy with the light."

"Glad to hear that."

The server brought their food over as a peal of laughter from Dylan's table snapped her attention.

"You look as if you'd rather not be here." Brody speared his fork into his baked potato a little too harshly. Her gaze had strayed to the other table again, and she'd been trying to catch snippets of their conversation. "You're listening to their conversation."

She looked at him with guilt. She couldn't deny it. She was. "They're being loud."

"Why don't you join their table?" he suggested. An underlying irritation hummed beneath his words.

She sensed a subtle shift in their dynamic. Somewhere between their meeting outside the florist shop and now, they'd gone from being politely civil strangers, to this; they were starting to have opinions and feelings about each other.

Brody was a good-looking man. She had tried not to see it, had tried to push the idea out of her mind, but sitting in front of him, having lunch across the table from him, she couldn't help but notice this more strongly than ever.

The old Leah would have jumped on a man like this and dug her claws in from the get-go. She'd been so needy before, she hadn't been successful, and maybe that was the problem. Her neediness had deflected men away.

But ever since meeting Brody, and the circumstances of their meeting, her neediness was shot to pieces, like the cancer with the radiation. Just when she hadn't had the mental capacity to think about a man, he'd come along out of nowhere and at a time when she didn't want company, but needed it.

"I don't want to join their table."

He slid her a disbelieving look.

"I'm sorry."

"You say that a lot."

"Don't get annoyed. Please don't. I'm sorry about you having to deal with your mom's will."

"Some things have to be taken care of."

A peal of laughter from Merry's table made her glance over at them again.

"I think you'd rather be with your friends than here with me," he said, his voice hard.

She lowered her gaze to her food and toyed with it. "That's not true."

"You haven't stopped eyeballing them. Why don't you go over and say hello?" She couldn't tell if he was mad about it or okay with it. She glanced at Dylan then looked away. The diner owner, Roxy, had gone over to their table, which resulted in more laughing and talking.

"That's wonderful," she heard Roxy say. Merry had her back to her so she couldn't see and confirm her suspicions.

"Leah, seriously?" He set down his cutlery.

"How was your baked potato?" she asked, toying with her tuna niçoise.

"Amazing, just amazing," he replied sarcastically before picking his fork up again.

How was it possible that they were bickering already? Was he moody? Miserable? Controlling? Fear took a hold of her heart and gripped it tightly, making her breath hitch sharply. She was reminded of the fact that she hadn't known him for too long.

They ate quietly. Between the pair of them, they made a miserable-looking couple. She hurriedly wolfed down her food. This wasn't at all how she had envisioned their lunch going.

From the periphery of her vision, everyone at Dylan's table got up. She heard the banter between them, heard Roxy congratulating them on their news again and then the other man and Roxy went over to the counter.

Leah lifted her glass of water to her lips as Dylan and Merry walked past, and that was when she saw that Merry was very big and very pregnant.

She almost choked on her water. She'd been right all along.

Merry was pregnant.

Brody's gaze pierced into hers. He looked angrier than he

should have, and she didn't understand why. Unable to hold her gaze, she looked away, straight at the couple who now stopped at their table because they'd caught one another's eyes.

She wished she hadn't looked their way. It would have been so much simpler to pretend she hadn't noticed them.

"Leah." Dylan looked genuinely happy to see her. Given his news, she imagined any happy parent-to-be would be ecstatic.

"Hi." She forced a sweet smile, then acknowledged Merry who also said 'hi.'

The other guy had walked over to the counter with Roxy.

She introduced Brody to them and vice versa.

"Have we met?" Dylan asked Brody. "You look familiar." Brody flashed him a smile.

"We probably have. I work all over the place. I'm an electrician first and foremost, but I double as a handyman."

"Maybe I've seen you at some of Reed's properties."

"Reed Knight?" Brody asked. "I know Reed. Yeah, I've done lots of work for him before."

This newfound link caused the two men to fall into an easy conversation. Merry looked at her shyly. "How are you, Leah?"

Dying. Worried, scared, lonely. Harsh thoughts lasered through her as she struggled to find the right answer. She didn't want to tell Merry that she felt jealous and wished she could feel happier for her than she did. She'd also forgotten her manners in the current rush of brain fog.

"Congratulations." She nodded at Merry's bump. "That's wonderful news for you both." She glanced at Dylan.

"Thank you," said Merry as Dylan slipped his arm around his wife's waist protectively. Leah's gaze swallowed it all up. From the corner of her eye, she felt Brody's eyes on her.

"It's wonderful news. I wasn't sure that time I saw you at the bookstore," said Leah.

"Yeah, congratulations," Brody echoed, shaking Dylan's hand. "Is this your first?"

"No," Merry replied. "I have a daughter from … before." Dylan's arm gripped her waist again. "But it's *our* first."

"We have a daughter, Chloe," said Dylan. "I'm a proud adoptive dad, and now we're going to double our children."

Merry made a face. "That sounds weird."

"But true." The deeply-in-love couple exchanged another adoring gaze. They didn't stare too long, or too longingly, they didn't need to. Even their fleeting glances reflected their deep love for one another. It was the way they were together. It made others feel the void that was missing in their lives. Leah felt this more sharply than ever.

Merry stroked her stomach lightly, proudly, tenderly. "We're so thrilled." Dylan's eyes filled with pride. A heaviness settled inside Leah and sadness collected in the pit of her belly.

She was happy for them. Watching this couple as intently as she had been, their love shone so clearly, so brightly, her overactive imagination didn't need to fill in the blanks. Merry and Dylan were meant for each other.

"It's wonderful news," Leah said again, after all, what else was there for them to talk about? Nothing could top news as lovely as this.

To think that she had hated this woman once. This stranger from Boston who had come here and claimed the man that Leah had had her eyes on. But watching them together, it was obvious that they were soulmates.

"When's the baby due?" she asked. Time had become a barometer of life. The cancer had made every second be meaningful. Every second counted. Mattered. Was hard won. She sometimes tortured herself by thinking about events that had yet to happen and wondering if she would be there to see them.

"Around the time of our one-year wedding anniversary, around Christmas," Dylan announced proudly.

"It seems to be a good time of the year for us now," Merry said, more to her husband than to the rest of them. Dylan moved his head closer to her, sharing an intimate moment that relegated her and Brody to the background.

"You mean that?" he asked her, in a voice so low that it was a miracle she heard.

"I mean that," Merry answered, her voice almost a whisper. "It's been like that ever since I first came here."

Then, as if they suddenly realized that they weren't alone, they turned and faced them. "It's nice to see you," said Merry. "We'll let you get on with your lunch."

"We're finished. Don't worry about that," Brody told her, something in his tone indicating that he was glad that he'd reached the end of the meal.

"See you around." Dylan lifted his arm as a parting gesture. Her eyes were still on the happy couple as she watched Dylan open the door for his wife. A baby this Christmas. How wonderful for them.

"You must have bionic ears," Brody said, giving her a dubious look.

She laughed, plastering a smile on her face. "Don't be silly."

"It must be part of a woman's skill set, eavesdropping on conversations."

"A woman's skill set?" She took a sip of her water, trying to calm herself down now that Merry and Dylan had left.

Dylan adopting Merry's daughter. A baby on the way. A lovely way to celebrate a one-year wedding anniversary. All the good things.

"Did your previous girlfriends have that skill set? Is that why you're referring to it?" It was a barbed retort, but she didn't like the idea of him thinking of her as being nosy. Even though he'd be correct, as in this situation.

"A few did."

A few? The idea of him with another woman, a *few* other women, pricked her more than it should have. She still couldn't comprehend why he'd never married.

Brody would be a great catch.

For other women.

She realized that when she saw the way other women gawked at him as she walked with him.

Big, strong, handsome, kind and thoughtful, too, with a hint of grumpiness thrown in. He would make someone happy.

She hadn't noticed this about him before, and now that she'd had time to think about it, she knew the reason why. The hospital visits had been laden with fear and worry and she hadn't had the presence of mind to notice much. Let alone a man who looked like Brody.

But lately, in her unguarded moments, she found herself thinking about him, and at times like this, when he was in front of her, staring at her like he was right now, it was impossible not to be mesmerised by those blue-gray irises.

"It always got …complicated," he answered, almost reluctantly.

"Complicated?"

She was aware that she was prying, but since they were talking about these things, it might be her only chance to find out things about him. How much more could they talk about Starling Bay, and the places to get lunch, and Peter or Hyacinth?

"It never happened."

This man also spoke in short phrases, that didn't tell her much. It was almost like talking to Peter, at times

"What never happened?"

He raised his arm and glanced at his watch. "We should get back. It's coming up to an hour."

That's how it was, was it? Mention of his personal life and he was ready to hightail it?

She sat back in her chair, wanting to know. "Hyacinth won't mind, and I'm sure you told me your boss was being lenient with you on account of your mom…"

He lifted his face, his strong jaw drawing her attention. Her heart leapt for joy. Strong jaw, a few days' stubble. His hair longer than she had ever remembered it. Salt and pepper, giving him a sophisticated, seasoned air, until you saw his work clothes; dark and dotted with dirt and dust, and goodness know what stains all over them. Big boots, too.

Enormous.

He didn't look like a fresh-faced young man, because he wasn't. He was older, wiser, seasoned and strong; a man who fixed things, who strutted around with that tool belt around his waist, fixed things.

An action hero of sorts.

Everything about Brody spelled masculinity, power and strength. He had protector written all over him. When he looked at her like that, her blood pooled south. Words and sense flew out of the window.

"What never happened?" she managed to ask.

"I never met anyone that … I guess … I was with for more than a few weeks or maybe—"

"A few weeks? You had hook-ups?" she blurted out, her mind racing to fill in the blanks. Her heart fearing what those blanks might be.

"Or months," he said, his voice quiet and a scowl on his face. She wished she hadn't been so judgmental. "I'm not that kind of man."

"Of course not." She shook her hand through her hair, her nerves frazzled beneath her calm exterior.

"You said you didn't know them too well, your friends," he said, gesturing with his hands towards the door through which Dylan and Merry had left. "But they seemed quite friendly. Which one's your friend? I'm assuming it's Dylan."

She didn't understand the question and pretended to gloss over it. "We should go." She looked over at the counter.

"So soon? You said Hyacinth is easy on you."

She clenched her jaw and eyeballed him.

It seemed they both were dancing around this conversation and neither one of them wanted to answer specific questions.

But silently, they got up and she settled the bill at the counter.

CHAPTER 13

This lunch hadn't been at all like he had imagined it would be.

Somewhere along the line, things derailed. It was odd, because up until now, he and Leah had been getting along just fine. Things were getting so familiar and comfortable between them that he looked forward to seeing her.

Carlyle was good to him, but the work on the town hall was routine and boring. He didn't like overseeing refurbishments and rewiring jobs. He liked getting his teeth into something meaty, like a new build that needed everything. Still, it was a job, and one for which he was thankful.

Going home in the evenings sucked, but Jackie and the kids would video call him almost daily and that added some lightness to his otherwise dreary day.

He didn't have much else going on, and he didn't have anyone else to share his thoughts with. It wasn't as if he could go to his mother's house and have dinner, tell her about his day and find out about hers.

Leah provided a way out of the dark tunnel. She didn't come

onto him, she was sweet, and headstrong, and interesting. She made a better lunchtime companion than his work friends.

Until today, things worked out well. He wasn't looking for romance, and neither was she, and that lent an easy vibe to their growing friendship.

She was a good listener, and easy to talk to, which was why he'd had such high expectations for their lunch.

But those expectations had been shot down almost immediately when they stepped foot into Roxy's. Leah hadn't been interested in making conversation with him and couldn't help herself from listening to the people at the other table.

That's when it dawned on him that he'd been an idiot. She'd gone to lunch with him because he hadn't given her another option. She'd done it because she *owed* him.

He didn't want or need anyone's pity, least of all hers.

"You go on ahead," he told her as they started to walk back to the town hall.

"Where are you going?"

"I need to make a call."

She detected a touch of ice in his voice and when he avoided eye contact, she didn't believe him at all.

"Oh, okay." She tried to read his expression, but it was like a blank wall. "Lunch was nice," she said as he was about to walk off.

"Yeah?" And before she could say another word, he walked off.

Lunch had been abysmal and Brody wasn't pretending otherwise. She often told Peter that there were two types of people—the radiators and the drainers. The drainers sucked your energy, such that after you had been in their company, you walked away with low energy, feeling downcast and deflated.

Maybe once upon a time, she had been a drainer.

The other type of people were radiators. They made you feel good all over, as if you could do anything. When you spent time with a radiator, you walked away energized and upbeat, your insides lit up like a flame.

She'd started to think of Brody as a radiator because he made her feel upbeat and her heart sometimes missed a beat or three when she saw him. Maybe her stomach flipped, once or twice.

But this lunchtime, the energy fizzled away leaving her feeling drained. He'd been quiet and moody, and their time together was tense.

Looking back, she realized that it had been her fault. She was so caught up in Merry and Dylan that she'd neglected him. She didn't think he'd notice, but she was obviously not so good at being sneaky.

If Brody paid more attention to people at another table instead of her, she would have felt insignificant. She would have been angry with him, too. She slumped back in her chair.

This was no fault of Brody's. He was annoyed with her and rightly so. He was so annoyed that he couldn't even bring himself to walk back with her.

She returned to her desk feeling down and sorry for herself. All she'd had to do was be in the moment, and be grateful that someone like Brody wanted to have lunch with her.

Instead, she'd ruined what could have been a great time for them both.

He'd been harsh. Walking off at the end, refusing to talk to her properly. People had bad days. He'd had a bad day, and maybe Leah had, too.

He relented, and before the day was over, he made his way to the part of the building where Leah's boss resided. He tried to remember what Leah had said about where she sat, and he wasn't sure if she was one door down from her boss or a few. Some of the doors were closed, and not all of them were numbered.

He knocked on a few doors, but there was no answer. He didn't even have Leah's phone number.

"Can I help you, young man?"

The hair on the back of his neck prickled to standing. He turned around and found himself staring into the face of a woman who was wearing way too much powder. So much so that it was the only thing his gaze fixated on.

"I'm looking for Leah."

"In what regard?" the old woman asked him. His eyes swept over her bouffant hair, light brown but more silver than brown. He shrugged. He'd be damned if he was going to tell her.

"Where does she sit?" He pointed at the door nearest to him. "This one?"

"I can help," she ignored his question. "What seems to be the problem?"

"There's no problem. I just … uh … wanted to talk to her."

She peered at him, deep rivulets rippling out from the corners of her eyes. "You are one of the workmen."

His hands went to his hips and he widened his stance. "Yes." He was usually polite to people, but he didn't like the way she appraised him, nor did he care for her tone.

"I'll talk to her tomorrow." He turned to go.

"Now that you're here, young man, you might as well make yourself useful."

He turned around and scowled. "I'm going back to work."

"I have a problem with the fluorescent light in my office."

"Ma'am, that's not my problem to deal with."

"You work for the company we have employed to take care of our refurbishment. Of course it's your problem."

"Yes, but—"

"In here, young man." She waggled her stubby little finger at him as if he were a child and disappeared into her office.

Because he wanted peace of mind, and to get the heck away from her, he obliged.

CHAPTER 14

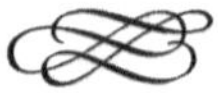

"What are you making?" The sound of Peter's voice, asking a question, no less, made her turn around.

"Pound cake."

"Pound cake?"

"So called because you need a pound of everything to make it. Flour, sugar, butter and eggs."

"It smells nice." Her son peered through the oven door while she stirred her chicken Alfredo.

Today must have been her lucky day. Peter had given her more than two words. Sentences, even.

"You can try some in a minute."

"You've made two cakes. You don't usually make *any* cakes."

"I used to make cakes, before ..." Before she got sick and making cakes wasn't a priority anymore. "It's for a friend."

"Who?"

"The guy who came over to fix the light." She watched his expression turn quizzical. "I thought he might appreciate it." There was no need to tell him that this was some sort of peace offering.

An apology.

She'd come home earlier than usual, causing Hyacinth to worry. She asked her if she was okay because Leah never went home early.

The more she thought about lunch today, the more obvious it became to her how rude she'd been paying so much attention to Dylan and Merry.

It was a mild obsession of hers, but one which was slowing slipping away now; a comparison of her and Merry's lives. She felt ashamed of being so wrapped in other people's business that she'd lost sight of her own.

She needed to fix that. She had a one-month scan appointment at the hospital tomorrow, and then, all being well and good, she would make a conscious effort to enjoy her life.

For now, she needed to do something for Brody to show him she was sorry. Lunch was supposed to have been her payment for him fixing the light.

"Do you like him?"

She almost dropped her wooden spoon. "What? No! I'm baking a cake because he was … he fixed your light."

"But you paid him for that."

"Uh …" She hated telling him lies, even little white ones, but she didn't want to have to explain that her payment had been lunch, because then she'd have to explain why she was now making him a cake on top of that.

There was too much explaining, and she and Brody were only friends. Right? "He lost his mom. He mentioned that she used to make pound cake and he loved it. I thought it would be a nice thing to do."

"How old was his mom?"

"Older than me." She glanced at Peter and saw his expression turn contemplative. She could almost hear the cogs whirring in his brain as he processed this news. "She was much older. She was a grandma."

Peter stared at the simmering pot, and frown lines crossed his smooth skin. Her son had the tiniest, faintest dusting of a thin mustache. A few zits popping up on his skin, too. Her once cherubic, cute and cuddly little boy was going through puberty.

Something in her heart snapped. Sadness iced over her, dark thoughts breaking through. She didn't know how much time she had with him. Healthy people never gave these things a thought, but she'd confronted these demons. The hourglass of life was now a constant visual in front of her eyes. A reminder that life was transient, could be fleeting, and was not guaranteed.

She wanted to be here forever, for Peter. She couldn't have forever, but she wanted to be around for when she could babysit her grandchildren. Brody losing his mother pressed upon her that nothing was for certain.

Forever wasn't a right. Things could go wrong. She'd looked it up online and discovered that young women died from breast cancer. They didn't always catch it and stop it from spreading.

What if *she* didn't make it?

She busied herself with clearing away the countertops. Peter saw his father twice a year and now he didn't even want to go at all.

If she died, where would he go?

To his father?

Or to her parents?

"Is he married?"

"Who?" She turned around slowly, lost in thought.

"The guy who fixed my light."

"Brody. He has a name, Peter. No, he's not married."

"Does he have kids?"

"No."

"Why not?"

"I don't know," she cried. "He's nice, but I don't like him. Not like that, in case that's what you're thinking." She felt the color rushing to her cheeks and started to get out the plates. Anything to avoid facing her son.

"Then why are you baking him a cake?"

"I told you. To say thank you." To apologize for not being present at lunch, but she didn't say that out loud. "It's what people do, when someone has done something nice for them."

"You see him every day?"

What was this? Two thousand and fifty questions before dinner?

"I see him at work, yes." She dished out the chicken Alfredo. "You don't talk much usually, and then all of a sudden, you have all these questions. It's only a cake."

"You've never made anyone a cake before. Just saying."

"Can you take these over to the table and get out the jug of water, please?" The timer went off, and she pulled her cakes out of the oven. They smelled heavenly and had risen perfectly. A rich, buttery, sugary aroma floated in the air.

"Do you think I should shave?" Peter ran a hand over his smooth jaw, and she noticed a smattering of hairs when she peered closer.

"I think, maybe wait a while?" The hairs on his face were so fine, they were barely visible.

"But Denny shaves, and so do a couple of the others."

"You're all going to get hair growth at different rates. I don't think you need to start shaving yet. I mean," she paused to think. What would Peter's father say? She didn't know. As a woman, she didn't know what advice a father would give, but she was Peter's mother and father figure all in one. She had to have all the answers. "Do you think you're ready to shave?"

He shrugged. "I dunno. Maybe I'll wait."

"Just a while, maybe."

"Can I have some cake after?"

"*May* I have some cake after? And yes, you may."

It wasn't such a bad day after all. This was the longest conversation she'd had with her son in a long time.

The next day, she strode into the town hall, carrying the cake she'd baked for Brody in a small bag.

She had baked first and thought about how to deliver it to him later. She wasn't sure how to get it to him and as she walked through the building to get to her office, she'd run into a few workmen. They were all dressed identically to Brody, though not all of them wore tool belts, and only some wore helmets. The problem was from a distance they all looked the same.

Brody had mentioned that the men had a small area at the back with temporary bathrooms and a small kitchen area, and that they often gathered there.

It was into this area that she walked and felt immediately conscious of the stares that greeted her.

But there was no missing that broad back and those hard-as-iron arms. She caught sight of him talking to someone. As if he'd known that she was looking for him, he turned around, his face breaking into confusion, before softening to a smile. He walked towards her.

"Are you lost?" he asked, giving her a cryptic look.

"Not at all. I specifically came looking for you."

"Why's that?"

"I baked something for you." She handed him the bag. "It won't be anywhere near as good as your mom's but I tried my best."

His face lit up, and he didn't even look in the bag. "You made pound cake for me?"

She nodded, the surprise on his face priceless.

"Leah," his eyes met hers, shining with happiness. "You didn't have to."

"I wanted to."

"Thank you." He peeked inside the bag. "It's all wrapped up."

"I wanted to make sure it would stay intact."

His face melted into a heart-warming smile, and the memory of yesterday's awkward lunch was instantly erased.

"This is really kind of you."

"It's for yesterday. At lunch. I was rude."

Still carrying the bag, he led her away. She was grateful to be away from prying eyes, and out of the view of the other workers. "Rude?"

"Listening to the conversation at the other table."

"Oh, that," He shook his head as they faced one another in the corner of a hallway. "Don't worry about it."

She owed Brody an explanation because he'd been good to her. In a town where she sometimes felt as if she didn't belong, Brody made her feel a part of it. Yesterday she'd ruined what should have been a pleasant time for them both, and now she had a duty to explain. "She moved here a couple of years ago."

He blinked, not understanding. She lowered her voice and looked away as a couple of workmen walked past. "You could say I'm in awe of that woman."

"Hyacinth?" When his brows snapped together, she was forced to explain.

"Meredith. Merry. Dylan's wife."

"Why are you in awe of her?"

His tone made her wish she hadn't started. She'd backed herself up into a corner and there was no way out of it without explaining, yet how could she without making herself sound needy and desperate?

"Don't judge me." She closed her eyes and squeezed them tightly for a few seconds. "I used to like Dylan, once."

Brody's eyebrow lifted a few millimetres.

"He was in charge of the Christmas pageant and Peter used to take part. I'd tried for a long time to get Dylan to notice me. I wasn't the only one," she said quickly; hearing herself say this out loud sounded worse than in her head. "The other mothers all thought he was hot, too." She couldn't gauge Brody's reaction but noted that a muscle flexed along his jawbone.

Her insides turned queasy. This was harder than she had thought. Not just hard, but cringeworthy. She was a grown woman, and she was confessing about a crush.

Talk about pathetic.

She pursed her lips together and stared at him.

"Go on, I'm listening." Either he was going to burst out laughing, or he would avoid her from this moment on. Nothing good would come of it.

She winced.

"You might as well tell me," he pressed, as she struggled with the weight of her explanation. She should have handed him the cake and walked away. But she'd started now, so …

She braced herself. "Nothing was ever going to happen, he didn't even notice me, and then Merry came along, all the way from Boston, with her daughter in tow. She was taking a break, so the rumors went. She didn't like Christmas. I think her husband died or something."

His expression dulled. "Poor woman."

"I know. Sad story." She drew in a long breath. Making this confession felt strange, but without it, Brody wouldn't understand her compulsion to eavesdrop yesterday. It seemed more important for her to let him know that she wasn't a nosy woman.

Just sad and pathetic.

"Merry came along, it was supposed to be a short Christmas break and she was supposed to go back to Boston after, but she came, she conquered, and she stayed. Somewhere along the way, they fell in love and got married, and now … now they're having a baby. That's why I was preoccupied. I couldn't help but overhear—"

"You were being nosy."

"I call it 'eavesdropping.'" She faked a smile. But a part of her felt lighter, as if she'd confessed to a priest. "I could hear them talking excitedly, and I kind of suspected she might be. And she is."

"You are obsessed by her."

"I told you."

"Are you not happy for them?"

"Of course I am. I *am* happy. I can see they're so good together."

"And Dylan ..." His eyebrows raised slightly, his cool gaze assessing her.

"I'm not dreaming about Dylan Fraser anymore, believe me. I'm not. That stopped soon after Merry came on the scene. It's just that ..." She looked away, pausing to consider her words carefully. "Life feels unfair, sometimes. Really unfair. It sucks like that."

She might have sounded jealous, but she wasn't. Not of Merry, not anymore. She was sad and feeling hopeless for her life, and for Peter's.

Gone were her dreams of finding someone, and maybe settling down one day; of giving Peter a family, and of making their future safe and secure.

Cancer had opened her eyes to the fragility of her life. Of how she was the only one on whom everything depended. She was the breadwinner, the caretaker, the person responsible for her son.

Everything she did, it always came back to Peter.

He was her life, her world, her everything. He didn't know it, this testy thirteen-year-old boy, but he was the epicenter of her world, and the idea that she might not have as much time left with him broke her every time she thought of it.

What ate her up most of all was not knowing if her body was cancer-free. She worried that the poison was lurking again inside her, and that it was only a matter of time …

Living in fear was no way to live. She looked at Merry and wondered what having that kind of life would be like.

"It sure does," he said, agreeing.

"It's been a difficult time for you as well," she said, realizing she'd been so caught up in her own problems, she hadn't thought that he might be hurting too.

"Takes some getting used to."

She waited for him to say more, but the man didn't speak as freely. A shiver rolled through her and she wondered if he was judging her, seeing her as clingy and desperate.

A weak and lonely woman.

"I'm not like that anymore," she said, needing to fill the empty silence between them. "I don't want to be with anyone. I don't care about those things. I don't have the time or the patience, and …" Her word vomit had trapped her. "I won't allow myself to be a burden to anyone."

"You're not a burden to anyone. You're not a burden to me, and this," he nodded at the gift she'd given him, "this makes me appreciate having you in my life even more."

Appreciate having her in his life?

She gave her head a shake, as if something had gotten stuck in her ears. She couldn't have heard right, because what he'd said had made her feel all warm and fuzzy inside. She was hearing things, surely?

"And you care about me otherwise you wouldn't have baked the cake my mom used to bake for me."

A lump lodged in her throat.

This man.

This man.

He made her heart rate rocket. Her legs turn weak. "Yes, but we're friends," she whispered, her voice shaky and odd.

"We are friends," he told her, his gaze lingering over her face, sucking the air slowly out of her lungs. "but—"

"Hey, Brody. Carlyle's looking for you."

"Meet me for lunch?" he asked.

"Hyacinth needs me to help her with something then."

"The woman isn't letting you eat?"

She grinned, amused by his quiet anger. "She is. I just need to do a few things."

"He's hollering for you!" Brody's coworker returned, looking anxious.

"Tell him I'm coming," he growled back, then turned to her. "This conversation isn't over." His gaze settled on her face for a few seconds. "I'll see you later," he said, then marched away, obviously annoyed at the interruption. His colleague rushed to keep up with him.

Her heart was beating like a drum in a steel band, happiness bouncing through the air waves.

CHAPTER 15

She was still smiling by the time she'd turned on her computer and was getting ready to work.

Something inside her ribcage fluttered. She'd become so used to seeing Brody almost every day, she couldn't imagine getting back to a working life and him not being a part of it. It would all change when his project finished and he moved on.

It was something she didn't want to think about.

"It's lovely to see you looking so happy!" Hyacinth strode into her office in a flouncy red, purple and white floral dress. A choker of pearls adorned her neck.

"You look lovely," Leah remarked. She wore less powder and she really did look lovely today.

Hyacinth's hand went to the pearls and the other hand to her bouffant hairdo. "We have a department meeting this afternoon. I always like to make a bit of an effort."

Leah stared. Hyacinth was the most dressed, overdressed, person she knew. She was the queen of accessories. A purveyor of pearls and brooches, often dressed in brocade suits or flouncy floral or otherwise large-print dresses.

"Are you still okay for us to work through lunch? I want to make sure we have the most up-to-date meeting notes and relevant paperwork printed and stapled for the meeting."

"It's not a problem at all."

"Good."

She disappeared, and Leah got on with her work but her heart was still recovering from what Brody had said earlier, about him appreciating having her in his life. Those words were on constant replay in her mind. They were the reason behind her smile.

Even during lunch, when she was busy taking the sheets Hyacinth had printed and stapling them together, she could think of nothing but Brody. It was only her rumbling stomach that reminded her she was hungry.

She finished stapling the last of the booklets and delivered them to Hyacinth's office.

"All done."

She placed the pile down, then went back to fetch the next few piles of paperwork.

"Wonderful." Hyacinth flicked through one of the booklets. "Perfect. I shall now call the mailman to bring the mail cart and transport these to the meeting room."

"I can do that—"

"It's not your job. Speaking of jobs, there was a man looking for you yesterday. One of the workmen, I believe."

"He was?" It must have been Brody, but he hadn't mentioned it.

"I put him to good use," continued Hyacinth. "I got him to fix my light for me."

Leah laughed out loud. "You did?" She couldn't wait to ask Brody about it.

"Everyone has their job, and my place is to oversee it all." Hyacinth flashed her a smug smile.

"Let me know if you need anything," Leah said, as she left the office.

Not ten minutes had passed since she had sat down, when there was a knock at the door. Brody stood in her doorway, taking up all of it. The muscles in her mouth stopped working. Not only did he look sexier than ever, he was here, in the flesh. His dark work clothes looked cleaner and newer, and she couldn't help but rake her eyes all over him.

This conversation isn't over yet.

"Have you been to lunch yet?" he asked.

She tilted her head. "I was just about to go to lunch now, as it happens."

"Perfect timing," he said, folding his arms and leaning against the doorway.

"Come with me?"

She grabbed her bag and got ready to go. "To where?"

"To my mom's place. The neighbor said he heard a bang. I have to go check out what happened," he said, when she hesitated.

She opened her mouth to protest. It didn't seem right her going over. But then again, was it really so wrong? What was she afraid of?

"I can make you some tea, a sandwich even, and we can have some of that delicious cake you made."

"You didn't share it with your coworkers?" she asked, surprised that he'd kept it to himself.

"Are you kidding me? Share it with them? Heck no."

"Then how do you know it's delicious—"

"Because it smells like the one my mom used to make."

She wanted to clarify something. "You want me to come with you to your mom's place *now?*"

"You were about to go to lunch. I haven't had lunch either.

Hop along for a ride with me, Leah. Nothing to it, I promise." He did that thing again, lifting his hands up as if to show her that he wouldn't do a thing.

She shivered as goosebumps scattered all over her back. She was in the mood for doing something different. Why not?

CHAPTER 16

$\mathcal{H}$e silently chuckled to himself.

If he was a believing man, he wouldn't have put it past his mom to be matchmaking from heaven. Having Leah sitting in his car as he drove to check in on his mom's house was strange, to say the least. But his faith had been rocked by his mom's passing. He didn't know what to believe anymore.

She'd made it clear she wasn't looking for anything, and he understood that. Respected it. She was on the road to recovery, and he was healing in his own way, too. He wasn't going to make any moves, even if she was sensible and pretty, if a little guarded. She was a change from the women who gave him blatantly knowing looks as they walked past. The town hall was full of them.

But Leah baking him a cake—what did that signify?

Friendship.

Just that. Nothing more, and he'd do well to keep that in mind.

He parked outside his mom's house and eyed it carefully. It looked fine, but he needed to make sure it was all intact inside.

"Should I wait outside?" Leah asked, as he was about to open the car door.

"In case someone's broken in?" he joked. "You'd rather leave me to catch the burglar alone? Thanks."

Her brow creased. "Burglars. I didn't think of that."

He opened the car door wider but didn't climb out. "It must seem weird; you didn't know my mom, and now you're wondering if you should go into her house with a man you barely know."

"Is it that obvious?"

"That you're scared?"

"That I'm cautious," she clarified.

"Yeah, and I don't blame you, either. But you baking me a cake would have made my mom smile. It would have gotten her hopes up, too ..."

"Gotten her hopes up?"

He dipped his chin and grinned as he recalled their past conversations. "She was like that; always matchmaking if she could, but not in a laying-it-on-thick way." He climbed out of the car. "I understand you being wary, after all, we barely know one another. Tell you what. Why don't you sit over there on the porch, and I'll bring the food out when I'm finished inside? I'll go see what made that noise."

"I'll come and rescue you if I hear a scream." She got out of the car.

"A man like me?" He flexed his muscles bodybuilder-style. "I don't scream. Stay put. I won't take long."

He walked around the house, checking all the rooms and the windows. It wasn't long before he found the culprit. In one of the spare bedrooms, the stepladder had fallen and knocked a pot of screws and bolts over. The room's window was slightly ajar. No wonder the neighbor had heard.

He was relieved that it had been nothing else. He righted the stepladder, this time making sure it was secure and in place up against the wall.

Time to make Leah some lunch.

Sitting outside on the porch probably sent out a signal that she didn't trust Brody, but she was more relaxed than ever. And it gave her time to collect herself after he'd done that Mr. Olympia pose.

She'd have fanned her face if she didn't fear Brody coming out and catching her. Everything she had come to know about him was good. Her gut told her that Brody was a man she could trust, rely on even, and his actions backed up her intuition.

But she was also curious.

Pushing the slightly open front door, she walked into the house and stared at the walls of the long living room which were adorned with photos. They were old photos, taken when Brody was a child, with his sister. Baby photos, toddler photos, photos which ran the whole gamut from childhood to later life. She recognized Brody's mother, in her various stages of life, as a young mother, a proud parent at different birthday parties, then a proud mother-in-law and grandmother.

Brody's life, and that of his family was portrayed on these walls, and as she carefully examined the pictures, she got a good feel for his family and his upbringing.

"You changed your mind?" His rich voice startled her as he walked down the stairs.

"These are beautiful. You have precious family memories everywhere."

He stood by her side. "Hard to look at now."

"Look at the way you're looking at your mom," she said pointing to a photo in which Brody couldn't have been more than eight or nine. His mother was proudly holding up a small flower while Brody gazed at her adoringly, as if she were the center of his universe.

"It was Mother's Day," he said, his voice sounding strangled. "We'd made flowers out of cardboard at school, then cut them out and colored them in. She used that as a bookmark for decades." He sniffed. "I think she might still even have it lying around somewhere."

He kept staring at the photo, and from her side view, she wasn't sure if his eyes had welled up. Instinctively, she reached for his hand, her fingers wrapping around his big coarse hand, in an attempt to comfort him. "These are lovely memories, Brody. You'll have them forever."

He nodded, and she quickly moved her hand away. He cleared his throat.

"How about a sandwich, and some of your cake?" he asked, still not meeting her gaze.

"If it's not too much trouble." She gave the photos one last glance before following him.

He was washing his hands as she walked into a large bright and airy wood-paneled kitchen. It was of an old style, but homely, and cozy, and everything she expected it to be.

"Ham and cheese okay? Or did you want something else?" He walked over to the fridge.

"Ham and cheese is fine. Shall I slice some of the cake?" she offered, wanting to make herself useful.

"Go ahead."

Quietly, they got on with their tasks. This didn't feel odd, not in the slightest, and *that* was the oddest thing of all. Because it felt as if they'd been doing this for years, as if it was nothing for her to be here, slicing cake while he made her a sandwich.

She glanced at him a few times, trying to gauge his mood, but he seemed to be focused on making the sandwiches.

"You still have food here?"

He cut the sandwiches in two. "I live between the two houses, for now. I'm hoping it's temporary. It's not easy taking care of both places and working, but I like coming here."

"It's a lovely home. It feels cozy, welcoming."

"My mom was all about cozy and welcoming."

"Thank you," she said, when he put a plate down beside the plate on which she'd cut a few slices of cake. He pulled out a few cans of soda, and a bottle of water and two glasses and set them on the table.

"This is quite a feast," she mused, pouring herself a glass of water as he opened a can of soda for himself.

"Makes a change from the beach, huh?"

She nodded.

They ate quietly, and after a while she remembered something. "Did you go looking for me yesterday?"

"I did."

"Why?" After that lunch, when he'd left her and hadn't looked too happy, she wanted to know why he'd sought her out.

He stared at her for so long that the color in her cheeks rose. "Probably for the same reason you baked me a cake."

"I was rude. You didn't do anything wrong," she threw back. Her heart was doing somersaults inside her chest.

"I shouldn't have been so grumpy. I'm not sure why I was." His eyes bore into hers like a heat-seeking missile and her heart thundered inside her chest as she found herself admiring the dusting of salt- and pepper-colored stubble on his face. It suited him so much.

She looked away, staring at her sandwich as if it contained some sort of cryptic code, then took a bite of it and prayed it didn't leave breadcrumbs around her mouth. Or cheese stuck in between her teeth.

Across the table, Brody reached for his soda, but all she could focus on were his wide shoulders and his thick corded forearms. His dark work clothes hugged his body in a way that gave her the kinds of thoughts she hadn't had for a while.

She tried to think of ice and Antarctica, trying to cool herself down. She forced herself to acknowledge the hard, cold fact: a man like that had to have a girlfriend.

The old Leah would have never let a chance like this pass her by, and here she was, sitting in his mother's house, eating a sandwich he'd made for her, and doing nothing to attract his attention.

"I went home early," she told him.

"Everything okay?" The way his eyes filled with concern touched her. He probably thought it had something to do with her health, not anything to do with him.

She hesitated about telling him that she'd had her one-month scan a few days ago, and she was waiting for the results of it. "Yes, everything is fine. I'd finished my work for the day, so ..."

"Your boss got me to fix her light."

She grinned. "Hyacinth told me."

He looked so peeved. "She told me I needed to fix it."

"But it's not your job. We have maintenance people to do things like that."

"I told her. I tried to," he cried, before telling her that luckily, he hadn't needed to change the light tube or anything, but that the connection to it was loose hence the flickering.

"Thank goodness it was nothing more. Hyacinth wouldn't have let you go home until it was fixed."

"You said she was nice to work for," he retorted.

"I said she was nice to me."

That made him chuckle.

Not long after they finished their lunch and quickly cleared up, he shocked her.

"I meant what I said earlier, about being friends. You're not a burden to anyone, Leah, and frankly, I'm surprised you would think you were."

She almost choked. It was the first time he had broached the topic that had warmed her heart and make her feel all light and fuzzy inside.

"Peter's father makes me feel like a burden," she said, after a while. "He's so wrapped up with his new family. I hate calling him to ask about things."

"New family?"

She told him about the new baby her ex-husband and his wife were expecting.

"You said he cheated on you?" Brody asked.

"I'm not sure." She suspected he had, he'd denied everything, and she wasn't the type to pick up the phone and shout accusations over it at the woman she suspected him of seeing.

Whether Tom had technically done anything or not, he had an emotional connection with this other woman. He'd obviously seen something in her because he'd lost interest in Leah and their marriage.

What had broken her in two was that he had chosen the mistress over *them*. Her and Peter. If there was one thing she always wanted, it was a family; a husband and children. Tom leaving had killed that dream.

Brody's eyes were locked on hers, as if he was waiting for her to say more.

"I could never prove it," she said finally, not wanting to discuss the matter. "I don't dwell on it anymore." There was no point. Her ex had moved on. It was history, and she and Peter were doing the best they could to move on, too.

"The camping equipment. When do you need it?"

She felt relieved that he'd switched to a safer topic. "I was going to ask you about that."

"Why don't you bring Peter over to my house this weekend and he can take whatever he wants?"

"Great, thank you. I will. Should we come at any particular time? You must have plans this weekend?"

"No plans. I'm free. Busy doing nothing." He paused, letting that sink it. "Come over whenever you want."

"Okay."

She stared up at him, and the pitter-patter of her heartbeat started again. She moved away, fearful that he might hear it.

"My address and my phone number, in case you need it," he said, scribbling something down on a piece of paper.

As they drove back, all she could think of was how her lonely mind drifted towards Brody in the evenings, when she'd be staring at the TV alone, and Peter would be upstairs in his bedroom talking to his friends or playing games on his laptop.

In those solitary moments, she would find herself thinking about Brody Holt and wondering what he was doing.

CHAPTER 17

She'd taken Peter over to Brody's place. It was a neat and tidy little home with a well-kept yard out front. Inside, it was minimalistic with good quality furniture, dark couches and a huge TV screen.

Brody led them to his garage.

"Here, kid. It's all in that backpack. Take whatever you need. Take the entire backpack if you want."

"Are you sure?"

"I'm sure. Why else would I tell you to come over and take what you want? You sound just like your mom." Behind Peter's back, Brody rolled his eyes at her and grinned.

She rolled her eyes back at him. "Thanks."

"When are you leaving?" Brody asked him, but Peter was too busy going through the backpack.

"He's leaving on Monday," she answered. Her nerves pinched at the thought of Peter going away.

"A week alone?" Brody sounded surprised. Or pleased.

"This is all I need." Peter held out a few plastic utensils, a small pan, a first aid kit, and a few other things.

"What about the backpack?" Brody asked.

"I've got one of those. Mom managed to get that for me."

She didn't like the way he said 'managed,' as if it was a great cost for her, but she was grateful to Brody for this. It helped, and he had stepped up when her ex had let her down.

"Thank you." Peter said.

"Thank you, *Mr. Holt*," Leah muttered under her breath. Her son's manners vanished along with his sweetness. Maybe a week apart would be good for both of them.

"Call me Brody." And then to her, he mouthed, "It's okay."

"Is that a fishing rod?" Peter cried.

"It sure is."

"Do you go fishing?" Peter went over to where the rods were affixed to the wall.

Brody folded his arms. "I do. I like it. You ever been, kid?"

"Never."

"Maybe I'll take you some time, if you'd like go to?" Brody suggested.

"That would be cool." Peter's excitement caught her by surprise.

"Really?"

Fishing?

Since when had Peter ever been interested in fishing? She watched happily as Brody showed him his rods and answered Peter's questions.

Later the following evening, she stood in the doorway to Peter's room with a look of horror on her face at the items of clothes and various camping things all over the floor. Determined not to fly off the handle, she inhaled a slow breath.

"Are you packed, sweetheart?"

"Can you help me, Mom? I can't get the sleeping bag back in." He looked at her helplessly and she couldn't stop herself from grinning back at her useless boy. He'd have left everything until the last moment if she'd left him to his own devices.

She crouched on the floor, trying not to make a face as she eyed everything that was spread out all over the floor. "It was nice of Brody to lend you his equipment."

"He hasn't even used it." Peter attempted to roll up the sleeping bag again. "Everything is like brand new."

"Lucky you." She tried to slide the storage sack over the rolled-up bag.

"I like him. He's cool. But why's he being so nice to us?" Peter asked.

"Because he's a nice man."

"He likes you, doesn't he?"

"Why did you take this out, sweetheart?" she groaned, struggling with the sleeping bag and hoping he would get off the subject. She'd never been good at getting the darned thing back into its little sack.

"You told me to check if it had holes."

"I asked you to check that last week. Does it?"

"Nah, it's fine," he replied.

"Well, good. Because if you'd found out now, I wouldn't have been able to get you a new one. Here," she motioned for him to hand her the sleeping bag. "Let me try." She unrolled the sleeping bag and then rolled it again, squishing it as tightly as she could. Together they struggled and finally got the bag back into its sack.

"Brody likes you, Mom," Peter stated.

"Hmmm." She busied herself with picking things off the floor.

"That's why he's always being so nice to you."

She looked at her son and hoped nothing in her expression would reveal her real feelings. "He's being nice, because he is nice." Brody was a rare find. He was like a friend, only male and gorgeous, and *there*.

In her sphere of work.

She ran into him almost daily, and when she didn't see him, her disappointment was sky high.

Did he feel like that about her? "He's hurting because he lost his mom, and … well, I'm trying to get back to my life, so … I didn't know you were interested in fishing," she said, switching the subject quickly.

"I've never been fishing, so I wouldn't know. Brody says we'll go once I get back from my trip."

She stopped what she was doing and stared at him. She'd heard them talking, and she'd assumed Brody was just being nice when he'd offered, but Peter seemed eager to try fishing.

"Let's get the camping trip out of the way first, shall we? And then we need to plan your birthday."

She had an appointment at the hospital tomorrow afternoon. It was a big thing for her, and she was worried; the outcome could only be one of two things—either she was in the clear, or the cancer was back.

She had to drop Peter to school at a crazy early hour of the morning, and then she planned to kill time by shopping for some paint. She wanted to surprise him when he came back to a freshly painted room. In the afternoon, she would go to the hospital. With so much going on before then, she wouldn't have to think too much about the actual appointment.

The next morning as she dropped Peter to school, she said, "Be good, be careful, and have a lot of fun." She hugged her boy, and then held onto him, not wanting to let go. To her surprise, he didn't seem to want to let go either.

"Bye, Mom."

She watched him get on the school bus, her heart filling with sadness.

She had one week without him. What would she do? She'd spent a week without him before, plenty of times, but he'd been with his father. This was a first, leaving home and going on a school trip for what seemed like an eternity.

Sadness welled up in her throat, until she remembered that she had other more urgent matters to deal with.

~

He was worried. He hadn't seen Leah all morning, and at lunchtime, he walked by her office and she *still* hadn't shown up.

He needed to get her number. He'd given her his but she hadn't given him hers. He knew she was dropping Peter off to school really early in the morning but he was certain that she would have come into work by now.

He had half a mind to ask her boss, but he didn't want to risk going down that route yet. The old sourpuss would find something else for him to fix.

He went out late for lunch, then came back and attended an urgent meeting that went on for much too long. A niggling feeling at the back of his mind made him uneasy. Peter would only have needed to be dropped off in the morning. Leah used to come to work after her treatments. She prided herself on not even taking a day off sick. Today's absence didn't make sense.

Unless something else had come up.

That's what scared him.

As soon as the meeting was over, he made his way to Leah's office, but as he approached Hyacinth's office—the gladiator pit he needed to get past—he heard Leah's voice.

She sounded ecstatic, and that in itself gave him cause for relief. She was back, and she seemed to be okay.

He took a few more steps in that direction, still out of sight but well within hearing distance. She was jubilant. Deciding that he couldn't listen in—eavesdrop would be the word Leah would use—he turned and walked away. Then heard a whisper a few seconds later.

"Brody?"

He spun around to find Leah staring up at him. "What are you doing here?" Her eyes were gleaming.

"Why are you whispering?" he asked.

"If Hyacinth sees you, she'll find you something to fix."

Taking her elbow, he gently led her to the end of the hallway, well out of harm's way. "You sounded happy. Good news?"

"Were you eavesdropping on our conversation?" she asked.

"I'd started to walk away," he replied defensively. "I was worried about you. You've haven't been here all day."

"I told you Peter left for his school trip in the morning, and then I had a hospital appointment in the afternoon."

She hadn't said a word about that. "You didn't tell me that part," he said grouchily. "I was worried about you. Is…is everything okay?" It had to be. She had sounded happy when she was talking to Hyacinth.

"The scan was fine. It was clear," she squealed, her voice rising at the end. "I'm sorry I didn't tell you. I was nervous, and I didn't want to jinx it."

That made him feel better. It made sense why she'd kept quiet about it. He was so filled with relief for her that he almost went to hug her but settled for a lame handshake. "That's great, Leah. That's great news."

The smile on her face slowly disappeared. "It's good, for now. They said it's just a baseline for future scans. It doesn't mean I'm in the clear."

"But it's a great sign." She had a tendency to underplay things at times, and this was one of them. He bent down to meet her eyes, seeing that her gaze was fixated on the floor. "Right?"

She looked up. "Right. It is. I'm happy. I really am."

"Did Peter get everything packed?"

"Yes, with a little help. He was very grateful for your camping equipment, and so am I. You saved me buying that stuff which we'll probably only need this once. I can't see us ever going camping."

"It was lying around in my garage. I'm glad it came in handy." His hands settled on his hips. She was here, and she was fine. There was nothing to worry about, but she was watching him watching her. And she didn't seem to be in a rush to get back to her work. "Why didn't you take the day off?" he asked. It was mid-afternoon. Any other normal person would have taken the afternoon off at least.

"And do what? I managed to go shopping for paint, and then I thought I might as well come back to work instead of going home to an empty house."

Buy paint? She sure knew how to party. "Paint for what?"

"I want to freshen up Peter's room. He says we live in a rundown house, compared to where his father lives now."

That kid needed a talking to. Or someone to tell him it was okay to be scared. "That's not nice."

"It's not his fault. His father is doing well, and … and we are getting by."

"But still…" It annoyed him that her son, as pleasant as he'd been to Brody, seemed to be giving his mom a hard time. "He seemed pretty interested in my fishing gear."

"I have no idea why. It's the first I've heard of his interest in it."

"I'd like to take him fishing one day, if that's okay."

"Isn't it too late to go fishing now?" she asked, raising her hand and moving a stray lock of hair away from her face. There was a glow about her today. Maybe it was that boulder of worry disappearing from her shoulders now that she'd had her scan results.

He shook his head. "We can still go fall fishing. Catch a striped bass and cook it."

Her eyes turned as large as saucers. "You'd gut it and …"

"We should definitely do it. I know a great way to cook it."

"We'll see."

"No 'we'll see,' we're doing it. Peter and I already made plans."

"I heard, but I thought you were just being nice."

"I don't make promises I can't keep when it comes to people I like. Peter's a good kid."

She smiled. It was always nice getting compliments about your child.

"We should celebrate your good news," he said, then waited for her excuses to roll in.

"Oh, I don't know about that."

"Peter's away, and you don't have to rush back to cook dinner, or feed the dog, cat, fish, hamster, insert pet name."

She laughed. "I don't have a pet."

"Therefore, you don't have an excuse." But he didn't want to impose. The last time he'd made a suggestion that she could take him to lunch at Roxy's, it hadn't turned out so well.

"Think about it. You know where to find me if you change your mind." He wanted to leave the decision to her. "News like that needs to be celebrated."

CHAPTER 18

The mailman had dropped the wrong mail to her office and she was taking it to its rightful destination on the first floor when Heather accosted her.

"What are you doing up here?" Heather asked.

She explained, but the slightly dazed look in the woman's eyes signaled that she wasn't interested in knowing.

"Every time I see you, you're with that workman guy." And *that* was the real reason Heather had accosted her. Leah laughed uneasily.

"Not all the time." They didn't meet every day.

Heather nodded eagerly. "Yes, all the time. Did you two just get talking?" Her tone implied disbelief that someone like Leah had managed to get talking to someone like *that*.

"Kind of." She hadn't told Heather about her cancer or the radiation therapy, and she didn't want to either. It was none of her business and that type of personal news was better contained to those who were affected, like Peter and Hyacinth. Which was why Heather didn't know the history about the hospital visits, or how entwined her and Brody's lives had been prior to meeting again at work.

"How?"

"What do you mean how?" If she could shoot venom from her eyes, she would have. "We got talking near the water coolers one day."

This wasn't a lie. There was no vending machine at the town hall, because Hyacinth wouldn't allow it, and as she was on the committee, and had God-like powers, all the many employees there didn't dare to fight for one.

But there were a few water coolers in the tiny kitchen areas on each floor.

"Is anything going on?" Miss Nosy Pants asked. "Did you finally find someone to break your dry spell?"

Leah narrowed her eyes, suspicion collecting in her core. Though she kept her private life private, especially with work colleagues, she'd always told Heather that she had sworn off men. She had often commented that Peter was the focus of her life. "It's not like that," she said slowly. It really wasn't. But ... sometimes the way Brody looked at her made her wonder.

"Is he single?"

"Single? I don't know."

"You don't?" Heather's eyes grew wide, as if she couldn't believe that it was possible for a woman to be friends with a man —especially one who looked like Brody. "You mean you're not ... together?"

Leah laughed. "No." But in her head, in her wildly overactive imagination, she had started to wonder what that might be like. It confused her. She was still getting over the shock of her cancer, and a part of her was always on edge, wondering and worrying when and if it might return. She'd sworn off men forever now, but Brody had put the spring back in her step.

"Then you won't mind me asking him?" asked Heather. Leah stared at her.

"Asking him what?" Her defenses shored up as it dawned on

her what this woman was after. She damn well did mind. There was no way she would let Heather get her paws on Brody.

"If he's single, and depending on his answer, asking him if he wants to go for a drink one day."

The forwardness of this woman never ceased to amaze her. "You'd do that?"

"How else am I ever going to meet anyone?" Heather whined. The question threw a lance straight through her chest and twisted it. She had allowed Dylan Fraser to slip through her fingers when Merry had appeared on the scene.

No way was she going to stand by and watch Heather Tuley do the same.

Instead of returning to her office, she went over to the area where Brody sometimes hung out.

"You just missed him," said one of his colleagues. "He's on the first floor, near the stairs."

"Thank you."

Making her way there with Heather's words still fresh in her head, she didn't know what she was going to say. He was in a group of men, talking, and she stopped, not wanting to charge right in and interrupt him. But as if he'd sensed her presence, he turned and stared right at her. Goosebumps sprouted along her skin.

She smiled. A frown on his face revealed his surprise. He came over to her immediately.

"Let's do it," she said, not giving him a chance to reply. "Let's celebrate."

For a split second, those gray irises stared at her, and then his face softened. "You want to?"

She nodded.

"What do you want to do?"

"I don't know." She shrugged. "Go for a long walk on the beach?"

"We can do better than that. See you outside at five?"

She spun on her heels and left, before she changed her mind and said something else.

"That's where you keep disappearing off to, boss," one of his colleagues said when he returned. Mischief swirled in his eyes. "She's got a cute—"

"You keep your eyes to yourself," he growled, yet inside he couldn't help but get excited at the idea that Leah had not only agreed to do something, but she'd come all this way to look for him.

He knew just the thing.

At the end of the workday, he found her waiting for him outside the town hall steps. Without actually planning it, this had become their new place to meet.

"Think of anything?" he asked, wanting to see if she'd come up with an idea. There was a sparkle in her eyes which wasn't there before. In the past, worry had dimmed those eyes.

"I don't know. I'm always at a loss when Peter's away."

"Does he go away a lot?"

"To his dad's. A week in the summer, and a week or two at Christmas time."

"And when you're all by yourself, what do you do?"

They started to walk, and because he had no idea where they were going, he let her take the lead.

"I read, and clean the house, and do some exercise." She laughed. "I make up for all the exercise that I never do on a regular basis."

"You don't meet up with friends or …?"

"I'm not good at making friends."

He was about to fix that for her. "You have some good news,

and Peter is enjoying himself. I have an idea." He led her towards his car.

Her eyes grew large, the way they always did when she was surprised. "Where are we going?"

"Do you trust me?"

"I think so."

"You think so." He threw his head back and chuckled. "Hop in."

"Aren't you going to tell me?" she asked, as they got in and set off.

"Trust me. You'll find out soon enough."

The sight of the big wheel in the distance, turning all different colors in the sky, gave away Brody's surprise. Lights, moving carousels and fairground rides gave away Brody's surprise.

"The fairground?" She had only come here with Peter and some of his school friends and their moms throughout the years.

"Something different, no?"

Her face broke out into the biggest smile. This wasn't even on her radar, and it would never have been. To her, the fairground was for children.

"Brody, I can't believe this is where you've brought me!" A huge grin clambered onto her face and stayed there as she climbed out of the car.

"You don't like it?"

Coming here with a grown-up, and no kids to keep an eye on, already felt like a whole other experience.

"I… I don't know what to say."

"Then don't say anything. Just enjoy it."

They walked towards the shining multi-colored lights of the different rides, like one huge jeweled cushion in the middle of a vast expanse of land. Fairground tunes played from various stalls and rides, and laughter and the cries of screaming children filled the air.

They went on a ride, sitting together, the plastic shiny seat secured by metal bars keeping them hemmed in as it spun from side to side across the shiny, spangled floor, tossing them together each time it then changed direction from one end to the other. She screamed, the motion and the speed making her insides tumble like a washing machine. He grabbed her hand, and she, grateful for it, held onto it for dear life.

After a few fuel-injected minutes, the ride slowly came to a halt, and they got out.

"You okay?" he asked, his hands on her shoulders as she started to sway. She felt as if she was onboard a ship in choppy water, swaying from back and forth. Her body dipped, and in a flash his hands were under her arms, trying to keep her upright. She wasn't sure if her legs turning to jelly had to do with coming off a fast-thrilling ride, or because his hands were on either sides of her arms.

She brushed the hair away from her face and imagined herself looking like a real wreck. Straightening up, she pulled herself together. "I'm … phew!" She rubbed a hand across her neck, felt the pulse pounding there. "I'm good!" she exclaimed loudly, nodding, more to convince herself than anything else. "That was … gut churning."

"Want to take a break?" Watchful eyes were on her.

"Maybe wait a while before trying that again."

"Let's walk around a bit."

She was thankful for that option, and used the time he was on the stalls shooting and trying his luck at all the different games to smooth down her hair and to steady her breathing.

Being with Brody here, at a fairground of all places, outside of work. That meant something, didn't it?

They wandered around, buying things, cotton candy, hot dogs and cans of soda. Pure junk food. Fairground food.

They went to different stalls. She won a coconut, he won three, which they gave back to the stallholder because they would be a hassle to carry around.

She never imagined a night out like this. Her brain would never have come up with something like this. A few months ago, if anyone had told her she'd be doing this, she'd have thought they were crazy.

And it was completely crazy, but she was having the time of her life. A while later, when she was ready to go back on the rides, they went on the Ferris wheel. When they were high up in the air, at the highest point, she gazed down at the lights twinkling below and illuminating the darkness all around.

"This is so much fun," she murmured.

"Beats painting, doesn't it?"

She laughed and elbowed him gently. He did the same back, very lightly. The spot where his elbow had touched her side now tingled. Real or imaginary, she didn't know. But it tingled.

"My news wasn't that big," she said slowly. He turned to her, his mouth open, those usually narrow eyes wide.

"What do you mean? The scan was clear. It's a win."

"It's a win for now." It surprised her that he didn't seem to grasp it. For a man who had lost his mother, she assumed he would.

"Now isn't enough. I don't want now. I want forever. I want a sure thing. I don't want to live minute by minute, day by day, depending on scans and biopsies. It is so much better to just grow old and then die ..." She stopped when she realized what she'd said. "I'm so sorry. I didn't mean it like that."

He grinned at her. "It's okay, Leah. I know what you meant."

"I'm so sorry."

"I said it was okay. But you can't think like that. You can't go through life thinking that only bad things happen."

"Why not? Because that's been my experience of it. Being a single mom hasn't been easy."

"You've done a great job, holding it all together. I know it can't have been easy. We used to see you come to the hospital all by yourself, and my mom always used to comment that you were alone."

"I *was* alone."

"You're not alone now." His voice was hoarse, the look on his face serious. He wasn't joking.

She smiled, because she didn't know what to say to that, or what to make of the bubbly feeling in her belly.

On the way back to the car, just before they left, Brody stopped by a shooting gallery and walked away with a bright purple octopus that was a nightmare to carry. He gave it to her. "For you."

"Oh, no. I can't."

"You have to. It's a gift."

She hugged the great big ugly-looking thing to her chest. It was so big, she had to put it in the back of the car as they drove back.

"Brody, I've never done anything like that before."

"I know." His expression changed, and she would have given anything to know what he was thinking.

"Thank you."

"You don't have to keep thanking me, Leah. I had a great time, too."

He dropped her back to her house.

"Thanks for such a memorable night," he said, pulling the window down and craning his neck.

Her breath stilled. Her eyes settled on his mouth, noting the generous fill of his lips. Her legs went weak. "I will never forget this," she murmured. It had to rate as one of the best nights of her adult life. Unexpected, spontaneous, and with an irresistible hunk. Since when did she get luck like this?

She almost put her key into the lock when he shouted. "Aren't you forgetting something?" He rushed over to her and held out the octopus. She grabbed it with a chuckle. "Thank you."

It was with a happy heart that she walked into her home, giving Brody one final wave before she closed the door.

This was what life could be like. They were the most unlikely of people, her and Brody, and yet they'd spent the evening together, having fun. With him, she didn't spend her time thinking of all the reasons why she couldn't have love in her life. He made her feel as if it was her right to be happy, to think of the future, to allow herself to dream.

Hugging the octopus to her body, she reflected on the perfect end to a perfect day.

"You have a friend," Hyacinth commented the next day, when they ran into her as they returned to the town hall.

Leah didn't know what to say to that, and before she could think of an answer, Hyacinth continued, "And about time too, I say. About time too."

Leah raised her right eyebrow a touch. "There's nothing going on."

"Days off work, longer lunch breaks—"

"I haven't taken any days off work except for my hospital appointment!"

"Oh, I'm not making a dig at you, my dear. You've worked too hard and made up your hours, even when you were having the treatments. You take as many long lunches as you want."

"I always get the work done, Hyacinth." She took another step closer to Hyacinth's desk, her arms folded. "But we are just friends."

Hyacinth laughed and looked at her as if she were a complete liar. "Don't worry. Your secret is safe with me."

"Hyacinth, I'm telling the truth. There is no secret. Brody and I are friends."

"I know you want to be careful and not make any rash moves, but for the love of Christmas, you don't have to hide anything from me."

Leah tipped up her chin. If only it were true.

Unfortunately, she and Brody were nothing more.

Later that evening, she allowed him to surprise her again. They'd left work a little earlier than usual, but they started to approach Glassmere, the upscale part of the town, she had to demand he tell her what they were doing here.

"We're going to light a bonfire."

"A what?"

He told her his plans. Before they had set off, she hadn't known what to expect when he'd suggested they try something new.

But a picnic and a bonfire at the beach? At this time of the year? It wasn't something that would ever have crossed her mind, and Brody was the last person she would have expected to come up with such an idea. It didn't quite go with his power tools-and-workman exterior.

"Are we allowed to light a fire here? Do you have a permit?"

"I borrowed one, shall we say."

"Can you?"

"It's legal. Don't worry about it." He looked around. "We'll be fine. Relax."

Anxiety balled in her stomach as they made their way to the beach. Brody's car was parked a short distance away, which made it easier to carry everything. She had a few light bags, but he went back and forth a couple of times returning with small bundles of wood, a shovel, the picnic hamper and a few other things.

They were on a secluded part of the beach, and the only buildings visible, dotted a good distance away, were the multimillionaire homes. The lights from them glistened like diamonds in the darkening night sky.

"Are you sure it's okay to have a picnic here?" It seemed quiet and private here. Nothing like the part of the beach they usually went to.

"We'll be fine. Don't worry. I don't like breaking the law." He started to dig. She set down the things she was carrying and took out a large picnic blanket.

"Here?" she asked, not sure how far from the fire would be good.

"That's fine."

She spread the blanket carefully to avoid getting any sand on it and then opened the hamper. "Wow." Inside were various jars and spreads and luxury food items. She pulled them out one by one, examining them carefully. She suddenly felt like a young girl opening a stack of presents on Christmas morning.

"I bought a couple of things from the diner," he explained, scrubbing his forehead with the back of his hand as he stopped digging.

"So you did." She pulled out the small batch of freshly made rolls and sandwiches. He'd thought of everything, and she was blown away by his thoughtfulness and organizational skills. She glanced at him from the corner of her eye, trying not to stare too much at his bulging biceps as he started shoveling again.

"That should do it," he said after a while. She'd set out the food and watched as he pulled out something from the bag. He threw what looked like sticks and twigs, and newspaper into the hole he'd dug.

"When did you collect those?"

"I went fishing on the weekend. I made a small fire then, too."

"You did?" she exclaimed. "You're a pro at this."

"I like the outdoors," he replied casually, lighting a match and throwing it into the pit. "It's nice to sit outside in the quiet sometimes. That's why I like fishing."

"We don't ever do things like this," she lamented. She would never do something like this, and her ex hadn't been an outdoorsy man either. Peter, with his interest in fishing all of a sudden, would have loved this.

Brody scrubbed a hand across his jaw. "I figured you might like it."

"I love it already." She smiled up at him. The night had only just begun but this was already so different than her daily norm, and she loved it. "This fire would have been more than enough, Brody." She didn't even need food on a night like this. The heat from the fire was so warm and welcoming, she settled herself comfortably on the blanket, cross-legged, and thankful that today she'd worn pants.

"I gotta eat. You have to eat."

She pulled out a bottle of something red, and then reached in and pulled out a similar bottle but it was white.

"Grape juice," he said. "Sparkling."

"The good stuff, obviously." She peered at the label. "It's non-alcoholic."

"No alcohol allowed on beaches," he reminded her.

"How? When?" She struggled to find the right words. "This is so … wonderful, and you threw this together pretty quickly. Is this part of your skill set?"

He chortled. "It's one of many."

They had everything they needed; picnic food, drinks, fruit, even little chocolate cheesecakes.

On a Tuesday.

"What's the occasion today?" she persisted. People didn't just wake up and throw together something like *this* for no reason.

"Do we need an occasion?" He settled himself at one end of

the blanket, with an island of food between them. His eyes twinkled in the firelight.

"But it's a Tuesday."

"Then let's celebrate Tuesday."

Puzzled, she tried to read his expression. "You're in a good mood."

"I feel happy. Been a while since I could say that."

She nodded, understanding. Given her scan results, and having Brody in her life, and things going well at work, she counted her blessings.

"Can we start?" he asked, picking up a paper plate and handing it to her.

"This is your picnic, you decide."

"It's not mine. It's my mom's."

She held onto the plate, not understanding. "Your mom's?"

"My mom won this in a raffle at the flower show a few weeks ago. I only just found out. They'd been emailing her and sending messages on her cell phone." His voice cracked for one short moment, but she had come to know him well, his moods and the timbre of his voice. She knew listening to his mother's messages must have been hard.

"This is all due to your mom," she said softly.

"I told you she's matchmaking from above."

"Bless her." Leah looked up at the star-studded sky.

"Are you thanking my mom?" he asked, a quizzical look on his face.

"I'm not sure. Maybe."

He gave her a smile that made her heart float. In the shadows of the dancing flames, his skin was smooth, he'd shaved today, she suddenly realized, and the golden light of the fire illuminated his face and strong bones perfectly.

"I'm joking, about the matchmaking. No way was I going to

share this with my work colleagues. I figured you would appreciate it more."

"I do."

They both filled their plates and started to eat.

"Have you heard from Peter?"

"No. The school doesn't allow them to have their cell phones, which is a good idea otherwise they'd be on them the entire time. But they told us the kids are all having fun." She smiled to herself. Hopefully, Peter was having as great a time as she was.

"I'm sure he's having a great time. You don't need to worry about him."

"With all of this," she motioned with her hand at the picnic hamper and at their surroundings, "I haven't had any time to worry about anything. You're so good at being spontaneous. Sadly, I'm not."

His eyes twinkled in the firelight. "But that's because you've had to be sensible and realistic. You're responsible for a child and for running your house. This year must have been so difficult for you."

"You have no idea."

She realized she was hungrier than ever. The food tasted amazing, maybe because she was now so warm and comfortable, and in a setting that was spectacular. She'd never done anything like this before, and she appreciated it all the more.

"I'll never forget this," she told him.

"It's great, isn't it?" he agreed, taking a sip from his cup.

She sipped her red grape juice, thankful for everything. "I know what we can celebrate." She lifted her cup in the air, towards him. He mirrored her movement.

"To our friendship." She touched her cup to his.

"That's a good one." He touched it back. "To helping each other through dark times, or something like that. I can't imagine I've been of much help."

She clasped the cup to her chest. "This," she gesticulated with her hand at the delicious spread of food before them. "This to me is you helping me to feel good about the small wins."

"Small wins add up to bigger things."

A silence fell between them, but it was warm and soft, and easy.

"The guys at work think we have a thing," he announced.

She cocked her head, lifting an eyebrow in surprise. "Hyacinth asked me if we were 'friends.'" She air quoted the 'friends.'

"What did you say?"

"The truth. That we were *just* friends."

Brody shook his head. "My guys don't believe me."

"I don't think Hyacinth believes me either."

Their gazes locked and they laughed. Gawking at his face that was lit up in a golden hue, as the flames licked and curled, she didn't believe those words either. They were friends, but the way her heart thumped and bumped inside her told her otherwise.

Brody was the perfect catch. She'd told him at the start that she didn't want romance, but now her statement was false and out of date.

She yearned for something more.

He was sitting across from her, with the bonfire to their side and the food spread out between them. Nothing could happen given the obstacles in the way, but she couldn't stop gazing at that perfect nose of his or those gorgeous lips she sometimes dreamed about.

He stared up at the night sky, giving her the perfect opportunity to admire his strong jaw, that thick neck, the heavy brows. She wanted him to move over to her, so that he was sitting by her side, but that would seem odd if she asked him to do that now, and she didn't want to spoil the moment.

What if he didn't feel the same?

So, she said nothing, and they stayed where they were. Her thoughts about him and the way she felt about him had changed slowly, and then all at once. She was none the wiser as to what he thought of her. But he couldn't have had a girlfriend, she reasoned, otherwise he'd be sharing this picnic with her.

He'd done so much for her and Peter.

That meant something.

It indicated that he liked her.

Didn't it?

"This is the most relaxed I've been in a while," he said, his voice sounding odd and tight, losing the easiness of a few moments ago. "I like your company. I like you."

The weight of his words didn't feel as heavy as the first time he'd said something like this to her. She welcomed them now.

"I like you, too." Now her voice sounded odd and strangled.

If he was surprised by her comment, his expression held, and he didn't reveal a thing.

"Leah?"

"Yes?"

She'd spent so much of this evening ogling his face, and there was a soap opera playing out in her now wildly stimulated imagination. His contemplative gaze fixed on her, making her heartbeat louder.

"I have a question for you. You can say 'no,' if you think I'm imposing," he spoke slowly, as if he was carefully considering his words.

Her ears pricked up. Her heart skipped a beat. Her body was a tsunami of emotions. He was going to ask her if she'd changed her mind about wanting to stay single. She had the perfect answer for him.

"How about I help you paint Peter's room?"

That's not the question she'd been expecting. Her hopes crash landed to the sand.

"Paint Peter's room?"

"You were going to do that, weren't you?"

She'd been thinking all sorts of light and fluffy thoughts, gazing at him as if he were her own Greek Adonis.

And he'd been thinking about painting Peter's room.

It was like a firehose of water all over her face.

He dipped his head, watching her carefully, waiting.

This picnic, this night, this connection ... it was just him being nice.

Nothing more.

"Leah?"

She rubbed her forehead. Shoot. Yes. Peter would be back in three days' time, and she hadn't even started. She'd been too busy trying to stop herself from falling in love with Brody, and failing.

"I was. I haven't found the time to start."

"It's my fault for whisking you away."

"I would choose you whisking me away over anything else." This man made the last two evenings more fun than she'd had in the entire year, and for that, she was more than grateful.

And now he'd given her another completely unexpected evening. Romantic even, a fool would say, with a bonfire, food, a glorious night sky, sitting beneath the stars on a warm woolly blanket.

It was heavenly.

Perfect.

An evening such as she'd never experienced before. Brody made her feel as if she mattered, and after the way her ex treated her, she needed someone to fuss over her the way Brody did.

But on a night when he could have made a move, indicated his intentions, he'd told her he wanted to help her paint Peter's room.

Brody was still being a friend, and she had to accept that.

Maybe he'd gone over the top last night, a picnic and a bonfire?

But who else was he going to share the picnic hamper with? The beach was the only place it made sense to have it, and he loved bonfires.

Leah had helped him, and she probably had no idea that she had but having someone around to talk to helped him to cope with his mother's passing.

He had to be careful that things didn't spiral out of control. She'd already warned him, she didn't want complications in her life, and he had to respect that. If he could help her in any way, he would.

Which was why he showed up at her house the next evening ready to help her paint Peter's room. He knew she'd wanted to paint her son's room and that he'd eaten up her time by taking her out these past few evenings. He'd heard the way Peter spoke to his mother, and he didn't want to give the boy an opportunity to have a go at her. She was clearly doing her best and he wished the boy would see that as much as Brody did.

"Gray?" He stared at the cans of paint on the floor.

"And white for the fourth wall. It's dull but …"

"He's a boy. I'd be worried if he'd chosen something bright and cheerful."

She giggled.

They got on with the painting. The first evening, they did the first coat of paint, and after a few hours, Leah ordered takeout, so they ate together in her kitchen.

"This means a lot to me. Thanks, Brody," she said, when later he helped her to clear away the dishes.

"It means a lot to me not having to go home and wallow around." It was true. She might have thought he was doing this for her, but the truth was he needed a distraction as much as she did.

With the nights drawing in and the days getting shorter, this first winter without his mom was difficult to bear. With Thanksgiving and Christmas around the corner, memories of last year's Christmas, and that of Christmases in the years gone by, came to the fore.

Jackie wanted him to come to California to spend Thanksgiving with her family. So much for her promise to come here and help him go through their mother's belongings and make a decision about the house. She promised that she would come over for Christmas, and what could he say to that?

"I'm going to take Peter fishing," he announced

He'd been thinking about it, and yesterday, with the bonfire at the beach, when Leah had mentioned that she never did anything like that, he detected a hint of regret in her tone. It was the kind of thing he'd tried to do with his nephews and nieces, but when they came over, it was never for too long, and they didn't like the idea of going out and waiting for hours to catch a fish.

If he'd been a father, that was the type of thing he would have done with his children. It was too late for that now, and Peter had sounded impressed when he'd seen his fishing equipment. Brody sensed it might be a good thing to take the boy out and spend some time with him. The three of them could make another good day of it.

"You are?"

"Not just me and Peter, but all of us could go?"

"You'd want to do that?" she asked him.

"He seemed really interested in it."

"He's never been."

"Then maybe it's about time he tried it."

"Fishing?" she said, as if he'd decided to take her to the moon.

"You might even like it." He gazed at her steadily as he put on his coat, ready to drive home.

"I don't know about that, but I'm sure Peter would love it. Thank you."

He opened the door to leave. "He's back on Friday?"

She nodded, a look of sadness clouding her eyes.

"I'll be back tomorrow. We'll finish the last of the painting then." He didn't want to leave Leah to do it all by herself.

"Are you sure? I don't want to put you out."

He turned and stood in the doorway. "Which part of this week do you think has put me out?" His voice became quiet, the way it always did when he felt as if he was imposing on her, trying to fish for information.

"You must have other things to do." She folded her arms, a pose at odds with the way she was staring at him.

"Like what?"

She looked up at him through her curly lashes. "I don't know … I assumed …"

"I don't know anyone else I'd rather spend time with … as friends," he added quickly. "I've got nothing better to do aside from keep an eye on my mom's place and watch TV."

Her expression told him she had many questions, but he doubted she would ask him.

"In that case, see you tomorrow, same time," she said.

They were the antithesis of that couple she was obsessed with —Dylan and Merry.

Unlike those two, he and Leah were two lonely people getting over a bad time.

CHAPTER 21

*H*e was going out of his way in order to make an effort with Peter. Something rich and warm trickled over her. Happiness.

This week had been like no other, and as much as she looked forward to her son coming home, a part of her was beginning to feel sad that after tonight, spending time with Brody outside of work would come to an end.

"That's it," he said, taking a step back and admiring the wall. They'd left the last one, the white one, until the end.

She set down the roller and crossed her arms. Brody came and stood next to her and together they surveyed the fruits of their hard work.

A huge smile spread over her face. "He's going to be so happy."

Brody nodded. "I hope this is good enough for him."

"Enough for him to call his friends over for a sleepover. I should think so." Peter had told her about his plans for his birthday, and after this long, hard and worrisome year, she wanted to make it extra special for him.

He hadn't asked for anything over the top. No party in the

house. He'd told her he didn't want a birthday present from her, and that having his friends over would be enough. But she'd caught him looking at a pair of sneakers on his computer and she'd made a mental note of them.

They were brightly colored, garish-looking, in her opinion, and they were expensive, but she'd bought them for him because she could, and especially because she was thankful that she was here to see this birthday.

In one of her darkest moments, when she had first been diagnosed with the cancer, one of her earliest fears had been that she might not live to see her son's next birthday.

But she had.

She was here, and she had much to be grateful for.

"I can come over again and help you move everything back into the room when the paint's dry," Brody offered.

"You've been such a huge help already, Brody. Thanks, but I'll get Peter to help me. It's about time my boy started doing something."

"I'm glad it's done. You'd have done it all yourself otherwise."

"I wanted to surprise him," she said, turning to him, her gaze falling to that thick broad neck, and those wide, wide shoulders.

Standing this close to him suddenly made her aware of every flutter in her belly, every beat of her heart. It was so loud, so pronounced, she was scared he'd hear it too.

He stared down at her. "It's a testament to how great a mom you are that you wanted to do this to surprise him. I'm glad I could help."

"I wanted to do something special for him, not just because he complained about the house falling to pieces–"

"It's not falling to pieces."

"It's not in great shape."

"There are small things here and there that need doing, perhaps ..."

She poked him in the ribs gently. "You're trying to be nice."

Had she really poked him there? It was the first time she'd done something playful, but she felt completely at ease around him, and he didn't seem to notice.

"I'm being truthful." He scratched his nose. "I can help you with those tiny little things that need fixing. I'm a handyman, Leah. Use me."

She would love to use him. She looked away, color heating her cheeks. In an attempt to stop herself from combusting, she blurted out one of her fears.

"I was scared I wouldn't be around for his birthday. It freaked me out."

"No. Really?" He turned to face her, his brows pinching together.

"This thing," she didn't like to name it, "it makes you think about life and death, and who gets lucky and has another chance, and who doesn't. I was forced to confront things I'd never had to think about before."

He lifted his hand and for one missed-heartbeat second, she expected his hand to cup her face, but he touched her hair, then moved his hand away. The look in his eyes said it all.

"I don't know what it's like to be in your shoes, but I never imagined that these are the thoughts you'd have."

Her shoulders sagged as she blew out a breath. "My greatest fear is that I could die. Not fear for me, but for Peter."

"No." He took a step forward, his face filled with worry. It was different, having someone feel this way about her. It was as if he cared, and she liked that. It was like trying on a new coat and feeling snug and warm, and so comfortable, you didn't want to take it off. That's what this new feeling was like.

"Once you know that death isn't a faraway event, once you

have that knowledge, it sinks in, and seeps into your core," she said, conscious of how close they were, the closest they had ever been with the distance from their faces no more than six inches.

So close she could feel the heat between them.

Brody didn't say a word, and his silence prompted her to get it out—the worries and fears she'd been harboring—holding them so tight to her chest so that Peter would never catch wind of them. "The shock is monumental at first, but then it stays with you and becomes part of who you are, like the color of your eyes and hair. I'm not afraid to die, but I'm scared of leaving my son alone. There's a difference."

A sigh escaped his lips. A pained expression haunted his eyes.

"I'm scared of leaving Peter. That was my greatest fear in all this, that I might not survive and he'd be left all alone."

"I never imagined ..." Lines checkered across his forehead. "All this time we've spent together, talking and sharing our experiences, I never thought your pain would be this deep."

He had no idea of the part he'd played in distracting her. "You've been a good friend, Brody. A really great friend and distraction, otherwise I'd have spent a lot of my time thinking things like this." The way she had been ever since she'd been diagnosed.

"I hate that he left you to deal with it alone, your ex," he said, surprising her. "You're better off without him. You deserve to be treated like you're precious, because you are."

His gaze dipped to her lips, and her heart almost jumped out of her throat in joy.

The way he looked at her, she thought he was about to kiss her. Her insides started to do the salsa. Sexy thoughts flashed through her mind as she licked her lips in preparation, staring at the juicy bow of his lower lip, wanting to feel it against hers.

But her thoughts soon changed course and flew to a different destination.

Fear set in.

She hadn't kissed a man in years. She was out of practice, and Brody had probably had a lot of practice.

She wasn't jaw-droppingly gorgeous. She didn't turn heads, but she could brush up pretty well if she put her mind to it.

Yet her femininity had taken a dent this year. Her self-esteem plummeted, and with it her belief that anyone would find her attractive. Not only that but she was recovering, and even though she was in the clear for now, her future was uncertain.

This not knowing, this living in fear—that she could get sick again at any time—it was like trudging through a vat of tar. She couldn't face the future with confidence and certainty, the way other people could.

"I understand you being wary of people, Leah, but you're wonderful. You're strong, and independent, and fun. I love spending time with you."

He was moving on, ignoring her earlier precedent. Her racing pulse set her body aflame. Something shifted in her belly, it wasn't the touch of butterfly wings, no tiny, light fluttering movements, but something big and heavy, as if a golden eagle had taken flight inside.

She was ready to throw caution to the wind, her fears evaporating like a puff of smoke.

Her body was ready, the blood pumping through her veins like a waterfall. Any moment now, she imagined Brody's lips would press against hers, fire on fire, sating a hunger that had started many weeks ago. His hand cupped her face.

She didn't dare breath.

Only, it didn't happen like that.

"Would it be okay if I planned a trip for us all to go fishing this weekend?"

CHAPTER 22

She hugged Peter as if he'd been away for months on a military tour.

"Where did you get this from?" he asked as soon as they walked into the house. He set down his backpack and picked up the big purple octopus Brody had won for her. In the haste of moving the furniture out of Peter's room before painting, she'd left the octopus on the couch in the living room and had completely forgotten about it. Or what she was going to say about it.

"The fairground?" It came out as a question instead of a statement.

Peter's brows rose. "You went to the fairground? With who?"

There was no way out of this. So, she tried deflection. "I'll tell you all about my week, sweetheart, but first I want to hear all about yours. You're the one who went away. How was camping? I want to know all about it."

"Why do I smell paint?"

"Come upstairs, I have a surprise for you." Glad to have something to change the topic of conversation, she rushed up the stairs with him following close behind. "Ta-da!" She gestured with her hand.

"Oh, Mom. You didn't!" Peter walked into his room, his face filled with joy, his hands on his head as he struggled to contain his surprise.

"Careful, don't touch the walls. It's still drying."

"Oh, Mom!" In the next second, he put his arms around her. "I love it!"

The emotion, the genuine enthusiasm—instead of the usual grunts and apathy— filled her with happiness. "You like it?"

"I love it. But the color, how did you know?"

"I guessed?"

He beamed at her. "You know me so well."

"Of course I do. I'm your mom."

"I love it."

He stared at the room, going over to the walls and examining them carefully. "It looks so much bigger now."

"Because everything has been moved out."

His eyes narrowed. "You didn't do this by yourself."

Her cheeks burned. "Brody helped me."

He looked at her and blinked a few times. She wished he'd say something, so that she could gauge his reaction. She hoped he wasn't still thinking about the octopus. Not that she had anything to hide.

Nothing had happened.

Unfortunately.

"I had a hospital appointment, sweetheart. I meant to tell you." She wrung her hands together, then saw the fear creep across her son's eyes. "It's nothing like that. It's good news. It's *great* news, actually. I'm in the clear."

"You are?" he whispered. His shoulders lowered a few inches, giving her an indication of his worry.

She nodded. "Yes."

"Forever?"

She couldn't answer that. She prayed it would be forever. "Let's hope."

He hugged her again, only this time he didn't let go as quickly. Sensing that something was wrong, she held onto him. "Peter?" And when he still didn't pull away. "Peter, sweetheart. It's fine. I'm fine. I got the all clear."

Slowly, he moved away, but his hands were still around her shoulders. "But what if—"

"Let's take it one day at a time. This is good news, sweetheart. This is the news we needed. Okay?" She willed him to smile. The last thing she needed was for her boy to worry about her. This burden and the stress weren't his to take on. She would do the worrying for both of them.

"Is that why you got the paint? So that you and Brody could do it together?"

Now she was going to look like a liar, when in fact, her getting the paint had been something she'd done before Brody had changed her plans for the week.

"Brody and I are friends. Nothing more. I wouldn't lie to you, but there is nothing going on."

"Is he the one you went to the fair with?"

"It was a spontaneous thing. He said he was happy when I got the all clear …"

"You told him?" Her son's forehead puckered.

"He already knows, sweetheart. Remember I told you that I used to see him with his mom at the hospital? We've been friends ever since."

"Friends?" He didn't seem to believe her.

"Just friends. It's possible to be just friends. We've both suffered in our own way."

She coughed lightly. She wasn't going to lie about anything. There was no reason to. She and Brody were friends and nothing more, and given the signals she was getting from him, it didn't seem as if he had any intention of wanting anything more.

Peter looked at her.

"He says he'd liked to take you fishing this weekend, if you want to go."

"Why's he want to do that?" The teenager's sullenness had returned.

"Because you looked as if you were interested when you saw his fishing equipment. Because he thinks it would be a nice thing to do. You don't have to. Brody wanted me to ask you."

"Maybe."

She wasn't going to push it. He'd only been home a few moments and already she'd thrown so much at him.

"So, you went to the fairground?" There was a book's worth of subtext behind that one sentence.

"And he won that octopus, and the next day we went to the beach and had a picnic and a bonfire."

"You did what?" Peter asked slowly, as if she'd told him she'd adopted a goat.

"I know. Imagine that. I had planned to start painting your room right away, but Brody … uh, me and him, we ended up making the most of this week. You were away and I hadn't had time to myself like that before, where I could—"

"You don't have to explain to me, Mom. I'm really happy you had a great time."

"You are?"

He nodded. "You look different."

Her head tilted to the side and she wondered what he could see imprinted on her face, because deep down, a part of her was disappointed. Although she'd once been happy to count Brody as a friend, she now wished that he could be something more.

CHAPTER 23

They went fishing off a pier which was about an hour's drive away.

Brody brought his fishing rod along and his fishing equipment, but it still didn't stop him and Peter from going to the tackle shop and having a good look at what was offeror sale.

She stayed where she was, though it was getting chilly. Brody had told her to bundle up, because it would be extra cold near the water, and it was. She'd made up a picnic just in case they didn't catch anything, and because she was dubious not about them catching something, but wanting to clean their catch and cook it, too. Peter seemed super excited by the idea, but she wasn't so sure.

As usual, Brody brought along some foldable chairs, and it was on one of these that she made herself comfortable and tried to read a book.

Tried, and failed, because being outside, watching Brody with her son, it held her attention. Soon enough, she closed her book and set it to the side, her eyes on the two figures in front of her and she rubbed her arms, feeling the cold.

For a man who didn't have children, Brody was better with

Peter than she thought he would be. Given that he probably only saw his nephews and nieces once in a while, he seemed to have a great knack for getting Peter to open up.

Her son took to him in an instant. Contentment warmed her, even if the cold in the air chilled her bones. She wished for the type of bonfire they'd enjoyed the last time on the beach.

Those were memories she carried with her, and dipped and dived into when she was faced with work and lonely evenings in front of the TV once more.

"I've got something!" Peter yelled. She heard Brody shriek in a congratulatory tone. "That's it, kid! That's it! Reel her in gently."

She got up and rushed over. "Have you caught something, Peter?"

"He sure has." Brody looked impressed. "He's a fast learner."

"Or lucky," she said, watching Peter's face, an expression of total concentration.

"Fast learner I'd say," Brody insisted, "though luck does have a small part to play when it comes to this. Yikes, kid! That looks like a big one. Now, focus on bringing her in."

Peter reeled the fishing rod until a big fat fish wriggled at the end of it.

She clapped. "Peter! You did it!"

"That looks like a mighty big one, kid." While Brody helped Peter to bring it in, she walked away, not able to face whatever it was they would do to the fish next.

She looked around the pier to find people scattered around, with their fishing rods in the water. To her it felt odd, people doing this for *fun*.

"He's good." Brody came over to her after a while and started to wipe the fish clean with paper towels.

She looked away, peering at him from the corner of her eyes, unable to face him directly. "What are you going to do with the poor thing?"

"Wrap it in waxed paper and store it in the ice box."

"And then?"

"Gut it. There are cleaning tables up ahead."

She moaned as if she were in pain.

Peter came over. "Yeah, Mom," Peter piped in. "We can clean it and cook it."

"You want to gut a fish?" she shrieked. Who was this boy? Peter seemed rapt in admiration when it came to Brody. While it lifted her spirits, the idea of gutting and eating that fish out here didn't sit with her too well.

Brody's eyes danced with amusement. "Would you rather I don't?"

"That you don't clean it and cook it?" she asked hopefully. "I would rather."

"Mom's squeamish like that," Peter explained. Brody smiled.

"What am I going to do with the garlic and minced shallots, lemons and a small bottle of white wine?" he asked. "I have a great recipe for striped bass."

She sat back down on the folding chair, feeling a little weak. Blood and guts she couldn't cope with.

"This is a great catch, kid," Brody said.

"Thanks. This is better than the camping trip I went on." Peter looked extremely proud of himself.

"Why don't you go see if you can catch some more?" Brody suggested.

She watched Peter walk away triumphantly. "He's having so much fun."

"I think he is."

She looked up at Brody, her heart full, her eyes filled with happiness. "Thank you for suggesting this. It was a great idea."

"I knew it would be. He's enjoying himself."

"Brody!" Peter yelled. "I've got another one."

"It can't be," Brody looked shocked. "He's better at this than me."

She watched as Brody left her side to join Peter. The image of the two of them together imprinted a new memory on her heart.

She'd been worried that Peter didn't have a male figure to look up to, and it was one of the reasons she'd wanted him to continue visiting his father for more than a few weeks in the year. But Peter felt neglected by his own father, and that broke her heart.

Brody stepping in, albeit temporarily, set her mind at ease.

CHAPTER 24

"*D*o you remember how we did it the last time?" Brody asked the boy, who was taking his new fishing rod out carefully. He'd bought one for him for a birthday present and had given it to him a week early.

"I think so."

In his experience, the best way for someone to learn something was to let them make plenty of mistakes, instead of hand-holding them every step of the way until you ended up doing everything for them.

"That's it." He watched Peter cast the fishing rod.

"This is awesome, Mr. Holt. Thanks for getting me this."

"Hey, you're welcome. A boy needs his own rod, and I didn't know what else to get you for your birthday."

"You didn't need to get me anything. I've had an awesome time just going fishing with you."

"Yeah?" A hole cratered open in his chest. He'd had such a loving upbringing, with parents who adored and loved him, and he sensed this kid had been short-changed. Not by his mother. It was plain for everyone to see that Leah's world revolved around her son, but that man, the father, her ex-husband, that piece of …

"I like you coming along, kid."

"It's been the best birthday present ever."

Brody raised an eyebrow, affection and protection filling him to the hilt. It was only a fishing rod. It made him wonder what gifts his father gave him. The slimy weasel. He was tempted to tell Peter to wait and see what his mom had bought him, but he didn't want to ruin Leah's surprise.

He liked this kid. He had a good heart. Leah was lucky. Scratch that. Peter was lucky. He was that way because of the way his mom had brought him up.

"I don't think your mom likes fishing much." She'd asked him if it was okay for just him and Peter to go because she needed to get a few things for Peter's upcoming birthday party. He was fine with that, and Peter was ecstatic. The kid seemed to look up to him.

"I'm happy to have my mom back. I'm glad she's okay now." Peter turned his head and looked at him. Remembering his own mother, and how the sepsis had quickly taken her, Brody understood the boy's worry.

"Your mom is going to be fine."

"Mom says your mom got sick, really sick …" Peter said.

Brody drew in a long breath, remembering that time. "She did. She caught an infection and … things quickly worsened."

"That must be the worst thing in the world, not having a mom." Peter's face crumpled, and he chewed his bottom lip.

"It is …" Brody stared at the ground. The scent of his mother was almost gone from her house. Now, there were only photos and physical things that pointed to the woman who had once lived there, but the tenuous reminders, like the lingering lavender scent she sometimes wore, were fading fast.

"Did you cry?" Peter asked softly.

Brody lifted his head. "Yes, I did cry."

"I can't imagine you crying."

Brody lifted his shoulders for a good few seconds before letting them drop again. "Doesn't matter how big and strong you are, your mom is your mom." He shrugged. "You can put on a face that you show the world, but in private, the tears still come. Somehow you learn to deal with it, because you have no other choice."

"I wouldn't want to live if my mom … if …" His head dipped, and he looked as if he was about to cry. Brody put his arm around the boy's slender shoulders. It hit him, how deeply Leah's illness had affected the young boy; how he had kept it in, all that fear and worry barely concealed beneath the surface.

Peter didn't look at him, and Brody respected that. Staring at the lake, he tried to reassure the boy. "Your mom has been given the all clear. Now they'll monitor her and keep an eye on her."

Peter sniffled. Brody cast a side-eye at him to check if there were tears streaming down his face. One lone tear rolled down his cheek. He squeezed the boy's shoulder again. "She's young, and she's going to be okay, son." And then, in a jovial voice, needing to lift the mood, "Doesn't she look fine to you?"

"She laughs a lot." Peter's expression slowly melted to a smile.

"She laughs a lot, huh?"

"She goes out more."

"Well, that's a good thing. How about we take this home and I'll show you how to clean it and cook it. That would be mighty impressive to your mom, don't you think?"

Peter's wide eyes indicated he was up for it. "Mr. Holt …" he hesitated.

"Yeah?"

"I wanted to ask you for a favor."

"Shoot."

"Could you help me with some painting, like you did Mom?"

"Painting?"

The boy explained how his mom had been talking to him about painting the house and giving it a little uplift. "I feel bad, 'cause I was angry one time and I told her our house was falling down." He chewed his lip thoughtfully. "I know stuff like that hurts her, I shouldn't do it but …"

"But you feel angry sometimes?" Brody suggested quietly.

Peter nodded. "So, will you help me? I don't want her to do it. I just want her to rest and get better."

Brody huffed out a contemplative breath. He wanted the same thing. With so much going on in this boy's life, it was no wonder he acted up with Leah, but times like now revealed how much he cared for his mother. He didn't have a bad bone in his body.

"Sure, I'll help you, but we have to discuss it with your mom first, okay?"

"Okay. She's so happy now, I know she's going to be cool with it."

She did look happy. Brody compared the expressionless woman he used to see sitting in the hospital waiting room to the vibrant woman who looked so joyous now.

"That's because of you," the young boy told him.

"Me?" His heart jolted with hope. "Did she say anything about me?" he asked, shrugging his shoulder dismissively, as if he didn't care, even though his ears were on alert.

"Just that you're her friend and that you're nice."

"Anything else?"

"Nah, that was about it, Mr. Holt."

Nothing. For all the effect she was having on him, that woman felt nothing. She was still focused on her recovery and couldn't contemplate anything else. She'd told him that, and he'd do well to heed it. "Less of the Mr. Holt, Peter. Brody will do just fine."

CHAPTER 25

"No way!" Peter cried, the look on his face priceless. "You got me these?"

"Aren't they the ones you wanted?"

He was so happy and so wrapped up in his new sneakers that he could barely reply. Leah did what any mother would do and caught the moment with her cell phone camera.

"Aww, Mom, thanks. But they're so expen—"

"I've been saving up," Leah told him. "It's fine."

Her son gave her a huge hug, holding onto her for longer than she expected, his hug tighter and solid. "Thanks, Mom. I really love these. How did you know I wanted these ones?"

She smiled and said nothing. Brody reached for her cell phone. "Let me get one of both of you. This looks like a moment that needs to be captured forever. Smile."

But she didn't need to be told to smile. Her heart was already full and when Peter threw his arms around her, it was close to bursting.

"You too, Brody." Peter motioned for him to come next to them. Leah lifted an eyebrow at her son. "Brody?"

"*Mr.* Holt ages me," said Brody, standing next to her.

"I can't fit us all in," said Leah, her nostrils suddenly assaulted by the fresh scent of Brody's aftershave. This scent lingered in her imagination for hours when she tossed in bed trying to sleep, trying to get him out of her mind.

"Let me take it," Brody offered. "My arms are longer, for now," he glanced over his shoulder at Peter. "You'll be overtaking me soon at the rate you're growing."

The easy banter between the two made her happy and she tried to focus on that more than the way Brody's hard body was pressed up against hers.

"Ready? On three." Brody counted down, but his zingy aftershave and the hardness of his body were the only things she could think of.

"Okay, let's get this show on the road," she said, moving away from him as fast as she could and picking up the wrapping paper from the floor. Peter's friends would be over soon and she and Brody were driving them to the gaming place where she'd booked a two-hour gaming session.

A morning of gaming was followed by a movie at the theater, with popcorn, nachos and hotdogs. But a group of healthy, hungry teens were now ravenous and they stopped for dinner at a pizza restaurant.

Peter had told her he was grown up now and that he and his friends wanted to be left alone as much as possible, even sitting by themselves at dinnertime. She'd laughed inwardly at this rites-of-passage request.

This year was tough for both of them, but she had never seen Peter look so happy. She continued staring at her son with pride, watching him with his friends, while she and Brody were at a different table at the other end of the restaurant.

"He looks so happy," Leah gushed. This had to have been one of the happiest days for her and Peter. He'd had a fantastic birthday.

Brody lifted a bottle of soda to his lips. "He's having a great time, and so he should. The kid deserves to."

Her boy who had turned fourteen today.

Fourteen.

She still remembered being in the hospital and giving birth to him while her husband was away on business. He'd called and told her how crushed he was to have missed it. When he arrived the next day, she presented him with their firstborn, feeling grateful and thrilled that he'd come at last. She hadn't seen it then, that she was second, maybe even lower down on her husband's list of priorities.

She'd been blind and oblivious.

Not so much now. Her life was so different now. She was so different.

After this, the boys were all coming home for a sleepover. She'd made up the beds and only needed to blow up the air mattress she'd recently bought. With the boys bringing their sleeping bags, she was sure they'd all find a way to fit into Peter's room. But she didn't expect them to sleep much.

Brody said he'd stay with her for a few hours, in case the bunch of boisterous teens got unruly.

She liked that. She liked the idea of not having to do everything by herself, but more than that she liked the idea of having Brody around. Someone that the boys would take heed of.

"He's a good kid, Leah. You've done a great job."

"He likes having you around," she countered. Brody was a steadying influence on him to the point that Peter wasn't as angry or as short with her anymore. Recently she'd caught glimpses of the younger and sweeter Peter shining through.

"I like taking him fishing. He wants to learn things, and that's an admirable trait in anyone, most of all in teens."

"I told you, we haven't done outdoorsy things like that, and I doubt his father would ever take him fishing or do much with him. He's too busy helping his wife change diapers," she grumbled, remembering that he'd done nothing for Peter. Her ex-husband used to leave in the morning and return late at night, when she was worn out from taking care of the baby, having been alone all day. She'd discovered that babies were demanding, and they didn't sleep all the time. They pooped a lot and needed constant attention when awake. When he'd come home from work late in the evening, he'd ask her what she had done all day, before running his fingers across the surfaces, and then he'd get annoyed that the house was filthy.

He'd never suggested a cleaning lady for *her*, but Peter had told her he had someone come in daily now to help clean his great big fancy house and to help his wife out.

Her body tensed just thinking about the disparity in how he treated his current wife and how he'd treated her.

"Did he send Peter anything?" Brody asked.

"A card and some money."

"Did he call?"

"I don't know. He might have called Peter on his cell phone. I didn't ask him. I didn't want to ruin his day. He'll tell me in time."

They glanced at each other, unsaid words floating in the space between them.

"Thank you for everything you do for him, Brody. It means a lot to Peter, and it means so much to me."

"Hey, you don't have to say–"

She raised a placating hand, wanting him to listen to her. She could talk about Peter and other things easily, but when it came to telling Brody how much he meant to her, her voice turned shaky, and tinny, and sounded weird.

"I do. I want to. You told me once that you appreciated having me in your life, but that goes double for you. I appreciate you … your help … so much. *So* much. I don't think

I can ..." She paused to take a breath because right now, with his gray-blues staring at her so intently, the insides of her belly were having a party, disco lights included. She tried to steady herself. "You won't ever understand how much you've done for us and what it means to me, to me and Peter, to have you around."

His lips twisted up at the corners, and it looked as if he was going to say something. She braced herself, hoping ... wishing ... he would say ... something. The longer the silence stretched, the more her insides churned. "What is it?" she asked, observing the struggle written all over his face.

"About that ..." He cleared his throat.

She sat forward, because he looked so serious, and it got her worried. "Yes?" Was he going to tell her that he'd soon be leaving the town hall?

"I'm going to Jackie's for Thanksgiving."

Her frown deepened. Thanksgiving? It wasn't so far away, but ... she let out a small laugh, relief letting her muscles unclench— the muscles she hadn't realized she'd been holding taut. "For a moment there, I thought you were going to say you'd finished working at the town hall."

His lips twisted some more and he released a sigh she didn't like the sound of.

"You're leaving?" Her insides pinched as if a pin had gone through her belly.

"The job ends before I leave for Thanksgiving."

Her shoulders slumped and she felt the weight of those heavy eyes on her. Brody gone and out of her life? She was only just getting used to having him around. She'd come to rely on him so much. And so had Peter.

"Hey." Her disappointment must have been palpable because Brody reached for her hand. It was warm, and big, and when he placed it over hers, it hid her hand completely. She blew out a breath, the movement so bold on his part that it made her feel as if they were stepping into new territory.

"It's not that big of a deal," he said, his voice oddly raspy.

"It's not?" Her voice lowered to a whisper. She was in shock, not only from his news, but the way his thumb was sweeping over the back of her hand, gently rubbing it. He'd never done that before.

Not. Ever.

Did he know what he was doing? Because she liked it, and she didn't want him to stop.

"No." He side-eyed her. Those thick lashes on dark hooded eyes; the color a thin ring now that his pupils had grown larger. Just when she was getting used to this, he stopped abruptly, guilt sweeping across that finely chiseled face.

"We don't see each other as much at work now as we do outside of it," he said, moving his hand away. This was true, but a fog had descended on her, and her brain was a soggy gooey mess, still processing the touch of his skin against hers. "We're friends now. We can keep in touch. It won't matter if I'm there or not."

She stole his words and packed them away in a corner of her mind to analyze carefully later. "Yes," she nodded, a little too aggressively. A little too fast. "Yes. We can still keep in touch. Peter would like that."

From the periphery of her vision, she saw Peter walking towards them.

"Mom, can we go home now? We wanna start our sleepover."

CHAPTER 26

"It's time we started thinking about our Christmas pageant."

Hyacinth's face lit up like a Christmas tree. And Leah's heart sank. She didn't mind doing it. For many years, it had been an event that had allowed her to meet people, and because she was in charge, the position brought with it a modicum of respect. People looked up to her for advice and guidance.

It made her feel important, which was why she continued to do it, and also in the needy hope that one day, one magical, life-changing day in the future, it was possible that she could meet a single dad who she might hit it off with.

She shivered as she remembered the ulterior motives behind many of her decisions in the past.

Those things no longer mattered. She was a different person, grateful for every day, and not concerned about finding a life partner. Her focus now was on being well and healthy, and staying that way.

But, with Brody around, things had changed.

In *her* mind only.

Brody was still as friendly and as helpful as ever, as gorgeous as ever, and their friendship was on an even keel. As flat as the horizon, unfortunately, even though for a few heart-stopping moments at the pizza place, on the evening of Peter's birthday a few weeks ago, she'd thought he was going to say something profound. Her heart had been waiting, but in vain.

He was also still on Heather's radar, because Heather always asked her if she and Brody were still friends. Leah always answered that 'yes,' they were, and told her that nothing was going on. It was the sad truth.

But her days weren't as empty now; they were filled with many happy moments. Brody took Peter fishing a few times and invited them over to his place where he cooked his and Peter's catch of the day.

It was a beautiful thing to watch Peter and Brody's relationship blossom. The boy needed someone strong and sensible in his life to look up to, someone who showed him that he mattered.

Brody was that man.

Her son seemed to thrive under Brody's tutelage. For a boy who'd left his bed unmade and his clothes strewn all over the floor, his transformation was a miracle to behold.

Once, when Peter and Brody went fishing, she'd gone shopping for herself, for the first time in a long time. She'd even had her hair cut, getting inches taken off at the ends, which were all dry and with split ends. She indulged herself, something she hadn't done in years.

Later, they announced that they had somehow decided to work on the house together and start painting some of the rooms. The news made her jubilant. She'd been thinking of starting on that project in the New Year but if Peter was offering, and Brody was happy to help …

So, when her boss brought up the Christmas pageant again, her response hadn't exactly been enthusiastic.

Leah patted the back of her neck. "The Christmas pageant? I'm not sure that I want to take on the responsibility this year, Hyacinth."

They still had a month to go before the rehearsals started in the first week of December. "Did you think about maybe asking Dylan if he wanted to …?"

Hyacinth's chest rose in indignation, or consternation, Leah wasn't sure which.

"That man has made it abundantly clear to me that he is far too busy to take part in our Christmas pageant. Although …" Hyacinth smiled slowly. "He and Meredith are expecting their first child this Christmas." She clasped her hands together in ecstasy, as if she were the happy grandmother-to-be. "Her mother is delighted. Absolutely delighted, I tell you. Meredith having another child, and having a reason to like Christmas again. It's a Christmas miracle for sure. I mustn't be too harsh on Dylan. I'm happy for him and his family."

Leah's hopes sank.

And after a careful pause, Hyacinth asked, "Are you not feeling up to it this year, dear?"

The way Hyacinth looked at her, with her saggy gray eyes full of concern, made Leah feel immediately guilty. This woman was so good to her. She couldn't walk out on the play. She would need to help out for most of December, but it would be a few weekends and maybe an evening or two a week. It all depended on how bad the cast were.

Her insides roiled at the thought of it. There was a chance that her month *could* be filled with lovely moments.

Fun times.

And maybe the promise of something more? Something seemed to have changed between her and Brody, especially after Peter's birthday. It was hard for her to put her finger on it, but Brody seemed more … at ease? Sometimes his hand would brush against her arm if he wanted to get her attention. Or he'd look at her as if he was about to say something.

Something had changed, but she wasn't sure what.

"It's not that ..." she said slowly. Brody had made a few suggestions. This—coming soon after he'd told her that he was flying to California for Thanksgiving—confused her. These mixed signals played with her mind and she was none the wiser as to what his true feelings for her might be. He'd suggested that they could go to Whisper Falls to the Christmas market there when he returned, and they could even go ice skating on another weekend.

If her heart could smile, it would be grinning like a joker. Brody had spent so much time with them, and he loved it as much as she and Peter loved having him around. And now they were making plans of things to do.

She'd fully expected her son to wrinkle up his nose. When she later mentioned it to him, Peter was all for it. Whenever Brody suggested anything, Peter seemed to think it was a good idea.

"I can find someone if you're not well enough—" Hyacinth started to say.

She couldn't let her down. Not Hyacinth. "Forget I said anything. I'd be happy to do it."

"Wonderful!" The older woman clapped her hands together. "Oh, I so love Christmas," she cried, her thin vibrant pink lips stretching into a worm-like smile. "All the smells and the sounds."

"The smells and the sounds?" Leah asked, and then she thought about it. Of course. Christmas did have smells and sounds. "You mean spiced wine and cinnamon? Roasted chestnuts and hot chocolate. Gingerbread and Christmas trees?" She was suddenly getting into the flow of it. "Open fires, and the crunch of freshly powdered snow, a lots of feel-good Hallmark movies."

Hyacinth's expression sobered. "I was referring to the

Nativity, to midnight mass, the scent of candles, and the singing of Christmas carols and hymns."

Leah's mouth opened and then closed again.

"And baking!" Hyacinth cried, suddenly excited.

"Baking?"

"I love to bake. Don't you?" the older woman asked.

"Sometimes." She used to bake before. She'd make things with Peter when he was little, they would bake cookies and cakes and then decorate them.

"There's nothing like a hot oven baking magnificent things, and a kitchen littered with the fruits of your hard labor," Hyacinth continued. "I love to bake in big batches, so that we have plenty to eat, and plenty to give out."

The picture Hyacinth painted was of huge family get-togethers, but as far as Leah was aware, Hyacinth was by herself.

Two hot dogs and a bag of cotton candy later, and Peter was still starving.

It was too cold to go fishing and, since Peter often hinted that he'd like to go to the fairground that Brody and Leah went to when Peter had been away, that's where they'd gone. After many hours of fun on all the rides, and spending lots of money on the stalls, they were now driving to a pizza place on the way home.

Days like that were what Brody looked forward to. Spending time with Leah and her son was becoming the norm.

The pizzas they'd ordered arrived and Peter started to polish his one off. The boy could sure eat. That's what Brody liked to see. It reminded him of his own appetite at that age.

In getting to know him, he'd discovered that Peter wasn't the way Leah described him. He wasn't angry or sullen.

With Brody, Peter was the complete opposite. He believed

Leah though, and knew, from what his sister Jackie often said, that children often misbehaved with their parents and were as good as angels with other people.

His time with this family filled his own empty hours outside of work. Sitting together at this table, to unknown eyes, they probably seemed as one family.

"Hyacinth mentioned the Christmas pageant to me," Leah announced.

Brody eyed her, noting that she had a new hairstyle which suited her. He'd wanted to say something, but he hadn't, always conscious of the words she'd said at the start.

But, darn it, if she didn't look more gorgeous each time he saw her. She'd been a quiet mousy woman with hair that looked unbrushed or thrown into a bun away from her face, but now, the transformation was hard to ignore.

These days she dressed in a way that showed off her slim legs, wearing tight casual jeans and blouses which she didn't tuck in. A touch of mascara and lipstick, made those brown eyes bigger, and those soft lips fuller. She didn't wear her hair up anymore either. It was always brushed, sleek, but wavy, and swept away from her face, framing it perfectly.

Each time he saw her alone, he wanted to broach the subject, but the risk of ruining their friendship prevented him.

How much longer he could suffer this torture, he didn't know.

"Are you going to do that again, Mom?"

"We're *both* going to do it." Leah gave Peter a stern look.

"I don't want to. I'm fourteen now."

"You're good with the lighting," his mother insisted.

"But I don't wanna."

Leah pressed her lips together. "Come on, Peter. I can't do it all by myself."

"Why does she keep asking you?" Peter moaned. He was

about to shove what must have been his sixth slice of pizza into his mouth.

"Because Dylan Fraser no longer wants to do it," Leah answered. "I stepped in for him once and I've been stuck doing it ever since."

"Is it so bad?" Brody joined in, the name of Dylan Fraser making his stomach turn.

Leah looked at him, her eyes softer, darker, like pools of melting chocolate. He couldn't look away if he'd tried. "Stuck is probably the wrong word." She broke off a piece of garlic bread thoughtfully. "I used to like doing it. We did, didn't we?" She turned to Peter for confirmation.

"It was okay."

She stared at Brody again. "I used to like it. It was nice being a part of something. There's a community feel about it all. You have all these proud moms and dads forcing their kids to enter." She giggled. "And then the final show is on Christmas Eve in the town square. It's really pretty. Everyone comes together."

He nodded, remembering. His mother liked going to see the Christmas pageant every year.

"I told Hyacinth to ask if Dylan would want to do it this year," Leah continued.

"Why would you do that?"

"I just wanted to have a break this year." Her shining eyes were on him again, probing for a reaction. "I wanted to spend my free time doing fun things. You mentioned the Christmas market and Peter's itching to go ice skating now so …"

The way she looked at him, he didn't need to worry about Dylan Fraser. Leah sounded excited about spending some of the festive season with *him*. The three of them.

That's what it *sounded* like to him.

One day soon, he was going to have to find out for sure.

"It looks lovely." She stepped back and admired the new color of her bedroom. Brody and Peter had just finished painting one wall, and they'd called her to have a look.

"It's better than the dirty white," Peter agreed.

She'd managed to do a bit of painting, until they'd asked for snacks and she'd disappeared into the kitchen. Secretly, she believed that this was their way of getting her to do *nothing*.

Pale pink was the color she had chosen, so light it was bordering on white with a hint of rose.

She loved it. It was a change from the off-white, almost yellowing, hue of before. Change was good, and she welcomed it. Because everything around her was changing. She was starting to feel like a bloom unfurling, coming to life and bursting with color. There was a vibrancy in her step, and a desire to spring out of bed and be out there in the world. Her self-esteem was rocketing. Her body image, her health, her life, were things she was starting to feel good about.

Over the last few weeks, they'd tackled the rooms in the house with gusto, and now hers was the last one to be painted.

Slowly, she found out that Peter had asked Brody for help.

Her son was so pleased with the transformation of his own room that it spurred him into wanting to spruce up the rest of the house.

She'd felt bad about Peter asking Brody, because she knew that man wasn't going to turn Peter down, and even when she'd insisted that she could do it, and that she wanted to, Brody told her that being busy helped him, otherwise he'd sit around moping at weekends.

His life seemed to be emptier than she had first thought. There was no 'significant other,' and Heather was still sniffing around him whenever she saw the two of them together.

Brody being there and helping with the painting was a thrill for her because she got to see more of him. He was in her house. How much more informal could it be?

She'd noticed that he'd also fixed a couple of minor but annoying things around the house, like a rickety table, and uneven bookshelves. A doorknob that had come off. To make things even better, Peter had taken an interest in home DIY, and Brody started teaching him the basics.

This put her mind at ease. She could change lightbulbs, had changed fuses, had even learned to catch spiders and get rid of them, but anything more advanced set her back and these things went unfixed.

"What do you think?" she asked Brody, who remained silent.

"It's ..." He scratched his stubble.

She sensed he didn't like it. "It's?"

"It's a girlie color." He made a face, then turned his head, bringing his right ear to his right shoulder, and then did the same with the other side, as if he was easing out the tension in his neck and shoulders.

She watched from the corner of her eye, because they were magnificent shoulders indeed. When he painted, she found herself transfixed, staring at his broad back, at those strong, muscular arms as he angled the roller on the wall. Tiny, snatched, sneaky moments that were delicious.

"That's because it's my room." She raised an eyebrow. "If it were your room, I suppose you'd paint it blue or gray or something?"

"You bet I would."

If this were his room … she shivered, and then killed the thoughts before they mushroomed into flights of fancy.

Sometimes, she thought he liked her. Not like a friend, but maybe something *more*.

And sometimes, she knew this was just her dreaming. Because if the man had liked her, he'd have made a move by now.

CHAPTER 28

They'd been shopping for Christmas trees.

He hadn't even wanted a tree. Not this year, but Leah said she needed to get one, and he decided to go with them because, for some reason, he didn't like the idea of Leah wrestling with a big tree all by herself.

It occurred to him later that Peter would have helped her. Leah must have bought a tree before, many times. But he liked being around them, and helping them if he could.

It wasn't as if he had anything better to do.

And now they were at his *mom's* house decorating the tree she wouldn't be here to see. All three of them. If it was left up to him, he wouldn't have bought *a* tree, let alone *two*. He didn't need one for his mom's house, and he most certainly didn't need one for his.

Leah could be sneaky like that, he'd come to realize. She often managed to coax him into doing things he didn't want, but which he needed to do because ... they made him feel good.

Like now.

From the garage, he'd bought out the boxes in which his mom kept her Christmas decorations and now, opening each box with its carefully wrapped baubles, with lights and Christmas ornaments strewn all over the floor, it was like having his mom here with him. He'd helped her put up the tree every year, and this year, Leah was getting him to keep that tradition going.

Just like his mom would have wanted...

What she wouldn't have wanted was for him to wallow in self-pity and be swallowed up by a tsunami of sadness.

Yet spending time with Leah and Peter ensured that none of this happened. He hadn't been looking forward to Christmas, and even the idea of going to Jackie's felt like a lot of trouble. He didn't want to do anything. He was settled here, what with work and … Leah.

Things were still up in the air with regards to Peter's Christmas plans, and depending on those, Leah would either spend Christmas with Peter or alone. Brody didn't like the idea of that.

It wasn't his business but still, he didn't like the idea of her being by herself. As for himself, Jackie was determined to have Christmas at their mom's place despite him telling her that it was pointless since their mom wasn't even here.

As soon as Leah found out, she'd more or less convinced him that he needed to have a Christmas tree there.

"It will be good for Jackie and the kids, Brody, and even for you, to have this house all dressed up and ready for Christmas. You're doing the right thing," she said, as she carefully hung a delicate red ornament.

"Mom would have liked it," he agreed, seeing the tree come to shiny, glittery, sparkly life.

Men didn't have the feels, they weren't tied to places like women seemed to be. Jackie and Leah shared the same belief, that this was what his mother would have liked: to carry on, to spend time and celebrate Christmas as a family.

Watching her, he was tempted to say something, about how

right she was, and how much this meant to him.

But he also wanted to say more.

The words were untested and uncertain, but the feeling in his heart was undeniable. For too long, he had been patient, watching, waiting, wondering.

"What do you think of it so far?" She glanced at him over her shoulder. "No?" She took his silence to be a sign of his displeasure. She looked at the tree, stepped back a few feet, then angled her head as she examined the decorations carefully.

"Uh …" He cleared his throat.

"Brody, can I get something to drink?" Peter asked suddenly. He'd finished untangling a string of lights which were yet to go up.

"Sure, kid. Go knock yourself out, there are plenty of cans in the fridge," he answered.

Leah's hands flew to her hips defensively. "I think they look nice. What don't you like? Too much red?"

"It's not that …" he said slowly, the words poised on the tip of his tongue now that the coast was clear. There never seemed to be a right time, and he was always wary of what he was going to say.

Things with Leah were … new. Different. Easy and laidback. She had no agenda. She wasn't looking for anything—she'd made that perfectly clear—but while this had been easier to heed in the beginning, he was struggling with it now.

He couldn't read her as well as he could most women. Not like he could read her annoying friend Heather. That woman was so transparent, she might as well have had a love heart tattooed to her face with his and her names on it. The brazen hussy had eyeballed him for months and had recently asked him if he was going to the town hall Christmas party. He'd told her he wasn't invited before letting her know that his work at the town hall was coming to an end.

Her eyes had shuttered rapidly as if the shock of the news had short-circuited her brain. "You don't have to be invited. You can go as my plus one," she'd said.

"And why would I do something as crazy as that?" He'd looked her coolly in the eye and tried to get that one sure fact through that brainless head of hers.

He and the other guys had their own little farewell party at Quinn's, a rowdy bar just on the outskirts of the town.

That was the kind of place his guys preferred, and it was fine by him. They didn't care for appetizers and informal social events. No fancy sit-down meals or champagne. Just a good old beer or two and a couple of games of pool.

"Then what?" Leah's long eyelashes fluttered at him, and he was quickly shaken out of his reverie. "Gold," she said, not waiting for him to answer. "Maybe I need more gold." She crouched on the floor and started looking through the ornament boxes. "Give me a hand, please?" She stared up at him through long, long lashes. Was that mascara? Or had her lashes grown even longer overnight?

He crouched down, and opened a few of the boxes, searching for the one that had the gold-colored baubles.

"Here," he held out a box for her.

Her mouth dropped open. "These are so gorgeous!" she squealed, her slim fingers hovering above the different shapes; a reindeer, Santa's carriage, a snowman and a Christmas tree.

He wanted to take that hand and put it to his lips. She hadn't flinched that time he'd put his hand over hers when they were sitting at a restaurant. He couldn't remember why he'd done that, but it never left his mind that she hadn't minded.

Careful of what she'd once told him, he'd stopped, regained his senses, and decided that now was not the time.

Just like *now* wasn't the time. He was flying to California in a few days' time. He couldn't say something and then disappear.

It would be better to leave it until he got back.

CHAPTER 29

She pummeled the dough into shape but her arm hurt. It was a pain similar to the one she'd felt when Heather had mentioned Brody.

"I asked Brody if he wanted to come to the Christmas party," Heather had said earlier. Leah was too shocked to answer at first. Then, as calmly as she could, plastering on a nonchalant expression she didn't feel, "What did he say?"

"He said he'd think about it."

She hadn't believed her, until spiky, niggling, pernicious thoughts tasered their way into her mind and stayed there.

She couldn't easily broach this subject with Brody either, because his work was done. He and his men had slowly but surely vanished from sight. The town hall was brighter, cleaner and shinier. It was amazing what some new paint and touching up could do to a place; make it look like new.

She'd walked past the small temporary area where the workmen used to gather, where she'd often find Brody. Her heart hurt seeing that space bare and empty.

There was no more Brody. No more catching him at lunchtimes or running into him in different parts of the building.

No more plans to be made.

Maybe putting up the Christmas tree at his mom's place was the last goodbye? She was aware of his plans for Thanksgiving and Christmas, but she had no idea when she would see him again.

"Are we still going to see Brody?" Peter asked, when a few days had passed and there was no sign of him.

"I don't know. We won't see him now until after ..." She stopped kneading the dough for her pizza base. She didn't know when she'd see him next. "I'm not sure when."

"Where's his next job?" Peter asked.

"I have no idea. I don't think Brody has any idea either." She tried to rotate her shoulder, but the pain was sharp.

"You okay, Mom?" Peter stared at her, a deep vertical line between his brows.

"I must have pulled something when we moved my bed back in."

"I told you we should have waited for Brody."

She'd managed just fine without him, and it would be for the best if she stopped relying on him as much as she did. He wasn't going to be around much anymore. He'd said he would, but she was wise enough to know that what people said and what they did were two different things.

Seeing more of each other at work had allowed their friendship to evolve fast and easily, so that when she'd mentioned she'd needed to get a Christmas tree, Brody offered to come along with her.

It was because of that she'd ended up at his mother's house helping him, the Christmas grinch, decorate the tree there. He didn't want to do anything, but with his sister and her children coming over soon, Leah knew that the once warm and inviting house full of memories would be the opposite with nothing festive in it. She'd convinced Brody to change his mind.

"We can't always wait around for Brody to come and fix things. Goodness knows the man has done enough."

"But he likes helping, and he does this stuff for a living."

"Not moving furniture."

"You know what I mean, Mom. Look at you. You're in pain. I can make dinner, if you want."

Something warm and sweet, like honey, poured over her heart. She loved this new version of Peter, and she hoped he would never change.

"That would be great. I'll make the dough and you can roll it out and put the toppings on. Thanks, sweetheart."

Her arm would be okay in a few days' time. She needed to start exercising and taking care of herself; something she had gotten from Brody. He had a pretty good regimen going on and she'd been in awe when he'd told her about his daily exercise routine.

"Is it only us two for Thanksgiving?" Peter asked, sounding disappointed.

"Who else is it usually?" she asked, laughing. "If not us, then you with your father."

"I'm not going for Christmas either."

She huffed out a breath. She wanted Peter to herself, but she had to play fair. "Your father won't like that."

"I wonder why," Peter grumbled under his breath. "He just wants me to babysit his other kids."

"That is not true."

"How do you know? You're not there to see it."

She didn't want to believe it, because to do that would mean she'd done the wrong thing by sending Peter there. Tom had been a lousy husband to her, and he'd never been a great father either, but he was trying.

That's what he told her.

That's what she wanted to believe, for Peter's sake, that his father wanted to have a relationship with his son.

"I want to spend Christmas here with you, Mom."

"I would like you to stay here, too, sweetheart, but we have a deal, Peter. Your father gets you for one of those occasions."

"I don't want to go, Mom. I don't. Can Brody come over?"

"His family is coming here for Christmas, you know that."

"Aren't we going to see him at all anymore?" His voice was thick with shock.

"I told you, sweetheart. I don't know what Brody's plans are. His company has finished the project at the town hall. We might not ever see him again. People get busy with their own lives."

"But …" Peter's forehead was a question mark. "He can't just leave."

The pain in her shoulder, coupled with Peter and his questions, and Heather, were starting to grate on her. "People can, and they do."

Your father did.

"It's not fair." He marched out, reminding her that his hormones and temper were still all over the place. She understood it, though. His reaction. After growing up without a good male role model, he'd finally found one in Brody. For him to stop coming over would be a gut-wrenching experience for them all.

She couldn't think about life with Brody in it. Now was the time to do the opposite and get used to life without him.

Just like it had been before. Just her and Peter.

She was peeling potatoes for dinner the next day when the phone rang, and a few seconds later the doorbell rang.

Peter had answered the phone, so, wiping her hands, she opened the door, only to find Brody's cool, hard face staring back at her. The face she'd been seeing in all her empty moments ever since he'd been gone.

"You're supposed to be in California." Her heart mushroomed with glee. Had he changed his mind? Was he going to be here for Thanksgiving? A smile the size of the moon slowly spread across her face.

"I'm going tomorrow." He dipped his head. "I thought I told you?"

He had? She'd assumed he'd left over the weekend given that she hadn't heard from him.

And why would she?

Her foggy brain couldn't deal with dates in this moment. "I thought you'd already gone."

He shook his head dismissively. "Too many things to sort out. When projects end, it gets hectic, believe it or not."

She opened the door wider. "It's good to see you again, stranger. Peter will be pleased." Him here, now and unexpectedly? She'd take that any day.

He stepped inside. "I was passing by, so I thought I'd say 'bye' before I went."

"I'm making dinner. Peter's been chewing my ear off about when we'll see you again. I think he's missing you already."

"Just Peter?"

"What's that?" she asked, as she led the way to the kitchen.

"Is Peter the only one who's going to miss me?"

She reached for her vegetable peeler before giving him a side glance, trying to gauge his expression. Brody liked to joke around. "Peter?"

"Yeah. Is he the only one who's going to miss me?" The timbre of his voice changed, dropped down to super sexy again.

How was she supposed to answer that? Her insides were beginning to heat up. Brody showing up unexpectedly had kindled all kinds of emotions in her. She'd prepared herself for him being away, all the way in Cali, and she'd intended to use this break to mentally distance herself from him.

But now that he was here, filling out her kitchen with his Hulk-style presence, she was feeling on edge.

"Not just Peter." She peeled her potato fast and with fury. "I'll tell you someone else who's going to miss you." She pointed her peeler at him as a smile settled on his face. "Heather."

"Heather?" His brows crashed together.

She knew Heather was nothing and no one, and she'd heard Brody complain about her whenever they were accosted by her during lunchtime, she *knew* this, but even so …

"I don't care about Heath—" he started to way.

"Are you going to the town hall Christmas party?" She tried to level her voice. It was a simple enough question. Not accusatory. Not loaded with anger. But her voice somehow didn't sound normal.

"No," he stated firmly, as if she'd asked him if he wore a wig. "I'm not invited."

"Heather told me she invited you."

"Is that why you're all worked up?"

"What? No! Who says I'm worked up?"

"Your cheeks are red."

"It's hot in here." Her casserole was cooking in the oven, and she needed to make the mashed potatoes.

Of course it was going to get hot in the kitchen. She fanned her face. She was flummoxed, frazzled, losing her cool. If she wasn't careful, she'd revert back to clingy, needy Leah, and she was better than that. "You didn't mention it," she said, feigning casual nonchalance.

"Should I have?"

A myriad of emotions ricocheted through her. This slow-building, emotional connection to Brody, a blossoming, burgeoning, mind-twisting, schoolgirl crush which was nothing more than a flirty, frothy, flimsy souffle of feelings, it had to stop. And now.

"I don't know. Should you have?" she replied, hating the way her voice was quaking.

From the corner of her eye, she could make out that Brody had folded his arms and was staring at her as if she were the main attraction in a museum of freaks.

"What's going on?" His voice was quiet.

She was sinking, even if she had ten life buoys now, they wouldn't be enough to keep her afloat, not the way Brody's news had weighted her. Like iron chains around her ankles.

She couldn't answer that. Where would she even begin? How could she tell him how she felt about him? So, she focused on steadying her breathing.

"Leah?" He touched her arm. A sizzle crackled across her skin. Clenching her teeth, she faced him, tensing her muscles in an attempt to stay calm.

"Everything okay?" His blue-gray eyes pierced through her like an X-ray machine and soon enough he'd find evidence of her jealousy. She breathed slow, slow, slowly, trying to regulate her breathing. "Heather took great pride in letting me know that she'd asked you."

"I imagine she did," he answered in that slow, assessing way.

"She seemed to think it was a sure thing." Peel, peel, peel.

"I'm sure she did."

She threw the peeled potato into a pan of water and picked up another potato. It wasn't the Heathers of this world she was worried about, it was the other nameless, faceless Heathers this man was sure to meet. The ones he might like and want one day, the way he didn't want her.

Her belly quivered.

"Does it bother you that she asked me?"

"No, why would it?" she asked, her voice tight.

He cleared his throat. "I can't stand the woman. You should know that by now."

She kept her gaze on the potato and tried to still the beating of her heart.

"Now, if *you'd* asked me, that might be another thing."

Had she misheard?

"I said if you'd asked me to come, as your plus one, I would have."

"Why's that?" she managed to say, her pulse rocketing like a missile.

"Why do you think?" He stared at her, that simple action making her heart go funny. This man's superpowers were impressive. He didn't even touch her, yet he affected her physically. "Why do you think I'm here?" he continued, his voice soft as silk now, gliding over her easily. "There's something—"

"I don't wanna come at Christmas! I don't wanna come ever!" Peter's anger reached her ears and her heart cracked.

She rushed into the living room to find Peter pacing around, running his hand through his hair, his face red, his lips curled. "You don't care. You don't care about me."

"Peter," she hissed. "Give me the phone." What had gotten into this boy? Her thoughts were all over the place. She'd shared this heartfelt moment with Brody and now she was dealing with Peter and his father; a dysfunctional relationship if ever there was one.

"Hey, kid," Brody whispered. Peter looked up, his eyes widening as he saw that Brody had come. The boy couldn't give her the phone fast enough, letting go of it as if it was a hot potato.

Clutching the phone, she did her best to speak to her ex, while watching Peter high-five Brody. Then Brody led the boy back into the kitchen, out of earshot while Tom started to lay into her, blaming her for turning Peter against him.

"It's not like that, I've told him he needs to see you either for

Christmas or Thanksgiving," she tried to explain.

"You've turned him against me. I knew you would. My son hates me."

"He might have had a better relationship with you if you'd treated him like a son."

"What are you trying to say?" Tom shrieked.

"I'm not *trying* to say anything. I said it, and I know that you know it's true. Peter says you don't care about him. He says you get him to babysit your other children."

Silence sliced through the air like the rage coursing through her veins. Tom hadn't denied it. "It's true then?"

"They're his half-siblings. He needs to get to know them better."

"Peter's growing older now, Tom," she said in a calm and level tone, "and I can't and won't dictate how he spends his vacations."

She hung up, not wanting to waste any more time on this man. Walking back into the kitchen, she saw Peter and Brody sitting at the table, talking.

"I'm not going—" Peter started to say as soon as he saw her.

"You don't have to. I told your father you're old enough to make your own decisions."

"I asked Brody if he could spend Christmas with us."

She and Brody stared at one another. He looked as shocked as she felt. "Peter—" They had shared a moment, something verging on almost intimate, as if he'd been about to tell her a secret. But having Brody come over and spend Christmas with them? She wasn't so sure. Nor did she know why her heart was starting to race again.

"He can't, Peter."

"Sorry, kid. My sister's coming over with her family."

She hated seeing her son down, but Brody spending Christmas with them? That would be odd.

CHAPTER 30

He'd tried to tell her.

He'd had a perfect moment to say something, but Peter's outburst had prevented that.

The boy had told him that his father called to wish him a happy birthday two days after his actual birthday.

Brody understood the boy's pain, not feeling as if he mattered. He was more aware than ever of how much Peter looked up to him and he didn't want to let the boy down.

Which was why having to turn down his request to join him and Leah for Christmas was hard to do.

Leah had been odd that day, peeling potatoes but everything about her body language told him she'd rather poke his eyes out with the peeler.

He'd seized that moment to try to tell her how he felt ... using what he perceived to be a bout of jealousy.

Over her friend Heather?

Had Leah not paid any attention to what he'd said?

He couldn't stand that interfering, desperate woman.

"Here you go," Jackie's husband shoved a beer in his hand.

"Cheers." Brody lifted the bottle.

Jackie rushed into the room, where he and Ian were sitting with their armchairs in a recliner position so that they were almost horizontal, watching a football game on TV.

"Want me to give you a hand?" he asked, as his sister's slightly flushed face stared down at him.

She'd been preparing for the great big Thanksgiving feast tomorrow, and she had the children helping her.

Ian had ordered takeout for tonight. Now he felt guilty sitting here having a beer and watching TV.

"You can have today off, Ian, seeing that Brody's here, but there's a heap of vegetables that need to be peeled."

He heard Ian's deflated gasp beside him. "I was being a good host."

"After dinner."

"Want me to give you a hand right now?" he offered.

Jackie smiled at him sweetly. "You get today off, but tomorrow..." She nodded and disappeared.

"Slave driver," Ian muttered under his breath, before quickly adding, "But I wouldn't have it any other way."

They carried on watching TV, and all Brody could think of was what Leah was doing.

"You can't hate your father, sweetheart." She hugged a pillow to her chest, now that she had an opportunity to say something to Peter about it. He'd been so worked up when he'd had that argument with his father over the phone, and then after Brody left, she still hadn't wanted to say anything until her son calmed down.

"I wish he was more like Brody," said Peter, when the two of them were lounging in front of the TV after their small Thanksgiving feast.

"You shouldn't have asked him to come over for Christmas

day, sweetheart. It's not ... we're not that close, and he has family."

"How can you say that, Mom? We spend more time with Brody than we do with Dad, and its better time. We have fun. He's a nice guy. You have fun. He makes you smile."

She turned to see the expression on Peter's face, but her son's eyes were on the Christmas movie on TV.

Her son had stated a fact. She had laughed a lot more, smiled a lot more, around Brody.

And now she wondered what he was up to, and how his Thanksgiving was going, and when he would be back.

She also wondered what would have happened if he'd been able to finish saying what he'd started.

With all the suggestions he'd made and gotten Peter excited about, she was sure she'd find out soon enough.

"But Grandma's house won't be the same without Grandma." His five-year-old niece made the saddest-looking face.

He held out his arms, beckoning her to come over to him. She ran into his arms, and he swooped her up and sat her on his lap. "It won't be, but she'll see us when she looks down and—"

"From heaven? Is that where she is?"

He nodded. "She'll see us all together and it will make her so happy."

"Grandma will be happy?" his niece parroted.

"Yes."

"But how can she be happy when she's not with us?"

His heart deflated. He glanced at Jackie, seeking help. He wasn't used to dealing with such raw and direct questions. Questions he had no answer for.

"We won't see her, honey," her mother said, "But we'll *feel* her there. She'll see us all together, and it will make her happy, even if we can't see her."

His niece's tiny little brows quirked together, and then

smoothed out, as if her mother's answer made sense. She turned to him again. "Does Grandma have a tree?"

He could answer this one. "She sure does. It looks awesome. I think Grandma would have loved it. You are going to be seriously impressed." He tapped his finger on her button nose.

"I am?"

But before he could answer, Jackie asked, "You decorated the tree at mom's place?"

He glanced up at her. "I sure did, with a little help."

"How big is it?" his niece asked.

"It's huge." He used his hands to show her. "And it's got so many pretty lights, and ornaments, and –"

"Presents?" his niece asked innocently.

He chuckled. "I expect so. Have you been good?"

She nodded, her eyes wide and shining. "Then I see no reason why Santa would not leave a huge pile of presents for you all."

She squealed with joy, then jumped off his lap and ran off, screaming to tell her siblings that good news.

"What help?" Jackie asked, settling herself back into the comfy couch.

He opened his mouth. This was going to be tricky if he wasn't careful.

Very tricky.

But he had the perfect explanation. "You remember the woman Mom and I used to see at the hospital?"

"What woman?" Jackie's eyes narrowed, and her hands rested on her stomach. "You never mentioned anyone."

"I didn't?" He scratched his ear, then told her about Leah, and how he'd met her at the hospital, then explained that he'd ended up working where she worked. From there, he proceeded to tell her that he'd helped her with a few DIY tasks around the house, but left out that he'd also helped paint all the rooms in her house.

No need to mention the picnic or the fairground or the many other things he and Leah had done.

"You've never mentioned her before." Jackie's quiet eyes pinned him in place like a drill sergeant digging for answers.

"I haven't?" He tried to effect a nonchalant tone.

Jackie lifted an eyebrow, and he could just imagine her mind going full speed, filling in the gaps and jumping to conclusions. He hadn't ever talked about his friends, or relationships, no mention of personal details, because there hadn't been anything worthy to mention before. This had been a long-standing joke between her and Ian, and they'd often teased him about not being the settling down type, and now he'd confessed to having a strange woman in their mother's house, decorating her Christmas tree.

"No, you have not. Is there something you'd care to share?" his sister asked, her face twisting with what looked like horror.

Startled by her drastic reaction, he straightened his spine, standing taller. "It's not what you think."

It really wasn't, unfortunately.

"I hope we get to meet her when we come—" Jackie's face twisted, as if she'd tasted something bitter. In the next moment, she clapped a hand over her mouth and ran, almost hurtling into Ian who'd walked in. "I don't feel so good—" she started to say, before running out. The sound of Jackie throwing up filled the air, and he was sure he heard another similar sound coming from the other bathroom.

"Mom!" one of the kids shouted down from upstairs. "Mom, I'm going to be—"

It was the sound of vomit hitting the floor.

Peter was out with his friends and she was home alone with nothing to do but watch Christmas movies on TV.

And dream.

What if she, too, could have a happy ever after like the characters in these movies? She tried not to think about it, or Brody, but she was sure he'd told her he'd be back a few days after Thanksgiving.

He was the one who had suggested they go to the Christmas Market at Whisper Falls. He'd gotten her excited about going ice skating, too.

But he hadn't called. He hadn't shown up unexpectedly. He'd done nothing about those plans.

It sucked to be thinking about him when he so clearly had a life and was happy without her.

But he'd been about to say something. It didn't help her to imagine that the thing he was going to say would be romantic. Who knew?

Knowing Brody, he'd probably been about to tell her of a new place for him and Peter to go fishing again once the weather got better.

She turned on her side, slipped the pillow under her head, and reached for the box of chocolates on the coffee table.

She'd popped a hazelnut and dark chocolate creation into her mouth when the doorbell rang. When she answered the door, her eyes nearly popped out of her head to find Hyacinth standing there with a large octagonal tin in her hands.

"Well, hello," she boomed, and stepped right inside, thrusting the metal tin into Leah's arms. "I've been baking. Cinnamon buns and some peanut chocolate chip cookies for Peter."

She was too speechless to reply at first, then, "Why, th-thank you. I think." She opened the lid and to her surprise the beautiful smell of freshly baked food wafted to her. She was tempted to pick up the sweet-smelling and still warm buns and devour one. But she was also curious.

"This is so sweet of you, Hyacinth. You didn't have to—"

"Nonsense. I love to bake."

She vaguely remembered Hyacinth telling her.

"How was your Thanksgiving?" Leah asked. "Please, sit down." She hurriedly moved her cup of coffee and box of chocolates to one side, then offered the box to Hyacinth who turned her head away, wrinkling her nostrils.

"Thank you, but no. I can't stay long."

Why was she even here?

"These are ... these are lovely." She nodded at the box which the elderly woman had brought.

"Good. Make sure you eat them."

Eat them, as opposed to what?

"How was your Thanksgiving?" she asked again.

"It was fine. And yours?"

"Oh, it was wonderful. It was just Peter and me." She folded her arms. "But it was good. It was ... nice. Did you ... were you ... what did you do?" She didn't like to pry, but she was also curious.

"I spent it with my sister, as usual."

"Your sister?" Leah gasped. Hyacinth might as well have told her she was a serial murderer, for the shock she'd given her. She'd never heard Hyacinth mention any family.

"Yes. With Dorothy. We mostly spend it together. Her children and grandchildren come to visit, you know. It's wonderful. But sometimes I feel like I get in the way."

"I'm sure it's fine," said Leah, nodding as she took in this new morsel of news that changed her perception of Hyacinth. Now she no longer imagined her being alone, but the idea of her sister surrounded with her family while Hyacinth looked on, somehow didn't sound that much better.

After a pause that had grown long and uncomfortable,

Hyacinth rubbed her hands, as if she'd managed to get some dust on them, and announced that she was leaving. She had things to do and people to visit. She moved towards the door.

"But ... but... wouldn't you like to have something to drink?" Leah blurted. "And maybe stay awhile?" Hyacinth had visited before, when Leah had been just diagnosed with her breast cancer. She'd come with flowers and a plate of cookies.

"I have things to do and people to see, and it's December." She clapped her hands together in a theatrical manner. "We are going to be busy." She waggled a finger at Leah. "I've put out an announcement on the Starling Bay forum, and I've sent out word, we start the rehearsals next week. Are you prepared?"

She'd been bracing herself for this. "Yes."

"We start next weekend. I expect a flurry of children to come hurtling through the doors of the theater."

Leah grimaced. Hurtling wasn't a word she'd used to describe the children who came to the Fitzsimmons Theater and were herded there by proud parents.

"Make sure you're ready," Hyacinth told her.

"I am."

"If you could check the costumes in the theater, see what needs a good wash, and what needs to be replenished ..."

She always ended up with the costumes. "I'll take care of it."

"I don't know what I'd to without you, my dear." And, just like a hurricane that had trampled across her quiet and cozy afternoon, she vanished.

CHAPTER 32

The whole house had come down with a viral bug.

Jackie refused to believe it had been her Thanksgiving dinner. It could have been the takeout they'd had the night before, but he didn't see how that would have taken all but two of the younger children down with a severe vomiting and diarrhea bug.

He'd come down with it, too. The entire house lay quiet, except for the five and seven-year-olds.

He'd been too sick to travel and had flown back days later than he'd originally planned.

But now that he was back in Starling Bay, he had things he needed to put right.

Things that needed to be said.

And no number of interruptions were going to stop him.

It was late afternoon when he drove over to Leah's house. Now was the time. Tomorrow, he had a new job, a smaller project this time, but it was out of town, meaning it would be too late when he got back from work to see Leah and set things straight.

"You're back?" It was Peter who opened the door when he knocked.

"Got back this morning, kid." He walked inside, his eyes scanning for signs of Leah, while Peter asked him how his Thanksgiving was.

They talked, and he waited, hoping that Leah would come by. Surely, she'd heard his voice by now?

He told Peter he'd been sick and that's why he was only now returning home. The boy asked about ice skating. "Can we go?"

"Sure. That's why I'm here. I was hoping to ask your mom what her plans were."

"I didn't mean go now," said Peter. "You've only just flown back."

"There's no point going now," Brody agreed. He had other plans, but he noted how Peter's expression dropped. "We need to make a day of it. How about next weekend?"

"Can we?"

"Sure." He looked around. "Where's your mom?" She was likely annoyed at him, because he hadn't gotten in touch. He'd caught the bug bad, as bad as Jackie, and it had rendered him useless with no energy given how much he'd thrown up.

Not being able to see each other at work, and with the festive break, meant that a hint of frustration had crept into their friendship; at least, he felt that way. But he'd also noticed the last time he'd been here, Leah had gotten all hot and bothered for no reason, about someone as inconsequential as her friend Heather.

"Mom's in town."

He jerked his head back so fast it was a surprise he didn't give himself whiplash. "What's she doing in town?"

"She's at the theater, something about sorting through the costumes for the Christmas pageant."

"The theater? The Fitzsimmons Theater?"

Peter nodded. Brody knew where it was. "I should go."

"Why don't you wait for her here?" Peter suggested. "We can play a video game. Mom'll be back soon."

As much as he wanted to do that, hearing the plea in Peter's voice, he needed to see Leah more. He lifted his hand. "I'll be back soon, kid. Won't be long."

Her head was inside one of the trunks filled with costumes.

The costume room at the Fitzsimmons Theater was medium-sized with a line of clothing racks against two walls and a large chest of drawers. Along one side were a couple of trunks which contained the props and costumes for the Christmas pageant.

She'd finished going through the props. The manger was still in good shape, as was the baby Jesus and a few other items.

It was the costumes that needed to be checked for rips and tears, and to see if any of them needed washing.

She didn't have anything better to do on a Sunday afternoon, and she had promised Hyacinth. Having devoured two cinnamon rolls for breakfast, she'd decided that she ought at least take a look.

It wasn't as if Brody had kept his promise. If they were going to the Christmas market, or ice skating, or doing other fun stuff, it would have to be just her and Peter.

Tom hadn't kicked up a fuss after Peter's call. The man likely didn't want to have to take care of Peter, especially when their third child was nearly due.

Kneeling on the floor, Leah had her back to the door, and her head in one of the trunks as she went through the costumes.

Holding the sheep's costume up, she wrinkled her nose in disgust. It smelled musty and sweaty. Like moldy cheese.

The door creaked open as she pulled out the donkey and cow costumes, fearing that they would need a good wash.

"There you are."

She stayed frozen in place, shock icing the blood in her veins.

Brody?

She turned around, and slowly got up from the floor, holding a donkey costume in her hands.

"What are you doing here?" she asked, as he strode towards her. Two steps and he was within inches of her. His face looked gaunt. Dark circles that he'd never had before now ringed his eyes.

"I wanted to see you." There was a firmness behind those words.

"When did you get back?"

"A few hours ago."

He was standing so close. So unusually close. It wasn't just his aftershave that her body welcomed, but the heat that rolled off him.

She stood her ground. Whatever game he was playing, she wasn't going to step back in defeat, letting him think he'd won.

"Good Thanksgiving?" she asked, noting that he looked quite pale. If he'd landed only a few hours ago, what was he doing seeking her out?

"Could have been better." He seemed agitated, as if something was eating at him.

"Why are you here?" she asked.

"I never got a chance to tell you something."

"Oh, really?" Her voice was light and airy, the complete opposite of the catastrophic upheaval taking place inside her. She crouched back on the floor and started to sift through the trunk again, pretending to look for something. What she needed was to put some distance between her and Brody. "I need to get this done today."

"What are you doing?"

"Sifting through the costumes for the Christmas pageant."

"Hey," he said, reaching for her elbow, and gently trying to get her to stand up. "I didn't come here to watch you look through these clothes."

Heat rose along her cheeks, and something sweet and sultry sizzled in the air of this room which suddenly felt small.

She stood up slowly, curious to hear what he had to say. "What is it, Brody?"

"I didn't get to finish saying what I needed to say to you."

"I don't have a lot of time. The rehearsals start next week."

"The pageant can wait." An urgency turned his voice raspy. Lifting her chin defiantly, she looked up at him, into the soft and inviting depths of his eyes. She was in danger of taking a deep dive into them, and a part of her felt like doing just that.

"What, Brody? What do you have to tell me now?"

His brow lifted, as if he wasn't expecting the sharp tone of her voice. "We got sick. Some bug or something. We all caught it except two of the kids."

"You got sick?" she echoed. It would explain why he hadn't been in touch like she had hoped.

"I was sick, so was Jackie. The others didn't get it too bad, but that's why I didn't call or come back sooner."

"I'm glad you're better," she said, her voice softening.

"I know we had plans."

"I wouldn't call them plans," she said, "I mean, we were talking about doing stuff, you were talking about doing stuff, and ..."

"I hated being away from you, and I missed you."

Her stomach hollowed out, like one of the rides she and Brody had gone on at the fairground.

He had missed her? She clutched the donkey costume harder than ever. His eyes bore into hers, his gaze bouncing from one eye to the other, as if he wanted to figure out what she was thinking.

But she couldn't think because his hands were on either side of her arms. And he was only a few inches away. She could feel a sizzle, something crackling in the small space between them. It made her woozy, as if all the bones in her body had turned to jelly. She was aware that he was waiting for her to say something, but she couldn't. Her nerves, like the synapses in her brain, were all jangled up like last year's Christmas tree lights.

"I was at Jackie's and all I could think of was that I wanted to be here, with you, and Peter."

He'd said another sentence, and it was nice, it was a sentence that the men in the cheesy Christmas movies she'd gorged on all weekend said to their soulmates.

Only, this man was saying it to *her*.

And he wasn't her soulmate.

He'd taken up a huge space in her head ren- free, but … she somehow didn't believe what he was saying.

"Peter missed you," she said finally, in a voice that sounded hollow and unsure.

Brody shook his head, letting out a sigh that signaled his frustration. "I wish Peter's mother would miss me as much as I missed her."

She swallowed. And when he raised his hand to her forehead, his thumb sweeping away a lock of her hair, she swallowed again. The furry fabric in her hand made her fingers sweaty and it was suddenly getting too hot.

"You told me you weren't looking for anything, that you didn't want to complicate your life. You said you'd sworn off men. I respected that. At least, I tried to. But as I've gotten to know you, I find that harder to do each time I see you. I've tried to fight it. I have, because I don't want to ruin our friendship, but I want more than friendship now, and sometimes, I feel as if you do, too."

She opened her mouth, not because she had the words to say what she felt in her heart, but because she was in awe. His words were the words she had always longed to hear.

He touched her lips, outlined the upper lip gently with his thumb. Electricity crackled along her arms and along her back. Goosebumps snapped to attention, and with it the tiny hairs along her arms.

When he cupped her face, bringing to life a fantasy she'd often imagined when she lay her head down on her pillow, she dropped the donkey.

It was going to happen. He was going to kiss her, just as she'd been hoping and dreaming about.

He dipped his head, his arms encircling her waist and pulling her towards him. She felt as if she was floating on air. Her heart jack-knifed inside her chest. And then it happened, in delicious slow motion at the start, and then all at once. His face zoomed in, his scent intoxicating her. That first brush of their lips swept her into a universe of stars, up, up, up and away into the galaxy, where she danced in the inky darkness.

His touch sent her into a tailspin, and she slowly, tentatively, slid her hands up his hard-as-steel arms, so big she could barely wrap her fingers around them. His mouth pressed more firmly, and she sank into him further.

This closeness, once the stuff of dreams, still felt like a dream even though she could feel him, touch him, taste him.

"Is that you my—" The door creaked open and they sprang apart, like two teens caught in the classroom. Only to find Hyacinth staring at them as if they were naked.

The jewels in her brooch glinted under the light, and in the uneasy quiet, her jaw dropped. She was speechless, a feat Leah had never before witnessed.

"Not again," she heard Brody mutter under his breath, and then he did the unthinkable. "Ms. Fitzsimmons," Brody strode to the door, placed his hand on the knob, causing Hyacinth to take a step back. He advanced again and, to her surprise, Hyacinth stepped back until she was on the other side, outside the room.

"If you don't mind ..." Brody's voice dripped with silent anger, but it could just as well have been lust, it was so low, so raspy. "There's some unfinished business I need to take care of. I'm really sorry to do this but this is more important."

He closed the door on her.

Leah gasped. He turned around, his chest heaving as if he'd run a marathon.

"You can't do that to Hyacinth. Nobody ever shuts the door on her. *Ever.*"

"I just did." He reached behind him and locked the door. "Nothing is going to interrupt us now. Nothing is." Then, as if he'd realized what he'd done, he put his hand out in a placating gesture. "I didn't mean to ... this doesn't look good ... I'm not holding you hostage ..."

His words, his confusion at what she might think, it only endeared her to him even more. She was locked in a room with Brody, and she didn't care. She welcomed it. They'd been stopped so many times, and he'd just told her how he felt.

Her heart hammered against her chest, seeking escape, as if it were tied to a helium balloon and wanted to fly away.

"Come here," she said, her voice turning desperate with need. He took a few sure steps and reached her side.

"I locked the door because this is more important. I want you to know—"

But she didn't need Brody's explanations. Not in this heated, sultry, long-awaited moment. He had ignited a deep buried burning fire inside her, and she needed him. Wanted him. Springing up on her toes, she curled her hand around his neck and brought his head to hers.

That was all the confirmation he needed before he kissed her. She kissed him back. They were like two starving people who had hungered for each other and were now let loose in the pantry. He cradled her head, his fingers raking through her hair, while she reached for his jaw, felt the stubble prickle her fingers.

They were a mess of hands and lips, breathing one another's air, kissing as if this was their one and only chance.

She couldn't think, but only *feel*. Feel the stone hardness of his muscles against her, taste the sweetness of his mouth.

She moaned against his lips.

This had been months in the making.

CHAPTER 33

If it were not for the scan she had to go to the hospital for, Leah would have floated on air from the moment she left her home.

Anxiety swirled with dread inside her as she set off, but she calmed herself down, reminding herself that everything had gone well the last time. She felt well and was full of energy, and the reason for that happiness was the tall and gorgeous workman who had given her a kiss, or five, that she would never forget until the day she died.

She rushed into work, noting that Brody had finished here, but things had changed and she didn't need to worry. What they had was solid. Etched in stone, it was not the stuff of flimsy memories or airborne wishes. He'd kissed her, made her feel the way she hadn't felt in ... ever.

Tom hadn't been a great kisser. He hadn't been a great *anything*. What he had provided had been support, and a home, and she'd been blind and desperate to fall so easily for such thin promises.

But none of that mattered anymore.

She and Brody were at the start of something new and special.

She hadn't told Peter yet. This scan was a niggling worry, something she wanted to get over and done with, and once she could rest easy, she'd break the news to her boy.

Still thinking about yesterday, the smile on her face never left, so that when she walked past Hyacinth's office, she couldn't resist going back and knocking on the open door. She bounced into the room.

"Sorry I'm late, Hyacinth, I had—"

"I know. It's in my diary. All good?" The woman raised a hopeful eyebrow.

"I hope so. I'll hear back in a day or two."

The elderly woman looked at her, her lips moving as she if was about to say something, then thought better of it and didn't.

"It's going to be a good one, this year's Christmas pageant," she said, excited by the thought of it. This year's pageant had indeed gotten off to a spectacular start, what with her and Brody in the costume room. She would cherish those memories forever, and would remember them as the start of something. Desire had been blossoming inside her for weeks, and yesterday some of it was sated. She looked forward to the future and all it had to offer.

"You're all fired up and ready to go," Hyacinth remarked. "It's good to see you with a smile on your face, my dear."

At which her smile widened, if that was even possible. She had something to look forward to again.

"I'm happy." She nodded as she said it, the feeling bone deep.

Yesterday had been magical. When things got heated, because months of pent-up frustration could do that to people, she and Brody had walked around the town square, admiring Starling Bay's Christmas tree and decorations that lit up the square.

Christmas made her happy. Peter loved it, too. It was the one time of the year she really looked forward to. The bright golden fairy lights strung around the town square put a sparkle on everything, and the majestic Christmas tree in the center was a beautiful thing to behold. The air buzzed with excitement and anticipation. People were happy, busy, but happy, and there was hustle and bustle everywhere.

She was happy, too, and was suddenly seeing the world through new eyes. All because of Brody. Even running into Merry and Dylan hadn't dampened her spirits, and glancing at Merry's ginormous belly had made her feel happy, not jealous.

She'd been working at her desk for a few hours when her phone rang. She answered it quickly, thinking that it might be Brody but the doctor's voice—something she wasn't expecting— sent chills down her spine.

"Ms. Shriver, we need you to come to the hospital right away."

She slumped into her chair, her heart thudding.

"Why? What's wrong?" But she knew. Didn't need to hear the explanation because a distant part of her brain had already prepared for this result; had known it might be coming. And here it was.

"I can't discuss it over the phone, I'm afraid. You need to come here."

Her chest constricted, and something like a vise gripped her lungs so hard that she struggled to breathe.

"When?" she asked, feeling weak as she forced her lungs to let in some air, but the walls, like her fears, were closing in on her. The doctor told her to go directly to the hospital and meet with the team who was taking care of her before.

Less than half an hour later, she was sitting across the table from the consultant who had overseen her radiotherapy treatment. She smiled at the woman, trying to put on a brave face even though inside she was falling apart.

The doctor told her that the scan had shown a lump in the same breast, and while it was nothing to get too worried about, the doctor wanted her to have a biopsy right away. Just to make sure, she'd said.

So, she did, then went home.

For the next two days, as she waited for the results of the biopsy, she was more withdrawn, wanting to cut off from the world. Peter didn't notice a thing, but Hyacinth did, and so did Brody. He was too busy to meet her until the weekend, he said, because he was starting work on a new project. She'd told him it was okay. What she didn't say was that she didn't want to see him yet. She cited tiredness, and that she had a lot to think about and juggle, what with work and the Christmas pageant.

"I'll help you with that," Brody had answered.

There would have been a time once, not more than a few days ago, when she would have been overjoyed at that. But she couldn't face Brody yet, and if the news wasn't good, she wasn't sure she wanted to face him at all.

She couldn't think about Brody any more than she could think about the Christmas pageant. The sheen had worn off those two things, and now worry mixed with fear and settled in her stomach like a loaf of two-week-old bread. Heavy and hard.

Two days crawled by in excruciating slowness and then she was summoned back to the hospital.

The doctor looked her in the eye and calmly announced that the lump was malignant.

She wasn't surprised. She'd already known before the doctor had told her, before she'd seen the woman's smiling face and somber eyes. The disconnect was telling.

It all turned dark so quickly. The future that was just within her grasp quickly slipped through her fingers, like the grains of sand in an hourglass. She was forced to confront the dark demons of death.

It wasn't just Brody she couldn't have, her future was on shaky ground too.

The next few minutes, as the news sank in, were the longest of her life. Leah's mind flew to another place. Images whizzed past in front of her, of Peter on his birthday, of his glowing face when he'd seen the new sneakers she'd bought him, and his expression when Brody had given him the fishing pole.

"But the good news is that it hasn't spread. This is a local recurrence," the doctor said. Which meant that the lump was in the same place as the last time. She suggested different treatments, talked her through the options and what each route would entail. Radiation wouldn't be enough this time and she would need to think of chemotherapy.

"A mastectomy is another option," the doctor continued. Leah stared back in a state of numbness.

"A mast…mast—" She couldn't even say the word much less think about it.

"A mastectomy. Some of our patients prefer this because it gives them the best chance of making sure all the cancer is caught."

"That's what you said the last time," Leah said. "You told me we'd get it all, after the lump had been removed and the radiation."

"It doesn't always go according to plan. That's why we monitor and check."

"You told me I was in the clear."

She felt cheated. Her happiness of these last few months had been an illusion. She'd allowed herself to find joy, to live, to have fun, all because of the all clear.

The doctor gave her a kind and empathetic look, one which she had probably given to hundreds of women. "Take a few days and decide on what course of treatment you want, but I would like to start your treatment as soon as possible."

"How soon?"

"As soon as you decide."

"But how soon? How long do I have?" She needed to speak to her parents and make sure that Peter was taken care of.

"I would like to start by next week." The doctor went on to explain in more detail but even though she listened, she wasn't sure how much of the news sunk in. Her mind gravitated to darker places, to Peter being left alone, to the worst outcome, to this being her last Christmas.

"But ... I have ... I have a Christmas pageant to do, and ... and ... my son, Peter ..." A chill entered her body, turning every limb, every muscle, every cell to stone. She was supposed to break the good news to Peter about her and Brody.

Not this.

Not about her cancer coming back. "My son ..."

"I understand," the doctor said, her kind eyes full of emotion, her voice soft, but it didn't dull the pain that sliced her flesh like a butcher's knife. "You take the time you need, but it would be better for us to do this no later than a week."

The warning in that soft voice wasn't lost on her. She was going to die if she didn't move fast enough.

Die.

All her hopes and sparkly, festive dreams smashed to pieces. Just when her life was starting to come together, when things were so much better with Peter, when she finally had a shot at love with a wonderful man, then this happened. "It's not fair," she squeezed her eyes shut, clamped her mouth shut to stifle the loud sob that stuck in her throat. Fat tears rolled down her cheeks. "It's not fair. I don't want to die, I have so much to live for."

The doctor whipped out a few Kleenex tissues from a box conveniently placed within reach, and walked over to her. "Leah," she said, handing her the tissues. "It hasn't spread. We have a good chance of getting this, with chemo or mastectomy, we have a better chance of making sure it doesn't spread."

She sobbed into her tissues. Chance? Is that what her life had come to? No guarantee. No certainty, but a chance. She keeled over, howling into her tissue, the floodgates had opened and she broke down. A reassuring hand squeezed her shoulder gently. The doctor didn't say anything else, but stayed there, perched on the edge of the desk, her hand on Leah's shoulder, being supportive and quiet.

She had recomposed herself enough to get home, but by the time she walked into her home, she was in pieces again. Collapsing onto the couch, she sobbed, clutching her pillow for comfort.

She tried to calm herself down, but she couldn't. It was impossible to, because nothing about this situation was good. She reached for her phone and called Brody in a state of panic.

It was mid-afternoon, and he'd still be at work, he was busy, he'd started at a new place; she knew all this, but it didn't matter.

She needed him.

CHAPTER 34

His face lit up the moment he saw Leah's name on the caller ID.

He answered the phone, his lips already stretched to smiling. The thought of this woman being at the other end of the phone was enough to make his heart swell.

"Hey—"

"Can you come over?"

"Why? What's happened?" Her voice was different.

"Come over," she pleaded.

And that was enough. She wouldn't have asked him if it wasn't something bad.

Peter.

"Is Peter okay?" he asked, scrambling for his car keys.

"Brody … I need you."

"I'll be right over."

"I'm at home."

Something had happened to Peter. Or maybe her ex had done something? It had to be something really bad for her to be at home.

He was worried that she'd changed her mind after yesterday.

That was another option. He'd put his heart on the line, opening up and confessing his feelings for her because he could no longer hold them back.

The way she'd kissed him told him she felt the same way. Being locked in that room having intimate, uninterrupted time— way past overdue. Her lips, her eyes, her sparkling face, she was all he had thought about.

Instead of heading to the first floor to check the wiring, which he'd been on his way to do, he headed straight out of the door to his car. He hadn't even told Carlyle or any of the others. He'd call someone on his team on the way because he didn't want to waste any time looking for them.

He floored the gas pedal, driving like a man possessed. It had to be bad news. The worst kind. And then it hit him, like a rock thrown at his face.

It was back. The cancer.

Maybe.

Couldn't be, another voice intervened.

It. Could. Not. Be.

He punched the steering wheel as he waited at the lights, his insides tying themselves into knots.

Brody was at her door less than ten minutes later.

"What's wrong?" he cried, his face a car wreck as he stepped inside, his hands reaching for her face.

She stepped back, didn't reply, *couldn't,* because all of a sudden her throat closed up. The contents of her belly threatened to eject. She was hollow inside.

Terrified.

Voicing it out loud was a confirmation that this was real.

She'd been in a state of denial, even when the doctor explained everything to her.

"Leah, talk to me." He seemed to have aged with worry.

"It came back."

"What did?" He peered down at her, his brows pushed together. His big, strong arms went around her, iron bands across her lower back and shoulders. "You're shivering."

She couldn't stop, not even when his arms squeezed her gently.

"The cancer. It came back," she said, speaking into his chest. She heard a shocked gasp fall from his lips, and then he hugged her again.

"Okay." Still holding her, he moved away a few inches. She lifted her face to see the million questions in his eyes. "We can deal with this."

We?

If she had known this was coming, she wouldn't have let him kiss her. She would not have ventured into something with him. Now was not the time. She stepped away, wriggling out of his arms, before folding hers, putting up a defense shield, needing distance between them.

"Tell me what happened." The puzzled look on his face told her he didn't like it, the way she'd pulled away. But he didn't come any closer.

She told him everything, and he didn't interrupt once.

"And so, they want to start the treatment next week."

The surprise in his eyes flashed through those blue-gray irises so quickly, she almost missed it.

"We'll get through this, Leah." This time he stepped forward. "You're not alone anymore. It will be fine." His words were soothing; a great comfort to know, but what else could he say? Brody wasn't the type of guy to walk out on her, but she didn't want his pity, or his niceness. She didn't want him to feel obligated. She didn't want to put that on him. What they had was so new, it was cruel the way life had worked out. What a difference a day would have made.

She stepped back as his gaze penetrated through her. In another life, it would have been hypnotic, but reality had torn the curtain off her dream world. This was real. It was her life, and he had no idea how it felt. "You don't know that." The devil was dancing in her head, and he was telling her she could die.

Words were cheap. But they didn't cure cancer. How did he know she would be fine?

He was being reassuring, as much as anyone would be, to someone who had just been told that their cancer was back. Something soft flickered across his eyes. Sympathy? Pity? Sadness? "I know you're scared, but you can't go into this being anything but positive."

Be positive? That was easy enough for him to say. He wasn't the one living with this death sentence. It was back, and it was growing inside her. Cells multiplying, spreading the cancer around. The doctor's words rang in her ears: if she didn't act fast, it would spread everywhere.

She'd woken up this morning feeling on top of the world, and in the space of a few hours, her life had changed. Now, she was back in hell.

"My doctor says I have a few days to decide."

"Decide?"

"I need to have chemo or … something else. …"

She had known which one she was going to go for. One was slow, and would make her sick, and then she would still have to wait and see. Or she could have the mastectomy, remove a part of her that made her a woman, and hope that it might increase her chances, and give her a better rate of surviving.

But she couldn't talk to Brody about these things. She tried to hold herself together, hugging her arms around herself in an attempt to stay strong, and hope that big, fat ugly tears wouldn't escape from her tear ducts and roll down her cheeks. She couldn't fall apart in front of Brody, because then he'd feel even more obliged to stay by her side.

If only she could have taken back yesterday. Yesterday had given her a glimpse of the type of life she could have, and just as she'd started to savor and cherish that little taste of happiness, it had all been snatched away.

This wasn't fair. Life wasn't fair, and she felt this so completely in this moment now.

She had been down this road before. Had to face the fear alone and get through it. She'd done it before, and she would do it again.

Brody moved towards her, questions flickering across his eyes.

"Don't. Please." She didn't want him to hold her, or comfort her, because she didn't want to get used to it. Didn't want him to think he had to do anything or react in any way. If she got the mastectomy, he wouldn't look at her like this again. Like the way he was looking at her now, as if her pain and misery were his to share.

As if he would stay with her every step of the way.

She hadn't been thinking clearly when she'd reached for her phone. "I shouldn't have called you," she said, her voice sounding hollow and faraway. The alien words fell from her lips as if they were in another tongue.

"Why not?" The lines crossed his forehead, and his narrowed eyes reached deep within her, as if he was probing for the meaning behind those words.

"I can't … I shouldn't have called you. This isn't your problem."

She had gotten so used to having him by her side that she

wasn't thinking straight. A few kisses in a locked room did not signify anything.

He didn't need her to burden him.

"What are you doing?" Brody's face turned stony, his eyes hardening as if he didn't like the way this was going.

"I'm trying to tell you something."

"I hear a woman who is scared." He took another step towards her. "But I've told you, Leah, I'm not going to let you go through this alone. I'm going to be by your side every step of the way."

"I don't need you to be." The words were easy enough to come out, but when they hung in the air between them, like a barbed wire fence that split them apart, her heart ached with longing.

His eyes narrowed further, he was appraising her carefully. "You're scared, it's only natural for you to feel that way. I would be too. I can't take your fear away, Leah, but I *will* be there by your side."

"Why would you do that?" she tossed back.

"Because I care for you. I have for a long time; I just haven't said it. But yesterday …"

"Yesterday was … I don't know. Getting carried away in the heat of the moment." She waved her hand dismissively. All these months they'd been together, doing so many things together, spending so much time together, and he hadn't made a move until yesterday. Maybe he'd missed her and the perfect opportunity had presented itself, him finding her in the costume room.

But she had missed him too. When he was with her, he made her happy, and when they were apart, she missed him. All this time and she hadn't been able to tell him how she felt.

But he had.

Yesterday had meant something.

She didn't want it, not like this. "I don't want you to pity me."

"This isn't pity. This is me caring about you, very much."

The key turned in the lock just then, and Peter walked in, his face turning pink as he saw her and Brody standing so close.

At first it looked as if he was going to make an 'ewww' face, but then something must have clicked, like, it being a weekday, and the fact that she was at home, and so was Brody.

"What's the matter, Mom?" He stepped inside and dropped his schoolbag on the floor.

She and Brody said nothing. Brody wasn't going to say anything, and if anyone was going to tell Peter, it had to be her.

"Mom?" Peter stepped forward, worry creasing his forehead.

Brody slowly let go of her arm, and it was only then that she realized he'd been holding it. "I'll go wait in the car," he said quietly.

"Mom?" Peter advanced a few steps closer, as Brody shut the door behind him. Had he said he was going to wait in the car?

The car?

The guy was serious about not leaving her side.

"I had a scan …" she said slowly, gauging her son's face for his reaction. "And it showed a lump. The cancer has come back, sweetheart." There was no way to break this type of news gently.

Her son stumbled backwards. "You're sick again?"

"Yes."

"Are you going to die?"

Her mouth fell open. She was startled by his question. "No." At least, she hoped not. She tried to sound upbeat, but his question posed the issue that had whittled away inside her brain.

No. She was not going to die.

Not if she could help it.

"Mom …" Peter whispered, his lips twisting. She thought for a moment that he was going to put his arms around her and hug her. She waited for it but instead he moved away from her. "What happens now?"

"I have to … I have to go back to the hospital." She'd made

up her mind about the mastectomy. She wanted all of the cancer gone, and if losing her breast meant she would have peace of mind, then that's what she was going to do. "I'm going to have surgery."

"Like last time?" he asked. She assumed he was referring to the lumpectomy.

"It's more than that. They're going to remove the entire breast. That should kill those damn cancer cells for good, huh?"

Her son scrunched up his face in disgust. Maybe she had shared too much, but she owed it to him. He needed to know, in case, in case … something happened. Peter needed to know the truth.

"I will probably need to start my treatment by next week."

"Next week?"

She rubbed her hand across her face. Next week. She didn't have long to go, and so many things were going to suffer because of this. She hadn't had time to even tell her parents or to ask them to come over to keep an eye on Peter while she went in.

Nor did she want that. The surgery would be for three days, maybe more, depending on if her insurance covered the reconstructive surgery. She wanted that, too. She wanted it all done at the same time.

"But what about me?"

"Come and sit down, sweetheart. I know this is a shock. Let's talk about it." She wanted to alleviate his fears.

"Can't. I've got homework to do." He picked up his schoolbag and went upstairs.

Now she was in shock, the way Peter had reacted compounded on top of everything else; the cancer, the surgery, the future.

This wasn't the response she wanted, but it was the response she had expected. There wasn't a shred of empathy in her son's body.

She'd been sitting on the couch for a good few moments in silence, contemplating the state of things, when her phone rang. Seeing Hyacinth's name on the caller ID, she declined to answer. It was probably something to do with the Christmas pageant and Leah couldn't think about that now.

When the phone rang again, she groaned inwardly. She would need to answer it just to get Hyacinth off her back.

But as she held the phone to her ear, it was Brody's voice she heard. "Are you okay? Is Peter okay? Can I come back in?"

Come back in? Where was he? Then she remembered, he'd told her he'd be waiting in the car. "I forgot you were still here."

Why was he?

"I'm coming in."

She was about to tell him there was no point, but there was already a knock on the door. No sooner had she opened it when Brody marched in.

He looked around the room and asked her where Peter was and how he'd taken the news.

"He's gone upstairs, and he didn't really say anything. He's more concerned about his homework."

"He's scared."

I'm scared.

There had been many times when she'd longed for the feel of his lips on hers, for his arms around her, and in the space of two days she had some of these things, but for very different reasons.

Yesterday they had celebrated their feelings for one another, and today, he was commiserating with her.

There was no other way about it. She didn't want a man who felt sorry for her.

"You should go, Brody. I have a lot to think about and a lot to do."

"Okay." His hands went to his hips. "What do you need me to do?"

She forced herself to look away. "I don't need you to do anything. This isn't your problem."

He cupped her face gently and moved her gaze back to him. The way his eyes narrowed told her he didn't share her opinion. "You can try to push me away all you want, but I'm not going anywhere."

"We're just friends. You don't owe me anything."

"Friends?" Disbelief was scribbled all over his voice.

"We've been friends," she clarified.

"And now I want more."

"I can't give you more."

"Not now, not like this, but we started something yesterday, and you think I'm here because I feel sorry for you. I don't. I care about you, and I hate to see you hurting. I want more, and the way you kissed me back tells me you want more too. This might not be the right time to be talking about wanting more, but this news today, it's something we'll overcome. We'll get through it—"

He didn't understand. He couldn't promise her a successful treatment, no more than he could promise her eternal life. "You don't know what you're talking about."

"I'm in love with you, and I'll do whatever it is you need me to do. You can take all your anger out on me. I don't care."

"I want you to go, that's what I want you to do."

He studied her face for a good few seconds, her response clearly throwing him for a loop. "Okay." He nodded, then backed away. "I'm here. Always. You call me."

She'd told him to go, but the man couldn't have heard her properly. He'd said he was going to be by her side.

He'd told her he was in love with her. How could that be? A few kisses and he was suddenly in love with her? They'd been friends for so long, she'd thought he didn't have any feelings for her. Going away for a few days maybe pushed him into realizing it. But he was in love with her?

It didn't make sense.

Later that night as sleep evaded her again, she tossed and turned in bed, thinking of how scared she was of the surgery, of losing a part of her body, of not being attractive.

A man like Brody wouldn't want to be with someone like that.

CHAPTER 35

"Let's go for a walk, kid." He'd come back the next evening to see how Leah was. More because he also wanted to know of her plans.

She was doing her best to push him away. But he knew her, moods and stubbornness and all, that was what she hadn't counted on. All this time together, he'd come to know her pretty damn well.

She wanted to prove that she could handle this alone, that she was fine, but one look into those doe-like eyes told him she was anything but fine about the cancer being back.

Who would be fine about something like that? He had backed off enough for her to think he was heeding her words, but he stayed close by. He made it a point to check in on her for a short while in the evenings, to see if he could glean anything.

She was about as forthcoming as a mule.

But he could see that Peter was worried. It wasn't too noticeable to the untrained eye, but he'd come to know the boy well, and his silence was revealing.

Peter was trying to put on a brave face, but in thinking back to his own reaction, when his mom had told him that she had cancer, Brody instinctively knew all was not right.

"We won't be long," he told Leah. She was sitting at the table with a notebook and a pencil, scribbling down some things. He didn't want to impose, and she kept her distance. He got the message, but she needed to get his: He wasn't going anywhere. When he told her he was going to be by her side every step of the way, he meant it.

Of course, if she really did hate him being around, she only had to say it, and he'd go. So far, he hadn't heard her say anything like that.

"Come on, kid," he said, holding the door open.

Wordlessly, the boy followed him out.

They walked along the lamplit street, the cold, frosty weather drawing swirly clouds on each outbreath.

"How are you feeling, son?"

Peter's chin was tucked into his jacket, his hands shoved into his pockets. His gaze on the ground.

No answer.

He didn't expect one. The poor kid was probably drowning in thoughts so heavy, he couldn't come up for air.

Brody knew. He'd been plagued by such things. He'd been by his mother's side when she'd been sick, but he'd hadn't been there when she passed. He hadn't expected her to die, because she'd been told that her type of cancer had a great survival rate. The news made them so happy. So when the infection swooped in and killed her, it shook the foundations right from under him. The guilt for not being there in her final moments never left him.

He knew all about dark thoughts.

But his mother had seen her children grow up. She had seen some grandchildren, too. Peter's situation was entirely different. Leah was young, as was Peter.

This wasn't how it was supposed to be.

He'd had a hard time ever since Leah broke the news to him. Sleepless nights, and a festering anger simmering inside him at the unfairness of it, but it was something he would never reveal to Leah or Peter.

"Your mom is strong, Peter. She's going to be fine."

"Don't tell me she's going to be fine. You didn't see her when she was sick."

Peter was wrong, Brody had seen her, but he'd just witnessed fleeting moments here and there at the hospital.

He glanced sideways, but Peter's face was still buried to his chin in his coat, and his gaze was downcast. "It's okay to feel scared, and I know your mom is scared, even though she's trying her hardest to act like she isn't. I'm there for her and for you, son."

They continued walking and then he heard it. The sobbing.

"Peter?"

All of a sudden, the boy stopped walking and put his hand up against a wall, as if he needed the support of it to lean against.

He was sobbing, body jerking. He put his hand on the boy's shoulder. Let him cry it out, that was the best thing. Because words didn't fix things, didn't make anything better.

Peter needed to get it out of his system. Brody understood. The boy couldn't cry in front of his mother.

After a while, with his back still to him, Peter said, "I'm scared. What if she doesn't get better?"

"And what if she does?" he asked softly. Peter turned around.

"But what if she doesn't?"

"I know that's a possibility, but there's no point in thinking about stuff like that now. No point at all, you understand me? It wouldn't help you, and it wouldn't help your mom."

Peter nodded.

"We cross that bridge if we ever come to it." Something caught in his throat. He'd finally found a woman that he was crazy about. Crazy enough to follow her, like crazy-Heather did to him.

Peter wiped his nose with the flat of his hand. "I don't want to go to my dad's. Mom wants me to, but I want to stay here."

"I get that she doesn't want to worry about you."

"She doesn't have to. I'm grown up now. I can take care of myself."

Brody stifled a smile. "Your mom isn't going to think of it like that."

The boy drew in a sharp breath. "She's always taking care of everyone else. I want to take care of her."

Brody nodded in agreement. "I'm happy to help out in any way, kid. You let me know, okay? We should head back. I don't want to leave your mom by herself for too long."

"You like her, don't you?"

Brody grinned and slid the boy a side glance. "Is it that obvious?"

"She likes you too. She's trying to pretend she doesn't."

They walked along quietly for a while, each lost in their own thoughts.

"The sneakers were pretty cool too, huh?" he asked, as they reached the house.

"Super cool. I don't how my mom knew. I never said a word to her."

"Moms are often good at finding these things out," he said softly.

Before he got out his house key, Peter turned to him and in a low voice said, "Don't tell my mom I was crying."

"I won't, son."

"Not ever?"

"Not ever."

The next day, aware that time was ticking by, he stopped by Hyacinth's office. He knocked on the open door, and didn't miss the double blink, or the bright orange flowery blouse that didn't quite match the bright pink lipstick.

"We need to talk," he said, and settled into the empty chair.

CHAPTER 36

The next few days were a blur. She hadn't gone into work after that bombshell news and only spoke to Hyacinth over the phone, telling her of her plans.

She'd called Hyacinth and had a good heart to heart with her over the phone, explaining the situation, and, as was to be expected, Hyacinth was supportive and understanding.

Over the next few days, Leah decided what she was going to do. She didn't want her parents to come to take care of Peter. She didn't want them here when she recovered. Hyacinth had offered to help out where she could, and she was going to take her up on that offer.

She would need to stay in the hospital for three days for the surgery, slightly longer with the breast reconstruction, and then she'd need about six to eight weeks to recuperate.

Brody had come by in the evenings, but she'd told him she was tired and needed to figure things out. She hadn't needed to spell it out to him that she didn't want him around. Him being around complicated things for her.

Surprisingly, he told her he understood, and he spent more of his time with Peter.

Her heart was heavy. She felt wretched. What could have been a wonderful Christmas had disintegrated to dust. She felt sorry for Peter, didn't have the mental capacity to think about the Christmas pageant, felt sorry for Hyacinth, who told her not to worry, had forbid her to waste any time thinking about it. She said she'd take care of it.

Today was the day. Her surgery was scheduled for mid-morning and she was scared. Then Peter walked in, looking at if he hadn't slept, and she knew she needed to put on a brave face for him. After that first time when she'd broken the news to him, she'd tried to overlook his reaction and had explained to him that she was going to be fine. She had a feeling that her words didn't have as much of an impact as Brody's did. She had no idea what the two of them discussed, but she trusted Brody with her boy.

"I'm going in this morning, once you've left for school, sweetheart."

"Can I come see you later?" He poured cereal into a bowl.

"You can come see me at the hospital later today." She'd made arrangements with Denny's mom for Peter to sleep at Denny's house for a few days. She hoped this would be enough of an exciting incentive that he wouldn't worry too much about her.

"What if something happens to you, Mom?" He hadn't touched his breakfast. She swallowed, trying to think of the right words to put his mind at rest. She couldn't, because she was scared herself.

"I'm going to be in good hands, sweetheart. You know that. I want you to be strong for me. Okay? Take a bus over to the hospital and come see me."

"It's funny how you're letting me have a sleepover at Denny's now."

She laughed. "It was either that, or you stay at Hyacinth's."

A knock at the door interrupted them. This early in the morning, she wasn't expecting any visitors, but she had a feeling who it might be. The man who wouldn't take 'No' for an answer was standing on the other side.

Brody's cautious but smiling face stared back at her. "I'll take you to the hospital," he said, walking in smoothly, and to Peter, "Hey, kid. How are you doing?"

Peter waved, his mouth full.

She followed Brody, confused. She'd expected him to show up at the hospital after work, but not this. "What about your work?" she asked. "Don't you have a job to go to?"

"I'm taking some time off." He sat down next to Peter, making himself at home.

"B-b-but ..." she stammered. "How?" And to herself, *Why?*

"I'm not going to Denny's place, Mom." Peter wiped his mouth with the back of his hand. He'd wolfed down his cereal, and stared at her as if he had an announcement to make.

"Did you speak to your dad?" Maybe he'd decided to go visit his father over Christmas, after all. That way, after almost a week in the hospital, she'd come home a few days before Christmas and would only need minimal checking in on from Hyacinth. She didn't want to mess up her plans to visit her sister.

"I spoke to Brody. He says he's going to stay here with me."

"And you're telling me this *now*?" She wiped a hand over her brow. This was not what *she* wanted. Brody was already driving her to the hospital, and he'd just told her he'd taken time off.

What was he?

A new part of their family?

She was still shaking her head when Brody muttered something under his breath that she couldn't make out.

"Brody said you wouldn't like it." Peter hefted his backpack onto his back, his hands on the shoulder straps as he faced her. "It's done, Mom. I asked Brody and he said he'd be happy to. I didn't want to worry you about it, and don't worry about Denny's mom, I explained it to her."

Explained *what* to her?

She gave him a look of displeasure. But she didn't want to say anything, didn't want to upset Peter, because she knew he worried about her. The boy had been quiet, even though she'd sat with him every evening and tried to explain that she was going to be okay. But whether she'd convinced him or not, she couldn't tell.

How could she, when she wasn't even sure of the outcome herself?

CHAPTER 37

She was in the hospital, wearing a gown, sitting in the bed, when Brody walked in. That hulking tower of a man looked even bigger with his black coat and gloves, which he now took off.

Gray hairs mixed with dark along his jawline. He looked disheveled, as if he hadn't shaved in days. Or slept, judging by the dark hollows under his eyes. She didn't miss the stab of worry that cut across his face, before he quickly erected a false smile. She'd seen too many of these smiles in the oncology department at the hospital, and she could recognize one right away.

He walked over to her side, did something he hadn't done in days, he reached for her hand as he sat down.

She saw it, the slight slip of the shoulders, the way his body seemed to fold into itself, as if he'd been punched in the solar plexus. "How are you feeling?"

"Not as nervous as you," she replied, seeing for the first time that he looked worried. Or scared. This hospital. His mother. No wonder his confidence had vanished.

"I'm sorry. This can't be easy for you. The memories of the last time …"

He kissed her hand. "It's not that so much." He managed a smile. He was lying. "I'll be waiting here when you come out."

"I won't be very talkative," she said, noting how it had taken this, a strange environment and situation for her to resort back to being familiar and at ease around him. Clutching for normality in a sea of distress. She needed his strength, and his confidence.

"Thank you for staying with Peter."

"He asked me to."

"Thank you. But you didn't need to take any time off work."

He tilted his head, as if he didn't agree.

She liked the feel of his hands against hers, had forgotten how safe and protected she felt.

But she was going to have a mastectomy. She wasn't going to be whole, not after this. Whatever feelings he had about her would disappear.

He kissed the back of her hand, squeezing it between both of his as if he needed something to hold onto. He looked up at her, lines etched on his forehead. She had gotten so used to staring into his face, she knew every line and wrinkle, and plane and crevice of that strong jaw line, those lips, she even knew the way the lines spidered out from the corners of his eyes. She took one long look at his face, hoped that she would remember it forever.

"You told me once that you weren't looking for anything. That you didn't want a romance and that you had a lot of things going on," he said, watching her closely. "I heard you. I heard you clearly, and the truth is, you were right. You were recovering from cancer. Two months of treatment, alone, and you being a single mom, juggling everything. You think I couldn't see the fear in your eyes back then? It was the only thing I saw. But I was grieving, too, and no matter how weird it was that we kept running into one another, then finding out that we worked in the same building together, to me it felt almost as if we were supposed to be together. Like maybe we needed each other to heal.

"You think I didn't have moments when I looked at you and wondered what it might be like to kiss you? You think I didn't think of you every night when I went home, or when I woke up in the morning? I did.

"Early on, way early on, you'd told me you didn't want to get close to anyone. Those words stuck with me, but when my feelings for you changed, I didn't think it was fair to test and see if yours had." He paused, his gaze sweeping over her face for the longest time, until she wondered if she had a few stray crumbs around her mouth.

"Brody, you're saying all these things ..." she whispered. Why was he telling her this now, moments before she was going in for surgery?

"Because I can't keep them inside of my any longer. I've been trying to hide them from you because I didn't want to ruin our friendship."

She was silent, her mouth open, her eyes wide. Hanging onto his every word.

"I wanted to be more than just friends, Leah. I knew you were the one. Maybe that night at the fairground when I gave you the octopus and saw your beaming face. I'd never seen you look like that.

"You were carefree, without a worry in the world. Or I knew at the beach the next night, when we were both staring up at the stars. It might have been when we were painting your house. I can't pinpoint the exact moment when I started to fall in love with you, all I know is that I am ... falling in love. Somewhere along the way I tripped, and it was too late to pick myself up and pretend I didn't feel the way I did.

"I fell for you and there's nothing I can do about it. And now, I can't even keep it to myself. I was waiting for you to give me the signal, to tell me when you were ready, but then Thanksgiving happened. We got sick, *I* got really sick. All I could think of was you, more than ever. So, when I came back, I told you. And then *this* happened. All I want to do now is be there for you."

"Brody ..." Her eyes turned glassy. "Oh ... Brody ..."

"I meant it when I said I was going to be by your side. I'll be waiting here when you come out, and I'm going to take care of you when you get home. Hyacinth and me, we've got it all worked out."

"What?" she whispered.

"You don't have to worry about a thing."

The door opened and a doctor and a nurse walked in. "Are you ready, Ms. Shriver?" the doctor asked.

"Wait for me." Leah looked at him, wanting to hold on to that image of his face. "This conversation isn't over," she said.

CHAPTER 38

*H*e couldn't sit still.

So, he walked around the floor where Leah was, somewhere in her surgery, and when he grew even more restless, he went back to the part of the hospital where he'd once come with his mom.

Memories swept over him, the nostalgia hitting him like a thick puff of steam from a sauna.

He'd been filled with hope for his mother. Had expected her life to continue along the same path as the one before she'd gone in.

Sadly, it wasn't to be.

What happened to her served as a sharp reminder that things could change in the blink of an eye.

He didn't want that for Leah.

Walking back to her office, he waited, staring out of the window, checking the messages on his cell phone.

He'd told Jackie that Leah wasn't well, and that their Christmas plans would have to be changed. "I'll explain it all later," he'd said to her.

His older sister didn't ask anything, but she would, in time.

He guessed that not having to fly with her entire brood was probably okay with her. Especially since they'd all been sick.

At least that was one less thing to worry about.

He and Peter had attended a couple of rehearsals for the Christmas pageant. Hyacinth was in charge, leading the show, and somehow she had miraculously convinced Hailey Ross to be the narrator.

They were a week behind, because of what happened with Leah, but bringing the Hollywood star into the show was a genius move. He had to hand it to Hyacinth. The woman was shrewd and clever and manipulative. She got things done.

He was staying at Leah's house and taking care of Peter while Leah was in the hospital; not that the boy needed much taking care of. But under Brody's watchful gaze, at least the boy wouldn't be as worried about his mom.

He knew from Hyacinth, because he wasn't going to hear it from Leah, that Leah was having a mastectomy. He couldn't imagine how debilitating the idea of removing a part of your body would be, especially to a woman. Especially *there*. It helped explain, maybe, why Leah had been so distant with him, why she'd wanted to push him away.

It wasn't going to work, but she could try all she wanted.

It was a few hours later, as he sat in the chair by Leah's bed, that the nurses wheeled her back into the room.

She looked pale, and was groggy, barely making sense. The doctor called him out and told him that all had gone well, and that Leah needed plenty of rest. She was on a heavy dose of pain meds and that it might be better for him to come back tomorrow.

But he wasn't going to do that. He told the doctor he didn't want Leah to open her eyes and see that she was alone. He walked back in and stayed by her side, holding her hand, stroking her skin on the back of it. Waiting for her eyes to open.

Peter came by later, and Leah stirred a few times, her eyes opening a little, fluttering open when Peter called her.

"Sweetheart," she whispered, before her eyes shuttered closed again.

After a while, she slowly opened her eyes, looked around, and recognition flickered across her gaze.

Peter talked to her, and she answered in monosyllables. Brody watched her, saw her looking at him, saw her face soften, but he didn't want to ask her too many questions, and he let Peter do all the talking.

One of the nurses had mentioned earlier that they would be starting Leah on her exercises as early as tomorrow, and that she'd need to rest before that.

When she started to drift off to sleep again, he told Peter they should go, and that it was important to let his mom rest.

The boy was contemplative on the drive home. "The doctor told me it went well," he said, wanting to lift the boy's spirits.

Peter nodded. "She wasn't talking much."

"She's had surgery, kid, as well as a reconstruction. It's going to take a toll on her. She'll be better tomorrow."

"Shall we go to the theater?" Peter asked after a while, interrupting his thoughts. He'd been wondering what to cook once they got home.

"You want to go to the rehearsal?"

"Hyacinth said she was gonna ask Hailey Ross to take part in the play."

Brody grunted. "Hailey Ross?" And then after a few seconds, he asked, "Is she Monica Martins? The one in those action movies?"

"Yeah. That's her."

He laughed out loud at Hyacinth's presumptuous leanings. "It's not happening, kid. Do you really think a Hollywood star is going to get involved with a small-town Christmas play?"

"Hyacinth said she asked her and it was almost done."

Brody snickered. "That woman has grandiose plans and ideas."

Peter looked annoyed. "Can we at least go over and see? We're supposed to be helping."

It was true. He'd offered his services, and Peter also wanted to step in because his mom couldn't.

"Fine. They'll almost be finished, but if you think you're going to see Hailey Ross there, you've got another thing coming …" he muttered, turning the car around.

CHAPTER 39

It was the oddest sensation. She was in pain, and yet it was dull, not a sharp pain. Her head felt heavy, and she felt weak, as if the muscles in her body stopped working.

There was a pulling sensation under her arm, and her chest felt numb, at times. She'd been told to sleep on her back for the next month and a half, and didn't relish the idea of that. But what freaked her out was having to look in the mirror and see the new part of her body.

She dreaded that.

A few hours later, after the consultant came to see her, she'd managed to eat something, and felt a little more human.

When Peter walked in, she was sitting up in bed, a little more of her normal self. To see Brody coming in behind her boy set off a memory which was slowly reeling its way back to her.

He smiled at her, and she frowned, trying to remember what he'd said.

"Mom." Peter rushed to her side.

"Careful, Peter," Brody warned.

"Hey, sweetheart." She moved her face from side to side so

that Peter could kiss her gingerly. "I can't hug you." Her heart broke a little at that.

"Hey." Brody was next as Peter slunk into the background. "How are you?"

"I'm good. How are my boys?" Had she said that? She blamed it on the effects of the medication.

Her boys pulled up a chair each and sat down, and asked her how she was feeling but she didn't want to talk about how weak she felt, or the soreness and pain, or the throbbing at the site of the incision. She didn't want to tell them about the surgical drain that was attached to her, the long tubes that got tangled up with her IV line and her bedclothes; a nightmare she had never considered. Or the humiliation that was worming a hole into her self-esteem—the thing she had started to build upon, but which was now lost, just like a part of her.

She didn't want to talk about any of this.

Brody could have his pick of any woman. There was no way he would want someone who was less than complete.

"Tell me about you," she said, her voice sounding weak. "I want to know what you've been up to."

Peter and Brody glanced at one another, and she wasn't sure if she imagined it or whether Brody really did wink at Peter.

But as Peter started to talk about how much fun it was to have Brody come for a sleepover, she listened, her insides warm and happy. Her son was in good hands, and if she tried not to let the bad thoughts intervene, then so, perhaps, was she.

Over the next few days, she was up and about, doing the exercises, learning how to drain the tube, and how to take care of herself. Her head was filled with medication and post-surgery care, and she was handed lots of literature on how to deal with the emotional trauma of a surgery that changed the way she looked.

It hadn't been too bad, when she'd finally looked at herself in the mirror. It was different, and took some getting used to, but it wasn't as bad as she had envisioned. It wasn't going to be easy, stepping back into normal life and facing the world. Luckily, she had at least a month to take off, and for her, Christmas had been canceled. She didn't have to face the community and the Christmas pageant was a long distant memory that Hyacinth was taking care of.

When it was time for her to go home, Brody and Peter helped her carefully into the car, fussing over her every minute. She felt not just taken care of, but cherished, as if they were scared she might break.

Brody drove so slowly on the way home and when she finally walked back into her house, she was so grateful to be back.

"Did you put up some more decorations?" she asked. Her son had walked her through the living room, but she was sure she'd seen more lights and ornaments, and a couple of ornaments around the fireplace. The room had looked more … busy.

"Yeah. We went to the Christmas market," Peter explained innocently, then he said they had something to show her. With each of them by her side, they slowly led her towards the kitchen.

"Ta-da!" said Peter, gesturing with his hands to show her the new changes. Brody's face was beaming. "What do you think, Mom?" His face was an expression of pride. "I helped Brody."

She blinked, because at first, nothing looked much different. But then she saw that a couple of the shelves and her hanging utensil rack had been moved down a good few inches.

"So you won't have to reach too high for them," Peter explained.

"You lowered everything?" she asked, looking at Brody. This wasn't something Peter would even have known how to do.

"It's best to have everything within arm's reach," Brody answered quietly.

How would he have known?

She glanced at the changes again, her heart blossoming. "I don't know what to say." The tears welled up in her eyes. His thoughtfulness, his care, his concern—all for her. This was one hundred percent Brody.

This man.

"I don't know what to say. It's … you guys …" Peter went to hug her, but then stepped away. She couldn't be hugged, and she missed that. Instead, she took Peter's hand and kissed it. "I don't know what to say."

"Say you like it, Mom."

"I love it, sweetheart."

She looked at Brody, his eyes narrowed, maybe because he could read her face, see her teary eyes. "Thank you."

He nodded. "We painted over the other holes so it wouldn't be messy."

She looked and saw the place where the earlier holes in the wall would have been had been filled in and painted over.

"And we made a bunch of food and froze it," said Peter, opening the freezer and gesturing at containers neatly stacked up where none had been before.

Her insides emptied in shock. "When did you do this?" she asked Brody. Peter had finished school for the holidays, but Brody had a new project. How much time did he have off?

"We've been doing it while you were recovering," said Brody, each time his eyes scanned over her, it felt as if he had a million things he needed to say. It was different, and she couldn't put her finger on what exactly it was, but something had changed.

"This is … this is incredible. Thank you so much, Brody. I don't know what to say."

"You don't need to say anything."

"I can handle it from here," she said, not wanting to put him out anymore. The man had gone above and beyond what she'd expected anyone to do. Not even her parents would have done as much as Brody had. Her mom would have made her food, but lowering the shelves? No way.

"I know." He nodded again. He was about to say something, when Peter shouted from the living room.

"You didn't have to do all of this, Brody. It's ... too much."

"For who?"

She was about to open her mouth and tell him that she didn't need him to stay now that she was at home, but Peter shouted, "Come and look at these, Mom."

She gave Brody a what-now look and headed to the living room.

"Look at these!" The boy's excitement was bursting from every cell. On closer inspection she saw that the extra ornaments and things near the fireplace and under the tree were gift baskets.

"What—"

Brody helped her sit down on the couch, while Peter brought the gift baskets out one by one and placed them on the coffee table in front of her. And when that was full, he started putting things on the floor.

She stared up at Brody, who had his big arms crossed and an expectant expression on his face.

"Who sent these?" she asked, as realization dawned and she read her name on a couple of the gift cards. "Hope you get well soon, Leah."

Merry, Dylan, Jenna and Reed, and other names she vaguely recalled. "Get Well Soon, from all at Books & Buns," said one gift card that came with a huge basket of cookies. And there was a flower arrangement in a plastic vase with water from Roxy's Diner.

She wasn't friends with these people ... and she didn't want their pity. Anger and irritation foamed inside her.

"We didn't tell anyone," claimed Peter, standing up and reading her unhappy expression.

"I didn't want anyone to know." She fought to simmer down her anger. This was such a personal surgery. Such an excruciatingly difficult time for her, and everyone in Starling Bay knew?

She didn't even talk to these people most of the time. They were not her friends. Who was she to them?

"Are you upset, Mom?" Peter's face fell, clearly this wasn't the reaction he'd been expecting. The doorbell rang and Brody disappeared to answer it.

"It wasn't something I wanted to announce," she started to say.

"I didn't tell anyone, Mom. We didn't. Brody said you wouldn't want anyone to know, but Hyacinth …"

"I'm here!" The voice, once bearable, but now irritating to her ears, boomed into the air. Hyacinth walked in, looking garishly overdressed in her pearls and brooch with a brocade jacket and skirt.

"Are you ready?" she asked Peter.

He had never been so happy to see Hyacinth Fitzsimmons.

He led her into the living room, where Leah's stormy eyes gazed at the woman who strode in as if she owned the place.

"You're home, my dear." She was about to march towards Leah, and no doubt crush her in an all-encompassing embrace, when Brody took a hold of her elbow, preventing her.

"You have to be careful," he cautioned. "Leah's pretty fragile right now."

"You are?" the woman boomed. "What do you think?" she gestured at the gift baskets, happiness lighting up her entire body.

"Did you tell them?" Leah demanded, quiet anger dripping from her voice in a way that only he and Peter would recognize.

"Of course I did!" Hyacinth sat down on the couch, leaning towards Leah, but still keeping her distance. "Isn't this amazing, the community coming together and showing their appreciation for you?" She placed a hand on Leah's knee, and he saw the small involuntary flinch as Leah shifted her upper body away.

He stepped in. "Maybe just move to the side a few inches, Hyacinth. Mind the drain tubes." He felt the heat of Leah's stare on him.

"My dear, I'm so sorry." Hyacinth picked herself up and moved to a different couch altogether.

"Why does everyone know, Hyacinth?" And then Leah cocked her head, in a what-are-you-doing-here way.

"Because I had to enlist the help of Hailey Ross, I mean, I was going to anyway, but it made it so much easier when you had to go in for surgery. I'm not saying it was a blessing in disguise, this is terrible, terrible, what's happened, but I have faith that it's all going to turn out beautifully."

Leah ran a hand through her hair, and Brody watched, sensing and feeling her agitation.

"Maybe you should go," he suggested, and saw Leah's head snap towards him.

"Go where?" she asked.

Peter shoved his hands into his pockets, a smug grin on his face. "We've got the last of the rehearsals—"

"We'll have to have a final one the day before the performance," said Hyacinth, getting up. She pointed to a large gold-wrapped gift basket. "That's from me. I wanted to come and see you at the hospital, but Brody assured me it was better I came to see you at home."

Leah looked at him. She had no idea what was going on.

"But the rest of these," Leah asked. "Why does everyone

know. I wanted to keep it quiet. It's not something I wanted to announce in the local paper. I didn't want people to know."

"But, Mom, Hyacinth managed to get Hailey Ross to take part in the play, and people were asking where you were, and ... I'm sorry, I told them you were back in the hospital, and that you had cancer." Peter's voice turned brittle, reminding her that her boy was skating on thin ice, that her illness frightened him more than she'd at first acknowledged. "I didn't want to lie to them. I'm sorry I told them, but you don't have to hide it, Mom."

She sank back into the couch.

Hyacinth stepped in. "When people heard, and then discovered that Hailey was stepping in—as a narrator, of course. Can't have her being a sheep or a donkey or anything like that—but when she did, people started to think it must be something more serious, if 'the' Hailey Ross was stepping in to save the day." Hyacinth gave her another one of her infamous smiles. "Word spread. Dylan found out, and he and Merry sent a gift basket, and then, one by one, we started to get gift baskets delivered to the theater."

She looked at her watch. "Goodness, we need to go. These fine young men are helping me; they have been helping me right from the moment you had to go in. Don't you worry, my dear," she waved a hand at Leah as she walked away. "Everything has been taken care of."

"Yeah, Mom, it's all cool." Peter kissed his mom on the top of her head. "I'll be back later."

"Hailey Ross, huh?" was all Leah said. Brody leaned against the wall, observing her reaction. Her hard eyes turned towards him. "Aren't you going?" A hint of steel spiked her tone.

"I'm staying here with you."

"You rest up, my dear," Hyacinth told her.

"Bye, Mom." Peter closed the door.

An uncomfortable silence whipped through the air.

She was mad about something, and he wished he knew what and why.

"If you're angry that people know, blame me. I should have stopped Peter from telling people." He should have interrupted him and he thought the boy would have known that his mother wanted this to be kept a secret, but that was the effect Hailey Ross had when she'd walked into the theater that day. Peter had lost all sense of self and blurted it out to her.

It made him wonder about Hyacinth's skills of persuasion, that she'd been able to get the actress to take part, albeit in the role of a narrator.

She didn't say a word.

"Don't you want to open the gift baskets?" he asked, moving towards her slowly. She was in a delicate frame of mind. He had expected this. Everything he'd looked up had warned about this. This type of surgery wasn't like most operations. This one took away a part that meant something, unlike an appendix or a gallstone.

"Or did you want to rest?" he asked softly, before crouching on the floor near her.

She looked down at him, an unreadable expression crossing her eyes. "Didn't you want to go?" she asked.

"I told you, I'm going to stay here with you. There's nothing much for me to do. Peter and Chloe seem to be running the show, Hyacinth thinks she runs the show but—"

"And Hailey Ross? Is she going to rock up here and ask you to give her a lift to the theater?" The fire behind those words was like a spotlight, and it revealed all.

"I don't know. I've seen her once. You'd be better off asking Peter about that. He seems to know her daily schedule better than her agent." He laughed, but Leah did not.

"Don't you want to be around her? Get her autograph? Get a

selfie?" The barbed wire in her words would have unnerved a lesser man. But he was prepared.

"No, I don't."

Her distrustful eyes looked daggers at him.

"I'm exactly where I need to be, where I want to be, with you."

She pulled together her oversized cardigan, so that the edges overlapped and covered her chest.

"I appreciate all that you've done, Brody, and with Peter, and taking care of him, and the shelves and the food you've made, all of it. I really do, but—"

"I knew there was a but," he muttered. He was surprised it hadn't come sooner. He was aware that she'd have outbursts of anger, and that the emotional insecurities would overwhelm her. He was aware of the worries that Leah was dealing with.

This was all new to him. Wiring and nuts, bolts and power tools were his domain, not mastectomies and reconstructive surgery. But he'd been reading about surgical drains and post-mastectomy bras, because he wanted to be better equipped to help her, and he didn't want to do or say the wrong things. He'd meant what he'd said, he was going to be there for her, all the way. "But what?" he asked, carefully watching her.

"I don't want to be your charity case."

"You're not."

"I don't want to get in the way."

"You're not."

She took in a sharp breath, displeasure written all over her face. "I don't want you to feel obligated towards me."

"I don't."

She huffed. "Just because we shared a kiss in the–"

"A couple of kisses, if I remember correctly." He put her straight and enjoyed watching her cheeks slowly turn pink.

"Things have changed since then, and now it's all different, so

I don't want you to feel—" She pulled the edges of her cardigan together again. "To feel … anything you don't want to feel."

She was struggling, because she wasn't even making sense now. "You can't tell me what to feel, Leah."

She closed her eyes, and he could see the tiredness in the circles beneath them. This was all too much to take in, especially for her. He didn't want to lay it on thick, but ...

He walked over and crouched on the floor, so that he was close by, but not invading her couch space. "I understand that you're feeling sad with everything, not just what's happened to you, but *this*," he waved his hand that the plethora of gift baskets. "... this is too much to absorb, I get that. Especially if it challenges everything you ever thought you knew.

"You think you don't matter, but you do. You think you don't have friends, but you do. What happened in your past might have closed you off to the good things, it might have made you see things through a filter, but this," he nodded at the gifts again, "this is not because we asked anyone to bring you anything. This is people wanting to show you that they care. I know you're on heavy meds, and you're dealing with the trauma of the surgery, and there are probably a thousand negative emotions flying through you. I know I'd feel adrift if I'd lost a part of my body… I get all of that, but you need to know something about me, Leah, about the way I feel about you." This gained him a blink, maybe two, as she struggled to absorb every word and commit it to memory, so that they would be imprinted on her heart, easy to recall when she needed.

"I don't care about the surface-level things, Leah. That stuff isn't important to me. If you're worried that I'll feel differently about you, don't be, because I'm not a shallow guy. If I didn't care about you, I wouldn't be here now. I could have walked, but I'm not going to.

"You can do everything you want to push me away, close me

off, be angry, be distant; you're entitled to it. But I'm staying put until you look me in the eye and tell me that you have no feelings for me and you don't want me around. I have no interest in Hailey Ross. All my interest is in *you*. You're the one, Leah. The only one."

CHAPTER 40

*I*t was the day of the Christmas pageant, and she was taking it easy. She'd never watched so many Christmas movies in her life as she had these past few days.

Between the two of them, Brody and Peter didn't let her lift a finger. In between going for walks, doing her exercises, reading, she slipped in as many Christmas movies as she could. Never in all her life had she had the luxury of doing nothing.

And it was because of Brody and Peter. Her boys.

Brody had been sleeping on the couch ever since she'd gone in for her surgery. She felt bad and told him it was okay for him to go home whenever he wanted to. She didn't want him to, she'd added quickly, but she hated that he slept on the couch. He'd refused. He told her he'd stay until a few days after Christmas.

If she wanted him to.

Of course she did.

So much had changed. Her life had turned upside down, and then again.

"Wish us luck," Peter said, rushing over to give her a light kiss on her cheek.

"Have you shaved?" She noted that the soft dusting of hairs above his upper lip had been wiped clean off.

"You've only just noticed now?" Peter angled his face from side to side like a model showing off his features. "I asked Brody, and he showed me how to shave. I did it last week, Mom."

"Oh," she turned her head to Brody, who was standing there with a screwdriver in his hands. "You did, did you?"

Brody shrugged, those heavy shoulders lifting and resting. He was a sight for hungry lovesick eyes. "I think he was ready. I did tell him to ask you first, but he was trying to impress Chloe or Hailey, I can't remember who."

He winked at Peter, who grunted a loud, "Ewwww."

"Chloe?" Leah asked. She remembered Dylan's stepdaughter. "How's her little sister?"

"Noisy," said Peter, making a face. "She says she cries all the time."

Merry and Dylan just had a baby girl a few days ago. They'd named her Brooke. Leah ordered a little gift for the newborn online and hoped it would reach the Frasers by tomorrow.

A car honked outside, and Peter looked through the window, before smoothing a hand through his hair. Leah frowned. "Who's taking you?"

"I would have," said, Brody, "but he told me he's already got a lift."

Brody peered out of the window at the front as Peter cried "Bye," again and rushed out.

"Is Hyacinth taking them?" Leah asked.

"Dylan is." Brody turned to face her. "And Chloe's in the car, too."

Leah was surprised. "The baby's only a few days old. Shouldn't he be helping Merry?"

Brody came and sat down beside her. Close beside her, on the other side to where she'd had her surgery. "He called and told me it wouldn't be a problem. Merry's parents are over, and I think he's glad to get out of the house. The guy sounded like he needed a break." He patted her knee. "He said it was no problem."

She was touched.

Have a little faith, Hyacinth had told her once. Everyone had come together to help everyone. It all worked out in the end.

Hyacinth had proudly boasted that Hailey Ross had been a huge draw for the town. This year would be the biggest audience ever for the Christmas pageant.

"Are you sure you don't want to go?" Brody asked. "We can give you a disguise if you don't want to be noticed? A scarf over your head, big sunglasses–"

She gave him a quizzical look. "In this weather? It's snowing!"

"Nobody will recognize you by the time I've finished with you." He understood her need for privacy, especially now while she was recovering.

She giggled, relaxing into the couch. Brody had spoken from his heart the other day. He'd made her see things the way he saw them. He'd blown away her insecurities. A man who didn't care would never have done all that he had.

Brody hadn't told her in mere words, he'd *shown* her with his actions first.

She was lucky to have him. All her life she'd dreamed of someone like him, and when he'd finally come into her life, she'd kept him at bay. And then, when life had turned on her, he'd refused to leave her side, even though she'd tried to push him away. He wasn't having any of it.

"I'd like to see everyone, to thank them for the gifts and cards, and for thinking of me, but I'm still a little tired. I'm not ready to go into town and stand outside. It's going to be super busy this year."

He took her hand and intertwined his fingers in hers. "It's going to be crazy."

"You can go. I'll wait here for you."

"And leave you? We've got an empty house," he said, using a dastardly devilish voice, before waggling his eyebrows. "I need to get something from the store for tomorrow. The prep for tomorrow seems to never end."

"Oh, now you understand?" The Christmas Day feast seemed to need an ever-growing list of things. She'd honed it down to a fine art, as had most women, but she'd known Brody would struggle. He'd refused to let her help him, not even letting her draw up a shopping list, and now he was paying the price.

"I was going to take you to the Christmas market in Whisper Falls …"

She made a face. "It's too long a drive and I'd rather not be out in the cold all day. Thank you for remembering."

"Next year, I promise."

He said that as if it was a certainty. That's one of the things she loved about this man. His certainty. She could learn a thing or two about that from him.

"I have to go to the store again."

"Again?"

"I forgot the cranberry sauce."

"I wish I could just run out for you and get it," she offered.

"No."

She couldn't drive for a while, but she'd seen Brody and Peter making lists for a feast, it sounded like. It was only Christmas dinner for the three of them, and the two of them were acting as if they were feeding a hundred.

He had changed his plans and told her that Jackie and her family weren't coming over. When she'd asked why, he'd sounded a bit vague, telling her that the kids just wanted to chill at home, and that Ian, Jackie's husband, had had a really bad bout of the bug.

So, Brody was having Christmas with her and Peter. Peter's wish had come true. As had hers.

"If you made a list ..." she said, hating that he kept going out because he forgot something. Men seemed to hate lists as much as women swore by them. Even her ex had been the same.

Her ex who hadn't sounded too happy when she'd mentioned Brody to him. He'd demanded to know who this new man was that was special enough for her to spend tomorrow with.

She'd been as vague as possible and had cut that conversation short.

"I know, I know, a list is the way to go, but ... I also have a surprise, I'm not sure you'll like it."

"We don't need cranberry sauce," she said. "These things never end. There comes a time when you just have to make do with what you have. I want *you*, and only you, at home with me now. Let's both of us take it easy."

"If that's what you want," he said, leaning over and pressing his lips gently against hers. He moved away too fast for her liking, leaving her high and dry.

"Mind if we go for a walk first?" She hadn't been outside today, and she wanted to get a walk in before it turned really cold.

"Sure."

He helped her slip her feet into her boots. She still didn't feel comfortable with bending over.

"Thank you." She gazed at his hair, mostly dark but flecked with white. Things were looking up. She was on the mend, and in time she would go back to work and get back to normal, whatever her new normal, with Brody in it, was.

Maybe life had a chance of getting back to normal? Maybe now she could watch her dreams come true, the way they had for so many others she had stood by and watched.

He helped her to carefully put her arms through her coat sleeves, and then he slid a hat on her head and looped a woolen scarf around her neck. Next, he slipped on his thick coat which made him look even bigger, and then popped on a beanie hat.

They stepped outside, and she linked her arm through his, because the snow had set from earlier this morning and she was wary of slipping and falling.

It was eerily quiet as they walked through an area where the trees, bushes and the entire street with its cars were dusted with white powdery snow. The street lamps had turned on and the day was turning dark already, even though it was still early in the evening.

"I must be the luckiest woman alive," she said out loud. What a thing to say, after all she had been through.

"If anyone's lucky, it's me," he said, stopping and turning to her. "I get to have you, and Christmas with you and Peter. That's the best present anyone could give me. Well, *you're* the best present … I thought I'd be alone at this time of the year, even if I was at Jackie's, but I haven't felt alone, not now, not for a while." He cupped her face with those big strong, slightly hard hands. She leaned her cheek into his palm and smiled like a contented cat. Then he dipped his head and pressed those gorgeous lips against her mouth. Her heart swooned; heat sizzled in her core. She gazed at him, wicked thoughts swirling through her mind.

"What was the thing you wanted to tell me?" she asked.

"We have another dinner guest. Sorry, I should have asked you first. I asked her yesterday when she told me what her plans were, and I felt sorry for her. It felt odd not to say something."

"To who?"

"Hyacinth. She told me she usually goes to her sister's place for Christmas, but this year her sister went to visit her family. She left a few days ago, and Hyacinth didn't want to go before the pageant was over." He drew back. "I also think she felt as if her sister should have time with her own family, without Hyacinth tagging along."

"She told you that?"

"No, not in words, but I'm pretty good at reading people."

She tugged her lower lip between her teeth and considered this. "Yes, you are."

"I felt sorry for her. I never thought I would, but ... I didn't like the idea of her being alone tomorrow, so I told her we would love for her to spend Christmas Day with us." He made a face. "I'm sorry. I should have checked with you and Peter first."

"No, I'm glad you asked her. It was the right thing to do. I would have done the same."

"You don't mind?"

"No, why would I? She's helped me so much."

"That's what I was thinking," he said.

She giggled, laughing at the change in his attitude towards Hyacinth. "I told you she's not so bad once you get to know her."

"She's growing on me like mold."

"That's not nice. She's not that bad."

His face sobered. "She's not, but she's an acquired taste, and one I'm still acquiring."

"What you did was nice, Brody."

"Hmmm." He made a thoughtful noise in the back of his throat. "But seriously. What you've been through, this is what people go through at the end of their lives, and we faced it at the start."

At the start? What was he talking about?

"What doesn't kill you makes you stronger, right?"

"Who said that?" she wanted to know.

"Friedrich Nietzsche."

"Ohhh-kay. You're a reader now?"

"It was a quote on my mom's apron."

"Awww, Brody. Your mom sounded so cool."

"She was quite a woman. You would have liked her."

"I did."

"I think she liked you."

The corners of his mouth quirked up and the lines on each side of his eyes deepened. In that moment, she was flooded by overwhelming love for this man, who had taken such good care of her. He wasn't just a friend, he was her soulmate, and even though it was still the very early days of their being together, she knew this truth fiercely in her heart.

If anything ever happened to her, Brody would be there to always keep an eye on Peter. Her eyes filled with tears at the thought, but it was bittersweet, the tears were also of joy. She was on the precipice of tomorrow. The doctor had told her she wouldn't need chemo, but they would need to monitor her progress carefully.

It wasn't going to be easy, and the next few years would be an obstacle course to traverse, but with Brody by her side, she could do it.

He hooked a finger under her chin, lifting her face to him. "Hey," his voice had dropped to that sexy whisper again. "We've got this. We'll deal with it. I'm not going anywhere, and neither are you."

He could read her mind, he knew her. The level of their connection was sometimes frightening in its intensity.

As if to seal that thought into her mind and heart forever, he leaned forward and gave her a long, soft, lingering kiss that made her toes curl. She tipped her head back, letting him deepen the kiss, because, goodness, once this man kissed her, she wanted more, more, more.

When soft flakes fell around them, they slowly pulled apart. Snow was falling, and it was sprinkled all over him. He stroked her face, wiping the stray flakes away.

"We should get back."

She nodded, and they walked in silence. She realized that she was not alone, and now never would be.

Brody was in her life, and by the sounds of it, he wasn't leaving. He was a handyman who fixed things, but he was so much more than that. He was a protector, a caretaker, a man who fixed so many hurts—of things she hadn't even realized she was hurting about.

He'd mended the lonely hole in her heart, and she sensed she'd done the same for him. He filled her life with meaning, took care of her son, loved him and guided him. Without knowing, Brody had stepped up and become the man her son looked up to.

Eight months later ...

Another clear scan, another piece of good news, another win. It had been a series of wins for her all year.

"Brody," she gazed at his side profile as he drove. "We don't have to do anything." He made it a point to celebrate every little victory. Each time she had a scan and it came back clear, he pampered, spoiled and indulged her.

"You always say that." He glanced at her, his gaze landing on her lips, warming her to the core. He was extra today, extra happy, extra exuberant.

He was up to something.

Again.

She'd had no end of his little surprises. An evening out, a day at the spa, an overnight stay in a fancy hotel. A few months ago, he'd surprised her by taking her away to a secluded cabin in the middle of the woods for the weekend.

She had no idea what he had planned for this evening. "We

have so much to do at home," she insisted. Not that she minded any of this, but her anxiety spiked to know that they hadn't packed a thing.

"Peter's got it all under control," Brody assured her. Brody's love of the outdoors had infected Peter and tomorrow they were going on a one-week camping trip, the three of them.

She hadn't exactly jumped for joy when she'd first heard the news. But she'd also never been before, and when Brody heard that, he'd made it his mission to plan the mother of all camping trips.

She hadn't known whether to be scared or to look forward to it.

"Eight people?" she'd shrieked, staring at them both as if they'd gone crazy when he and Peter had gone out looking for a large tent and returned with an eight-person family tent instead.

"Mom, it's going to be awesome!" Peter had been beside himself. Later that evening, Brody put his arms around her and told her that having two separate rooms and a small living area was going to be much more comfortable for her than a three-person tent. He'd told her to trust him.

She did.

She'd come to rely on him for support, and love and understanding. This man met all of her needs, and over time, their relationship had bloomed. Now she couldn't imagine a life without him, and neither could Peter.

"Hey." With his eyes on the road, he squeezed her thigh. "By the time we get back, Peter will have packed everything we need. We have to let go and leave it to him, Leah. We need him to know we can trust him to do things, otherwise, how will he ever learn?"

He was right, it was maddening how right he always was. For a man who had no children, Brody had a way about him that somehow made Peter want to do things and become more independent.

"I guess you're right, but did we have to do this *now*?" It didn't make sense. It was early evening, and on the eve of their trip. Even if Peter was taking care of things, she had things to do. She was getting jittery.

Maybe he was taking her to dinner. A *romantic* dinner for two. She'd been a single mom for so long, it had taken a while for her to get used to having Brody around. He cherished her so much, and made up for all the times Tom had let her down.

"We always celebrate the victories," he reminded her. He'd made it 'a thing.' She dreaded if one day the scan results weren't good. What then?

She stared out of the window, gazing at the scenery, not wanting to dwell on that scenario. But the needling thought was stuck in her mind now. What would happen then is what had happened before. Brody would be by her side. She knew it in her gut.

Brody had never left her side. He'd nursed her back after her mastectomy. He was there for her before, and he would be there for her and Peter now, should things go wrong.

She sighed, relief washing over her. When fear reared its ugly head, Brody was there to calm the monster down. This brick wall of a man was her protector, her lover and her best friend.

When sprawling mansions came into view, she glanced at Brody to find the beach on his side.

"Glassmere?" she asked, recognizing the place they'd visited only recently. "Did you need to see Reed?" Reed Knight lived around here, she'd discovered. Brody had done a few side projects for Reed, and a few weeks ago, Reed and Jenna had invited them to a barbeque at his place.

It was eye-opening to see how Reed Knight lived. The man had a manservant and a housekeeper.

She'd gotten to know Reed, Jenna and their friends over time because they'd run into one another at various events. She had gotten to know Merry and Dylan even better because Peter and Chloe had developed a friendship during the Christmas pageant.

Brody had hinted that it could soon blossom into something else. She'd been super watchful since then, but for now, the two teens seemed to be good friends and nothing more.

Between talking to Pennington and Cecile, Reed's home help, she'd spent a lot of the time at the barbeque with Brooke; Merry's little eight-month-old daughter was beautiful.

Leah had tried not to make it so obvious, but it had been years since she'd held a baby and she loved holding this little bundle of joy. Her heart ached most times when she'd see babies, because her time for that was over.

She was sure that Brody noticed her reaction—the one she hadn't been able to hide—when Merry announced, right there at the barbeque, that she was pregnant again.

Dylan and Merry were having baby number three. Dylan's friends joked that the Frasers weren't wasting time with producing their soccer team.

She'd been happy for them, and had held onto Brooke for the rest of the evening, telling Merry that she was more than happy to babysit their little girl if ever she needed a break.

"Nope. I don't need to see Reed," he answered easily. "I thought we could have another picnic."

"We're having a picnic?" she asked.

"I brought leftovers, and some drinks."

He parked the car and they got out. The beach wasn't as secluded as it had been the last time they'd come here; the first time she'd been here, when Brody had sprung that surprise picnic on her.

He pulled out the familiar hamper from the trunk. She smiled. "Well, okay. This could be fun." Now that she was at the beach, away from the worry of the camping trip and packing, she relaxed a little.

They walked hand in hand along the beach, and the warm summer evening, with the low setting sun kissed her bare shoulders. The strappy summer dress and pumps were perfect for this weather.

Everything was different and the same.

Brody was here, and she was still in the clear with her cancer. Monthly check-ups gave her peace of mind. What changed was that she and Brody were together. What they had was as firm and as strong as the roots of an oak tree.

He had stayed by her side since Christmas, and helped her every step of the way. When someone did that, stuck by you through the bad times, not just the good times, it said a lot about them, and a lot about their relationship.

"Please tell me you're not going to light a bonfire?"

"No bonfire." He gazed at her for long moment, a devilish look in his eyes, as he spread out the picnic blanket. "Remember the first time we came here?"

"It's something I'll never forget." She started taking out the plastic food containers he'd so neatly packed, and then she pulled out the drink bottles.

Some sparkling fruit juice.

Some champagne.

She lifted the bottle up. "Champagne? I thought we couldn't have alcohol on the beach?"

He frowned, looking puzzled. "I don't know how that got in there. Hmm." He shrugged and started opening the containers she'd handed him.

"At least we're making good use of last night's leftovers." She hated wasting food, and with them going away, she felt pleased that they wouldn't have to throw much away. She dipped her hand into the hamper again and pulled out some plates and cutlery. And then she pulled out a box.

It was the size of her hand, but unlike the other food containers. "What's this?"

Brody scratched his jaw. "Hmmm. I don't know."

She opened it, to find a cardboard box inside. Lifting an eyebrow, she pulled the box out and showed it to Brody, who looked as shocked as she did.

"Was that there the last time?" he asked, making a face.

"I didn't pack this the last time. You did."

"Open it and see what it is."

She opened the cardboard box to find another smaller box inside. "This is ... insane." She laughed, not understanding. "Did we ever take this fishing?" Maybe someone had accidentally left something in it.

"You took your hamper to our fishing trips, and you only went once," he reminded her. She opened the box and pulled out another smaller box inside that.

"This is ridiculous," she cried, her curiosity making her open that box even faster. Inside this smaller box was another box.

But it was dark blue plush velvet, with a silver latch.

And it looked like a ring box.

Her insides fell clean out of her stomach. She looked at Brody, and he looked right back at her.

Tears started to spring up in her eyes, but she tried to blink them away. This could be a necklace, or a bracelet, or a brooch. For no reason at all, Hyacinth popped into her head.

Her fingers hovered over the latch she was too scared and too nervous to open.

"Open it," Brody said softly.

She swallowed. She was too excited to move.

He'd known this. He'd planned it.

Of course he had.

Calm down and open it.

She couldn't let this moment drag out any longer and make it mean something it wasn't. This was probably a pair of earrings.

Not that other thing.

"It's something small ..." Brody said. "I wasn't sure." He was preparing her. This was just another piece of jewelry.

Nothing more.

She rushed to open it, just as he said, "I didn't know if I should wait a while, until we'd been dating a year, and then I thought, when did we start?"

The sound of waves lapping against the shore and the cries of children playing nearby suddenly faded away. She stood up, even though her legs were shaking, and her knees were like jelly. Her eyes gaped at the pear-shaped solitary diamond ring that sparkled back at her. Her brain sent a carousel of images flashing before her eyes.

And her heart? Her big, solid, dependable heart, now da-doom'd, da-doom'd, da-doom'd in sync with her pulse.

"Will you marry me, Leah?" He was on one knee. She blinked once, maybe six times. "I know you might think this is too soon," he continued, "but, that's okay. I can wait, we don't have to plan anything right now—"

Tears rolled down her cheeks, misting her vision as she fell to the ground and then against his strong wall of a chest.

With the box in one hand, and the ring in the other, she threw her arms around his neck. "Yes, yes, I will. I'll marry you." Her words were muffled against his neck. She pulled away, needing to look into his eyes. They were teary, too. Hooded, shining with happiness.

"You and your surprises, Brody." She sniffled, holding out the ring between them. "I love you. I love you so much. I can't wait to marry you."

He cupped her face. "Is it too much, is it too soon? We don't have to now, we have time, we can wait for whenever you want. Whenever you're ready."

She nodded, tears crashing down her cheeks as he slid the ring onto her finger. She held out her hand, admiring it. "I love what this ring means." She sniffled as she gazed into his eyes. "It means we belong together, forever."

This man adored her, told her all the time that she was beautiful inside and out, told her that she was the best part of his day. He always said the right things, and now he'd asked her to marry him.

"Do you like it?" he asked, his voice turning low, hoarse and sexy as her eyes settled on his lips.

Kiss me now, her heart begged. Blood pounded through her veins, and in the midst of this unforgettable moment, something came to her that she had forgotten. "Peter," she cried, only now remembering her son. "I have to tell Peter."

"He knows," Brody said calmly.

"He knows?" She shook her head, her brain dazed at this level of planning. The champagne, the picnic, the ring, and Peter had been in on it all.

"I asked him," Brody said, stroking her cheek. "I had to ask him if it was okay."

She was so touched she wanted to cry. "You were both in on this from the start?"

"He *is* packing," he assured her, "but I think he's maybe also waiting for us to get back home."

She clasped her hand to her chest. "Brody," she moved her head from side to side slowly. "I'll never get over your surprises. I'll never be able to do one better."

"You don't have to do one better," he said, reaching for her hand and wrapping his around it. "I like seeing you smile." His face turned serious. "I know I've sprung this on you, but you're the one for me. If you need more time, that's fine, too. This can be a think-about-it ring, before a stay-with-me-forever ring."

She didn't need to wait. "This is a stay-with-me-forever ring now. I don't need to think about it. I know."

Lines formed on his brow. "I saw you with Brooke at the barbeque. You were walking around with her in your arms all evening, and I saw that look in your eyes."

She sank back in surprise.

"You're the one, Leah. I never met anyone I could say that about. I like what we have, you, me and Peter, but ... I saw that look in your eyes when you had that baby in your arms." He cleared his throat. "I used to think it was too late for me to have children, but ... if that's something you want ..."

Her tears started to fall again. "A baby?" she whispered. She was young enough to try. "But Peter ..." He was going to be fifteen this year. "The age gap between them ..."

"Merry and Dylan are juggling a big age gap with their kids, and now they're having another one," he countered. "Peter's probably going to go away to college in a few years' time. You and I? We're young enough to start a family, if it's something you want."

"What do you want?" she asked, because he had given her so much, and she wanted to give him what he desired.

"I want you, and Peter, and a family. I've never had children, but with you, it's something I can see in my future." He gave her a smile that was wistful and yet filled with hope.

She'd always wanted more children but Tom had killed that dream. Brody had revived it again, as well as all her other lost dreams.

He'd given her everything.

"I love you." She stared at him, her heart in his hands, because at last, she trusted someone enough to let them have it.

"I love you right back." He pressed his lips against hers, and then their kiss deepened, a hunger awakening, and a knowing, that this moment meant so much. It was the start of a new phase.

He reached for the bottle of champagne and was about to open it, when she cried, "Won't someone see us?" She recalled how they'd been so careful the last time.

"Some risks are worth taking."

She fanned her face, needing time to stop so that she could process this huge life-changing moment which had just taken place. "Can we just lie down? I need to savor this."

They lay down, side by side, holding hands. She gazed up at the pale blue sky kissed with a hint of peach and yellow.

It was a beautiful summer day, and Brody had asked her to marry him. Things like this never happened to people like her, but Brody changed all of that. He made everything she'd only ever dreamed of possible.

At a time when she'd been so entrenched in her belief that she was incomplete, *less*, and therefore unattractive, he'd come along just when she'd needed him the most. And maybe, just a little maybe, he'd needed her, too.

She looked forward to her future, and was ready to face whatever it might bring, because she had a wonderful man by her side.

Thank you for reading A CHRISTMAS WISH! I hope you enjoyed Leah and Brody's story.

If this is the first book you've read in the STARLING BAY SERIES, you might want to read the first book, WINTER'S KISS. This is about a sexy gift store owner, a jaded widow and a Great Dane. Or get the boxed set, Escape to Starling Bay

. . .

If you're looking for something else to read, why not try THE BRIDAL SHOP which is about the lives and loves of three sisters who run a bridal boutique:

Sisters. Weddings. Secrets.

At the age of forty-three, two decades after the trajectory of her life was cruelly thwarted, Ashleigh yearns for the life not lived.

Filled with regret, she longs to strike out on her own so that she can regain the dreams of her past.

Unfortunately, her sisters have other plans.

SIGN UP FOR MY NEWSLETTER to find out when new books release and also get the prequel to the series, WHIRLWIND KISSES for free!
http:/www.siennacarr.com/newsletter

I appreciate your help in spreading the word, including telling a friend, and I would be grateful if you could leave a review on your favorite book site.

Thank you so much!

Sienna

PREVIEW: THE BRIDAL SHOP

"You look absolutely stunning," said Ashleigh. She watched as friends and family of the bride gasped, their hands clutching their chests as they looked at the bride in the wedding dress she had just put on. This was the last fitting, and everyone was in awe. Tears threatened to fall from many eyes. Murmurs of approval mingled with long sighs, creating a chorus of wonderment. The bride-to-be's mother looked joyous. "My baby girl," she cried.

"Mom!" Helena, the happy bride-to-be and, even more importantly for the Rose sisters, an extremely satisfied customer, fanned her face and at the same time admired her reflection in the large ornate mirror.

"I *love* this." She smoothed down the rich satin of her dress then adjusted her veil, turning to look at herself from all angles. Her friends and family took pictures on their cell phones.

"Oh, my word." Eloise, Ashleigh's sister and co-owner of The Bridal Shop, along with their youngest sister, Ginny, dutifully sighed and gushed. This had been months in the making; not the dress, it wasn't made by them, but the entire operation from consultations to helping the bride find her perfect dream dress, and making alterations and so forth, took a while.

Ashleigh and her sisters were less in the business of selling dresses and more in the business of selling dreams. The Bridal Shop sold ready-to-wear bridal dresses made by a variety of manufacturers and designers, and with Eloise's artistic flair and eye for fashion, they could find the dream dress that would make a bride look perfect on her big day.

The dress was indeed beautiful.

"You'll look stunning walking down the aisle," Ashleigh told her. She had watched this exact same scenario play out many times over the twenty-plus years of running the family's business. She had seen thousands of happy brides start their journeys here, and it always began with the dress.

"Where dreams begin," someone in the bride's party said. "It's true, it's so true."

"Yes, they do …" the new bride-to-be echoed. "Where dreams begin, they do begin here and *now* …" The smile on her face spread out as she repeated the slogan which was synonymous with The Bridal Shop, the business Ashleigh and her sisters all worked at, the one her parents set up so long ago.

Where dreams begin.

The words were written in cursive gold writing on a cream silk painted wall, and it caught people's attention as soon as they walked in, putting them in the right state of mind for fulfilling their dreams.

Unfortunately, those words didn't have the same effect on Ashleigh and she forced herself to smile and nod in agreement.

Her dreams hadn't begun here. They had died.

"It fits perfectly," said Eloise, fussing around the bride. Of the three of them, Eloise was the one who had studied fashion and design and was the better equipped to deal with the actual design and fitting side of things. The business had been started by their mother many years ago. She had been the real figurehead behind the company.

"I'll leave you to it." Ashleigh left the enraptured group and walked over to the counter in order to get away. Sometimes, happy brides were more than she could handle.

She waited patiently by the counter, then checked the appointment book to see if there were any more fittings for dresses later today.

"I love your shop." A woman, probably an elderly aunt, walked over to her. "It has such a lovely feel to it. We knew it was something special the moment we walked in."

"Thank you. That's exactly the feeling we want you to have," Ashleigh replied. Customer feedback, and compliments especially, told her that they were doing things right. Over the years, she and her sisters had strived to make The Bridal Shop the number one wedding dress shop in Whisper Falls and the surrounding areas.

"Not to mention that your dresses are amazing, so beautiful, such a selection and the service you ladies provide is out of this world. I will definitely be recommending you."

"Thank you."

"How long have the three of you been running this business?"

"Twenty-two years," Ashleigh replied, forcing a smile she didn't feel. Once upon a time, it had been true. She had loved it here, running and growing the business that her beloved parents had started, until the fatal car accident had shattered their lives. The shock of losing both parents, so young and so unexpectedly, had blindsided them.

Ginny had been a mere toddler. "An accident," her mother had said, when a third child had been born so many years later. "A *happy* accident." The eighteen-year age gap between Ashleigh and her youngest sister sometimes made their relationship seem more like that of a mother and daughter, than that of sisters.

"Twenty-two years! You don't look old enough to be running something for that long." The usual surprise followed. Ashleigh didn't look her forty-three years. She was still on the tall side, and slim and svelte, though maybe not having had any children was the reason why. All three sisters were tall but Ginny was voluptuous and more rounded. Eloise was the tallest of them all, with long arms and legs. The Rose sisters didn't look like sisters at first glance, except for her and Ginny who shared their mother's hair color, although Ashleigh had hazel eyes. Eloise's dark brown hair and eyes were similar to their father's.

Twenty-two years she had stayed, running a business she'd never had any plans to run, and living in a small town she had wanted to leave so long ago. And here she was. Stuck.

"Where dreams begin, I love that," said another member of their entourage.

"Thank you." Ashleigh had to bite her tongue. For twenty-two years, she had stared at those words knowing that they weren't true. Not for her.

But in the beginning, the grief of losing both parents had been a shock that had devastated all of their young lives. And over the years, especially during the last three, a simmering resentment had started to creep up inside her each time she walked into the shop and saw those words. It had gotten to the point that she found herself staring at the slogan with the stark realization that her dreams had ended the day her parents had died.

Her mother had been smart, and astute, and Ashleigh missed her sorely. Her heart had been shredded to lose her parents, but the loss of her mother—her mentor, guide and friend—that loss had ruptured and caused a gaping hole in her young life. She knew it was one she would never get over.

How different all of their lives would have been had that truck not jack-knifed across the highway, causing fatal collisions and a pileup of the cars behind it.

The sisters had changed things at The Bridal Shop in recent years, moving away from their original location on Main Street to bigger premises slightly away from the busy town center. Moving to a more picturesque building surrounded by trees and greenery had worked out so well. They had changed the look and feel of the shop, making it more upscale, so that it seemed more like a high-end boutique than just a regular store. The addition of red velvet chaise lounges and chandeliers had transformed The Bridal Shop into a place that many from out of town came to visit. Some of the dresses they sold were sourced from new and upcoming designers. In this way, they were positioned perfectly for customers who wanted 'exquisite' without the Rodeo Drive prices. Because of their special relationship with the designers and manufacturers, they were able to also provide tailor-made dresses at a higher price for the more discerning clients, like Ginny. As a co-owner, she got such perks.

Many customers, though, were happy with the choice of ready-to-wear dresses they stocked. Many customers visibly gasped when they entered and saw the mannequins dressed in organza tulles and silk and satin dresses in white, cream or ivory.

"Dreams really do begin here, don't they?" the woman continued, obviously eager to chat. "It's the absolute truth, a woman wears this dress for one day, and takes her vows and makes a commitment, and then she starts a new life."

Ashleigh held her smile.

"How long have you been married?" the woman asked her. Ashleigh always found it odd how people presumed that she was married, despite her not wearing a wedding ring.

"I'm not married."

The woman's' face dropped. "Oh, I ... I ... I assumed."

"People often do."

"You've never married?" The woman stared at her as if she'd caught the plague.

"Mom! Stop being so nosy," a young woman hissed before giving Ashleigh an apologetic look.

"It's fine. I get asked this a lot." People assumed these things. She had never married, though Eloise had tried it, for about eleven months, before that ended. "But Ginny's getting married." She nodded towards her sister. "Next month."

A chorus of approval and excitement rose up. "How lovely!"

"Your dress must be amazing," the younger girl exclaimed to Ginny.

"Oh, it is. It's beautiful," Ginny gushed.

Ashleigh let out a small breath. "Only the best for this one," she muttered to herself. Ginny's dress had taken twice as long to finalize as most. She kept changing her mind, for one thing, and always wanting something else the moment she saw the new designs from their suppliers. Finding the perfect wedding dress for Miss Genevieve had been a continuously moving goal.

But now, it was done. Ginny's dress was ready, and with a month to go before her big day, Ashleigh was biding her time before making her announcement. Or, perhaps, she would do it before then.

"I want to get my dress from here, Mom." Ashleigh surveyed the young woman and recalled being that age. Her own dreams hadn't had a chance to start. She'd given it all up, the plans to travel for six months before leaving to go to Boston where Ford, the love of her life, would start working at his uncle's firm and she would start a degree in journalism.

That had been the plan, until life happened and changed everything. She had abandoned those plans and done the right thing. She had stayed behind to take care of the business her parents had built up, and to keep the family together. With the help of Aunt Becky, her mom's older sister, who also never married or had children, she had kept her siblings together and done her best to maintain some semblance of family life, even though the people who had given her life were no more.

Watching everyone else's dreams begin while hers had stagnated was becoming harder to swallow.

It was time to change things. To fix things. To put things right. She was patiently waiting for Ginny's wedding to be over with and then she would make her announcement, because soon it would be time for *her* dreams to begin.

BOOKLIST

Starling Bay: Come to Starling Bay, a small coastal town with lots of lovely places, and meet memorable people you'll want as your friends. Small town. Big Romance.

Whirlwind Kisses

Winter's Kiss

Maid for Him

Love Letters

Escape to Starling Bay (Books 1-3)

From Faking to Forever

Winter's Vow

Guarded Hearts

Table for Two

A Bouquet of Charm

A Christmas Wish

The Rose Sisters: Meet Ashleigh, Eloise and Ginny, the Rose sisters, who run a bridal boutique in Whisper Falls. Sibling rivalry, forgotten dreams, new challenges.

The Bridal Shop

ACKNOWLEDGMENTS

I would like to thank my amazing group of proofreaders who check my manuscript for errors, typos and inconsistencies.
I am eternally grateful for their help and support:

Marcia Chamberlain
Dena Pugh
Charlotte Rebelein
Carole Tunstall

I would also like to thank Tatiana Vila of Vila Design for creating this awesome cover.

ABOUT THE AUTHOR

Sienna Carr is a pen name for an author who has been writing romance since 2013. She lives in the UK with her husband, three children, and a parrot.

Connect with Me

I love hearing from you – so please don't be shy!
You can email me at: sienna@siennacarr.com